Burn After Reading

Tina Kakadelis

Regina Kakadelis, Editor

Stratis Kakadelis, Cover Design

Ana Lucía Figueroa, Cover Illustration

ISBN 9781795304658

Carly Allen has finally made it into the real world...and it absolutely blows. She hasn't seen or heard from Mollie Fae in years, and her dreams of writing have long been forgotten. Carly's lost and alone, and her last-ditch effort to find herself again is to go on a 2,500-mile road trip across the country. Buckle up, throw some Springsteen on the record player, and join Carly one last time on her quest to find true love and the person she knows she can be.

To Bruce Springsteen.
Thanks for the magic, the music, and the dancing.

"You must know...surely you must know it was all for you."

Jane Austen, *Pride and Prejudice**

* The credit technically belongs to Deborah Moggach, writer of the 2005 film adaptation of *Pride and Prejudice*, but that doesn't sound as fancy, now does it? No offense, Deborah.

1

Once in a Lifetime
by Talking Heads

They say those who can't, teach, and those who can't teach, teach gym. What do they say about those who can't write? Those who can't write do what? Well, in my personal experience, they work at Target.

So yeah. I'm a college graduate. Have been for quite a while now. It's easy to forget. I don't have my framed diploma hanging on a wall because I'm not a doctor or an engineer or anything like that. It would look a little weird if my only attempt at interior decorating was a framed creative writing diploma. It's not like I have an office to hang it in. Failed writers don't have a need for office space.

I tried the writing thing for a little while. Took that youthful optimism and ran with it straight to nowhere. You know the new *Gilmore Girls* where Rory's a self-proclaimed failure, can't get a job, and is an adulterer? Move aside, Rory Gilmore, there's a new self-proclaimed, unemployable failure in town. But not an adulterer. Like, c'mon, Rory. And with Logan? The plus side, however, is that I finished watching this version of *Gilmore Girls* in a reasonable amount of time.

Look at me. Twenty-eight, single, careerless. Wearing khakis, a red t-shirt, and a name tag to work every day. Not even an engraved name tag. This one was clearly printed on a label maker. It's the kind of name tag reserved for people the bosses think might be just a little short on commitment. They only break out the engraver for those who bleed red and khaki.

Listen, there's nothing wrong with this job. I worked at a record store and a coffee shop in high school and college. God knows I'm not better than any of these people, and I know for a fact some of them really like what they're doing. It's just not what I want to be doing. This was supposed to be temporary, a means to an end. The problem is, I don't know what that end is anymore.

It's good money. I'm a manager who unloads boxes all day. Not the glamour of Spin Me, Baby, but I'm not going home smelling like McDonald's. I just go home with little flecks of cardboard stuck to my shirt.

"What age child does this shoe fit?" A woman appears out of nowhere, forcing me to yank the pallet I'm pulling to an abrupt stop.

"Uh, I'm not totally sure. I work in electronics," I say. "Let me find someone who can answer your question."

She gives me the once-over. "That'll take too long. I'll have to go ask a woman," she says, then storms away.

Does she think I'm a guy? I know I have short hair, but I've also got boobs. There's no denying I'm a female. Do all women know what size shoes fit children of every age? Don't kids vary in size, at least a little bit? Is that how you finally know you're a woman? When you pass the child shoe size test? Talk about unrealistic expectations. And also, by her definition, she's not a woman either. Whatever. Gender's fake anyway.

When I started working here, I justified it by telling myself it was a job I didn't have to take home with me. Just one to go to, do my work, and leave without any stress or dread so I could focus on writing. It made sense, my mom commended me on making such a reasonable choice, and my dad asked if I could get him a discount. I had the parentals' blessing and the youthful determination to write something great, so it was a done deal. I accepted the job, bought khaki pants for the first time in my life, and went to work every Wednesday through Sunday from 9 to 5, listening to Dolly Parton as I got ready.

That was years ago and I have nothing to show for it. Writing-wise, I mean. Target-wise, I'm a box-unpacking prodigy. An online order-shipping demigod. A rapid-scanning cashier hero. Also, do you know how many dates I've gotten from working as a cashier? I think I've found the answer to everyone's 21st century dating problems. Full disclosure, though, there can be a downside. A girl I went out with a couple of times came through my line after I called it off and threw a DVD of *Gone Girl* in my face. Talk about a dramatic movie choice. Am I Amy or Nick? Nobody faked their own death or anything, so I feel a little wrongfully accused. But that was a one-time thing. Most girls usually just use the self-checkout after we stop dating.

I know what you're thinking. You're thinking "Single? Carly Allen? Where the hell is Mollie Fae?" Honestly, I'd like to know the answer to that question as much as you would. Last I heard, she's a lawyer in New York. On track to make partner in a prestigious Midtown law firm someday. Thank you, Internet, for keeping me up to date. She's a New Yorker and I'm an L.A.-er. Poetic, isn't it? Both of us grew up into wildly different people. She ditched her pretty pastel summer dresses for black coats and business professional courtroom clothes. I ditched the East Coast for a place that would accept my Hawaiian shirts for the unironic fashion statement they are.

I know, I KNOW. It's a bit of a shock. Last time you and I talked, things were going great. Mollie and I had just finished our freshman year of college and we were better than ever. We stayed better than ever all through college and even for a little while after. I moved out to Los Angeles after graduation and she moved south to me. We got a cute little apartment and made it our own. We were two kids in love, but the world wasn't ready for us.

Or maybe we weren't ready for the world. We got into a big fight that I still really hate talking about, and we haven't spoken since. Absolutely nothing. Not even a late-night drunk confession text. No cordial happy birthday or Merry Christmas text. I genuinely have not seen or heard from her in years.

Ain't that a kick in the head?

****

"Carly to HR. Carly to HR, please," a voice calls over the intercom.

Sigh. Not exactly what I was hoping for today.

I pull the pallet to the back of house and head toward HR. My brain is going haywire trying to figure out if I've done anything in recent days that was a fireable offense. I mean, I'm probably always a little sassier than I should be to people, but it's never truly awful.

Sam is in charge of HR, and his office is as far back as you can go in the non-public part of Target. I rap my knuckles against the doorframe, and he looks up and smiles at me. If Annie was single and living out here, I would two thousand percent try to get the two of them together. He has a sweet baby face and curly hair that's never fully tamed.

"Sup, Carly Allen?" Sam beams.

He also perpetually sounds like a dad trying to make himself seem cool in front of his kids.

"Sup," I reply.

"Come on in and take a seat," he says.

"Am I in trouble for something?" I sit down, still trying to figure out why I'm here.

"No!" Sam laughs, then gives me a more serious look. "Why? Did you do something you should be in trouble for?"

"Um, no, but then why am I here?"

"I had the CCTV up," he says, tapping his pen against the computer screen. "I saw you talking to that lady. She looked, shall we say, unpleasant."

"Oh." I relax a little. "Yeah, she wasn't the happiest customer we've ever had."

"Exactly!" Sam points at me. "I figured you could use a little unauthorized break."

"Huh?"

"Dude, I'm trying to be nice. I'm giving you a ten-minute escape."

"That's so cool of you."

Sam's wide smile is back. "Coolest HR around." He leans back in his chair.

"You're also the only HR around," I joke.

"Cool by default is still cool." He pulls a packet of Starburst candy out of his desk drawer. "Want one?"

"Yeah. Pink or red please." He hands me one of each.

"So, and I feel weird saying this, but like, what's up?"

"What do you mean?"

I shift in my seat. "I mean, we don't really talk much and we barely know each other, so what's up?"

"I just think you're cool," he shrugs. "I wanted to fix the whole not talking thing."

"So," I say slowly, "you want to be friends?"

He wrinkles his nose at that. "Friends sounds so juvenile."

"You just gave me candy as incentive to be your friend," I point out.

"Okay, okay." He waves his hands. "Yes, I think you're cool and I want to be friends. Happy?"

"Ecstatic," I reply.

"As the first order of our new friendship, you've got to come to leader laser tag tomorrow," he says.

"Oh, I don't know about that."

"You've never been to any leadership nights." Sam sounds a little exasperated.

"It's almost like I'm actively avoiding any and all team-building activities."

"Well, as your friend," Sam begins, and I try to cut him off. Unfortunately, that only makes him talk louder. "As your friend, I'm overriding. You're coming to laser tag, we're going to be on the same team, and we're going to kick ass."

I let myself smile a little. "I mean, I do love laser tag."

"Yes! There we go," he says. "No one can resist laser tag."

I shrug and kick my feet up on his desk. "So, can I hide out here for the rest of the day?"

"Well, Jackson isn't in and it's a Friday, so—" he trails off.

"Did I just get permission to do nothing?"

"Just this once, okay?" Sam says. "You can help me with orientation paperwork for tonight."

"Done. Y'know, I think I like you, Sam. You're a good dude."

He tosses me another Starburst. "To friends."

I laugh. "You're right, it does sound weird coming from a grown adult."

2

Hit Me with Your Best Shot by Pat Benatar

As a rule, I tend to attempt to not socialize with my coworkers. Most of them take their jobs a little more seriously than I do. I don't care how much you pay me, there's only so much I can care about Hatchimals and whether or not people can buy them for their children. I'm sorry. I know that makes me a bad employee and I do pretend to care, but some of these people are genuinely concerned that these random, greedy parents can't buy Hatchimals for their whiny children. A coworker was crying yesterday, and when I asked if she was okay, she told me she was definitely not okay because we didn't have a copy of *The Princess Bride* for a customer. I just didn't care. I know. It's a miracle I haven't been fired yet. Notice I said yet.

After all that, it might be a surprise that I'm actually at laser tag, but I'm waiting in my car until the absolute last second before I go inside. On the bright side, with laser tag there's not a lot of talking and I get to shoot people.

There's a knock on the car window and I jump in my

seat. I look out and swear a little under my breath. It's Sam, grinning and giving a little wave. I offer him a smile that I hope doesn't look too much like a grimace and take the key out of the ignition.

"I really thought you'd bail," Sam says as I get out of the car.

"I thought I had to be here." I lock the car, kind of wishing I could have stayed in it.

"Yeah, but still," Sam responds.

"Come on! I thought we were friends. You don't have any faith in me?"

"Of course I do," he says. "I'm glad you're here. I don't really get along with a lot of the leaders."

"Wait," I say, stopping in my tracks. "Why don't you like them?"

"I feel weird talking about it." Sam scratches the back of his head. "Like, what if you're friends with them?"

"Sam, this is the first time I've ever gone to a leader's night of any kind," I remind him. "You think I'm friends with these people?"

"I guess not."

"Okay then, spit it out," I kind of yell at him.

"I still just feel weird."

"Listen, this is what friends are for! Talking about coworkers behind their backs! That's what the best workplace friendships are built on."

"They're too nice!" Sam says, then immediately claps his hands over his mouth.

"I didn't think you had it in you." I knew he had it in him.

"It's just that they care so much." Sam shakes out his body. "This feels good. I've just been holding it all in."

"Let it out, bro."

"Okay. So one day I was at work and I was wearing these khakis and yeah, they're a little lighter than the ones I usually wear, and fucking what's her face, Carrie, was like, 'are you sure those are Look Book approved?'" Sam says, mimicking Carrie's voice. "Uh, yeah, I'm sure, Carrie! It's not like it's my job to teach the stupid book to new hires or anything!"

"Tear 'em apart," I encourage him.

"Then there are the idiot customers. Half the reason I took the HR job was because I didn't want to have to be out there. On the floor, y'know? Listening to all the inane things that come spewing out of people's mouths," Sam continues.

"Yeah, tell me about it," I say. "I could afford to never work again if I got a dollar every time a customer said something idiotic to me."

"I could buy this whole laser tag place," Sam yells, gesturing toward the building ahead of us. "Oh my god, and the ten-cent bag fee!"

"The stupid bag fee!"

"Listen, I voted for the bag fee. I'm all for it. Honestly, I wish the fee would've been higher because the planet is dying. But the way people act, you'd think the fee was $100 instead of just ten cents," Sam gripes.

"One time, I was backing up on register and this person bought seventy-five dollars' worth of stuff. Small stuff. I asked if he wanted a bag and he proceeded to lose his goddamn mind about it!" I say. "Like, it's ten cents. You're spending seventy-five damn dollars. Ten cents isn't gonna kill you."

"Or maybe you could just bring your own stupid bag!" Sam's right there with me. "It's always the old people, too. Just trying to kill the planet before they finally kick the bucket."

I laugh. "See how nice it feels to vocalize."

"Whew, yeah. I've kept it all inside since I started. Everyone in there just cares so much," he says, pointing to the laser tag place.

"Yeah, well, I am not one of those people," I tell him.

"You want to bail? Get some pizza or something instead?" Sam asks.

I shake my head. "You know, I'm actually kind of looking forward to shooting these people with non-harmful lasers. Get out some aggression."

"We're teaming up to take those kids down!"

"Totally. *Charlie's Angels* style." I start walking toward the building.

"Wait, does that mean I'm an angel or Charlie?" Sam asks.

"Angel," I grin.

"Fine, but I call Lucy Liu. She kicks ass in every movie she's in," Sam says.

"Do you want to be Lucy Liu or date Lucy Liu?"

"I mean, why limit yourself?" Sam smiles.

We head inside, and all of our coworkers are there, happily chatting among themselves. A couple of them make stupid jokes about how they're shocked I'm here. More than one of them calls me a vampire, which is just a dumb thing to say. Vampires can't go out during the day. They literally only see me during the day. I'm the exact opposite of a vampire. I'm also too tan and spend too much time looking in the mirror to be a vampire. I'm not perfect, but I need my hair to be perfect.

The plan is to split the group evenly into two teams, but Sam and I aren't having it. We were both very serious about taking down all our coworkers as a team.

It turns out Sam's some sort of weird laser tag prodigy, and he confesses later that he played every single weekend in high school and college, and he's also in a laser tag league. So he's the brains. I'm more the run-and-shoot-first-then-maybe-consider-planning-later type. If there's a suicide mission, sign me up and I'll run right into the opposing team's base. I ain't afraid of no lasers.

Sam and I won two of the three games the group played. The only reason we lost the third one is because we did shots of tequila at the bar right before we were supposed to go into the arena place. Because running is my main strategy, I didn't let the tequila stop me and I continued on as usual. However, because running is my main strategy, I did end up puking on one of the ramps to the second floor of the arena. In case you're wondering, puke under a black light is not pretty.

After our victory, Sam and I ended up getting pizza at the sad little bar/café the laser tag place has. It definitely wasn't the best pizza I've ever had in my life (the crust was almost certainly made of cardboard), but, and it could be the tequila talking, it was one of the best pizzas I've ever had in my life.

Hours later, it's last call at the laser tag place and we're sober, but I don't feel so great. Surprisingly, though, joking around in the parking lot in the cool California night with this new friend feels right. It feels a lot more right than anything I imagined was going to happen tonight.

3

Jessie's Girl
by Rick Springfield

It's the Sunday morning after laser tag and I'm off today, so I decide it's time for a little housework. All my dishes are piled in the sink, and I've noticed the dust on my coffee table. It takes a lot for me to be spurred into action, both in cleaning and in life, which means my apartment is pretty nasty right now.

I wipe off my record player and turn on the speakers. Billy Joel's *The Stranger* is my go-to for cleaning because the B-side of that record is unreal. I mean, *Vienna, Only the Good Die Young*, and *She's Always a Woman* all on one side? Billy Joel was not messing around. Yeah, the first side's good, but that B-side goes on forever. Hit after hit.

I've made it through the kitchen and the living room when I hear my phone ring. Right now, I'm deep-cleaning the toilet because once I do get started cleaning, I kind of turn into a machine. And anyway, I can't remember the last time I actually scrubbed the toilet. Who scrubs their toilet regularly? Okay, don't answer that. And forget I said anything about how long it's been since I cleaned mine. I know I tell you guys a lot, but this feels like we finally hit the line on things I shouldn't share.

I pull off one of the rubber gloves and take out my phone. It's Annie. You guys remember Annie. Childhood best friend until the bitter end. Except there's nothing bitter about it. Quite the opposite.

"Well, hello, Annie," I say, sandwiching the phone between my shoulder and my ear while I take off the other glove.

"I can't believe Mollie Fae is getting married," Annie blurts out in lieu of saying hello back.

"Excuse me?" I drop the rubber gloves.

"Yeah, and so soon. December 17th in New York City."

"I'm sorry, I think I just had a stroke. I thought you said Mollie Fae is getting married." I sink down to the bathroom floor.

"She's marrying someone named Jessie Green. Sounds really Plain Jane to me," Annie continues.

"What the fuck!" I yell.

"Wait, you didn't know?"

"How on earth would I have known, Annie?" I ask, running a hand through my hair.

"I don't know. I figured the news would have made it to you somehow." I can imagine the way she's shrugging as she says this.

I shake my head. "Don't you think I would've told you if I knew?" My voice sounds a little squeaky. "You know we haven't talked. Not since, like, y'know—"

"Y'all never made up," Annie sighs. "I know. Even now, it's hard for me to accept."

"When did you become so southern?"

"It's Todd's family. Half of them are from Georgia, and with all this wedding stuff coming up, I feel like I'm on the phone with them every day."

"Geez, is everyone I know getting married?" How can Mollie Fae be getting married?

"Well, since Todd and I are your only friends, yes."

"Shut up. I have friends, Annie. Well, a friend. Named Sam. Kind of," I say. "Whatever. Also, I've been meaning to ask you this, but if you guys are moving to Nashville, why are you getting married in Chicago?"

"You know why. Todd loves the Cubs so much and the only contribution he made to brainstorming for the honeymoon was to say he wanted to tour Wrigley Field. So we'll do a tour the day of the rehearsal dinner and then leave for the rest of our honeymoon after the wedding."

"Gotta love men and their sports," I laugh.

"Tell me about it," Annie grumbles, but I know there's no actual animosity there. They'd move Mt. Everest for each other.

"Back to Mollie," I say, trying not to come across as

desperate. "How do you know she's getting married?"

"She invited us," Annie says matter-of-factly.

"Us? As in you and me?"

"No, Carly," she says gently. "Us, as in Todd and me."

"Why would she invite you guys and not me?" I know the answer, but I can't stop myself from asking.

"Oh, I don't know, because neither Todd nor I dated her. Nor did we—"

"I'm going to stop you right there," I say tersely, even though I did ask the question. "Today is not the day to open that can of worms."

"Okay, even though you've never told me the full story of your break-up," Annie replies. "Mollie and I swap Christmas cards and the occasional happy birthday on Facebook."

"You swap Christmas cards?"

"Carly, I tell you every year. I always say, 'I'm sending Mollie a Christmas card, do you want me to say anything on your behalf?' and you say, 'fuck that.' I don't know what to tell you," Annie sighs.

"I know, you're right. It's just that I guess I didn't think she'd actually marry someone." I shift my legs a little. The bathroom floor isn't very comfortable.

"You thought you still had a chance?" Annie asks quietly.

"I mean, kinda. In a roundabout way. I kind of always thought I'd bump into her on the street and things would be different. They'd be how they used to be," I say.

"Carly, life isn't a big romantic comedy. You have to know that by now."

"Why can't it be?" I ask, with probably a little more sincerity than I should.

"Are we eighteen again?"

I would like that. "I wish."

"Listen, I won't go to the wedding if you don't want me to," Annie says.

"No, no, you should go," I reply quickly. "She invited you."

"Are you sure? We don't have to go. I mean, New York at Christmastime, yuck."

"Annie, you'd be an idiot not to go to New York at Christmastime. Good for her. Throwing a wedding during the most magical time of the year in the most magical city in the world."

"Does she live in a Hallmark movie?"

I laugh loudly. "God, she probably does. The tough New York lawyer with a heart of gold doesn't believe in Christmas, but she meets a, a what. What does her fiancé do for a living?"

"Non-profit work," Annie answers quickly.

"Holy hell, this is a Hallmark movie," I grumble. "She meets a non-profit worker during a case she's working on and they fall in love while suing the asses off corrupt men.

I'd watch it."

"Carly Allen watches Hallmark Christmas movies now?" Annie teases.

"Year-round. How the mighty have fallen, right?"

"Oh, honey."

"You know, I wrote a shitty treatment for a Hallmark movie a few years ago. They said it was too good. Too good for Hallmark, not good enough for anywhere else."

"Have you written anything recently?"

"Why would I do that?" I ask.

"Oh, I don't know. Maybe because I listened to your plans through four years of creative writing school. You talked about how much you couldn't wait to graduate so you could finally write what you wanted to write. I could be mixing you up with someone else, I guess," Annie says.

"I think I'm gonna go to bed now."

"It's three in the afternoon out there."

I lie down on the tile. It's cold and hard. "I miss you."

"I'm always going to miss you, too," Annie says softly. "Are you sure you're okay?"

I brush some tears away. "I mean, it's not the most ideal outcome, is it?"

Annie has to laugh at that. "No, I can't say it is."

"It's just dumb luck," I tell her. "Pure, dumb luck."

"It will all be fine," Annie says, and I believe her for half a second.

"I really miss you, Annie."

"It's just a few days until my wedding, and then we'll finally be in the same state again."

"Yeah," I say blankly.

"Hey, I promise things will be okay," Annie says. "We can even get a voodoo doll of Mollie and get drunk and shit talk her."

"I'll call you, okay? I'm just gonna go lie down for a while."

"Sooner rather than later, okay?"

"Okay. Love you," I say.

"Love you, too," she responds, and then the line goes dead.

I hang up and throw the phone out the bathroom door. It tumbles across the carpet, far away from me. My brain is working a mile a minute thinking about Mollie. I still remember the last time we talked. It was when Mollie was finishing her law degree at USC. We were living in this very apartment.

****

"So you don't believe in me?" I yell at Mollie Fae.

"Carly, that's not what I'm saying."

"Well that's what it sounds like. Listen, writing's a hell of a lot different than being a lawyer. You do X, Y, and Z and boom, you're a lawyer! Congrats! You did it! You've got a fucking hundred-year, tried-and-true plan that's all laid out for you. You just have to keep checking things off the list and you'll get your dream."

"Everyone on the planet knows creative jobs are unstable. That should not be news to you."

"Yeah, well forgive me for thinking I was different."

"No one gets everything they want right out of college. If you read about any author, they'll tell you about how they kept getting rejected. J.K. Rowling, for god's sake. Look at where she is now."

"Fuck Harry Potter."

"Wow, okay, definitely don't say that when you do get famous unless you want to alienate 70% of the population."

"Whatever."

"For fuck's sake, Carly! Write something! You had momentum from that novella. Stop moping around this stupid apartment and write something."

"No," I answer petulantly.

"Fine." She goes to the bedroom and starts throwing clothes into a duffle bag.

"Oh, are you leaving?"

"Yes," she says, and I finally notice her tears. "I can't do this. I love you, Carly. I'm going to love you until the end of time, I'm sure of it, but this keeps building and building, and I just can't do it anymore. You're good at what you do. So, so good. For the love of god, just believe it. You dream all these things, but you do nothing."

"I thought you liked that I dream things," I spit out at her.

"More than you'll probably ever know. But that's not enough. You have to make a living somehow."

"What does that mean? You want me to put on a tie, sell out, and join corporate America?"

"It means I think we should take a break." Mollie's voice cracks. "I'm going to accept that job in New York. Alone. I don't think you should come with me, at least not now. I think you should be on your own for a while. Figure some things out."

"You can't be serious."

"Prove me wrong then. Write something you give a damn about. Write literally anything. Put the tiniest bit of passion into something. Anything!"

"I've got nothing to write. You know that."

"And that's where you're wrong. I don't know that. I've never known that. There was a time when you didn't know that either. That's the real you. The one I want to be with."

"Looks like we're both out of luck, then."

She sighs and zips up the duffle bag. "Looks like we are."

****

Do you ever wish you could go back in time and kick younger you's teeth in? Yeah, me too. Every day of my life. But clearly not enough to actually do anything about it. I've wanted to call Mollie so many times, but what am I going to say? "Hey, I took your advice, gave a damn about something, and that something is packing boxes for delivery." Yeah, because writing and Target are totally interchangeable dreams.

I know what you're thinking. "Carly, we had to suffer through hundreds of pages of you not believing in yourself about writing, you finally overcame it with the power of '80s music, and now we're in the same stupid situation?" Well, yeah, it seems '80s music isn't as powerful as I once thought. Maybe singers from the '80s were just corporate sell-outs in shoulder pads. Maybe they didn't give a damn about what they were singing about. No, heaven is not a place on earth, Belinda Carlisle. Heaven is a paycheck and a bottom line. That's all that really matters in this bankrupt world. I know that now.

Success is money. There's no room in the world for creative people. Art is nothing. Music is just garbage with enough gleam to make you believe it could be gold, but it can't. Make no mistake, it's the furthest thing from it.

4
Baba O'Reilly
by The Who

I am not proud of the events of Sunday night, so we're going to breeze right past them. Just know that I stayed up way too late, drank a couple more adult beverages than what's recommended, and stared at the Follow Request button on Mollie Fae's private Instagram account for a lot longer than a sane human would. So, to answer your next question, no, I did not add her on Instagram. It seems I have some self-restraint left. Not much, but I guess some is better than none.

"Carly to HR. Carly to HR," a voice calls over the PA.

I hope this is Sam attempting to further our friendship and not an actual HR thing. I get that I kind of smell a little like a distillery, but I sprayed a lot of Febreze on myself this morning in an attempt to mask it. I know. Febreze. Who am I? Someone who does not own perfume of any kind. But desperate times, guys. I smell like a rustic pile of fall leaves, so who's the real winner here?

"What's up, Sam?" I ask as I sit down.

"Just wanted to hang with my new pal," Sam replies.

"Cool, cool," I say. "Do you mind if your new pal takes a quick nap on this chair?" I wiggle around to get comfortable, then close my eyes.

"Long night?" Sam asks.

"You don't know the half of it," I mumble.

"Love troubles, yeah?" he asks, and I nod. "I feel that."

"You got love troubles, Sam?"

"Oh, no," he says. "But I did just binge watch *One Tree Hill* over the weekend, so I feel you."

"You don't strike me as a *One Tree Hill* kind of guy," I say, smiling at him.

"It's my sister's fault. We watch shows together on Netflix. It was her pick."

"Whew," I say. "She picked a doozy."

"Tell me about it. I usually watch more serious drama, documentaries on true crime. That kind of deal. But man, I really liked it."

"Here's an important question that's gonna make or break our friendship." I open my eyes again. "Brooke or Peyton?"

"We haven't finished yet," he says. "There's something like nine seasons. You can't finish that in a weekend."

"Doesn't matter. You've seen enough to make up your mind."

"I don't like that you're putting our friendship to the test like this."

"Better to find out now than later."

"I can't tell how much of you is joking and how much of you will take this answer way too seriously," he says, squinting at me.

I start humming the *Jeopardy* theme song.

"Fine." Sam takes a deep breath. "Brooke."

"Ladies and gentlemen," I say with a smile, "we have a friendship."

"Oh, thank god."

"So what are the odds of you letting me sleep here all day?" I ask. I'm starting to doze off.

"Extraordinarily slim, because it's Monday, which means Jackson is here and he's walking this way. Oh my god, please open your eyes and sit up and make it seem like we're doing something productive." Sam's words are so fast they're almost one.

I bolt upright. It's not that I'm afraid of Jackson, but it seems that whenever he sees me, I tend to be taking a shortcut of one kind or another. If it weren't for the fact that I'm very good at my job, I'm pretty sure he would've fired me by now.

"Good morning!" Jackson says as he enters Sam's office.

"Good morning," Sam and I say, trying to hide our fear.

"What are you two planning so early in the morning?"

"Uhhh," I drawl, then can't think of anything else to say.

I look at Sam, desperately hoping an idea will strike one of us.

"Carly wanted to talk to me about team bonding, isn't that right, Carly?"

"Yes, that is definitely exactly right."

"What about it?" Jackson takes a seat next to me.

"She just went to her first leadership event on Saturday and loved it," Sam says. I glare at him. "She loved it so much she wanted to pitch some ideas for our next one."

"Well that's wonderful." Jackson smiles. I think it's the first time he's ever smiled at me. "What did you have in mind?"

"Painting," I say.

"Painting?" Sam looks a little confused. Who can blame him?

"You know, like those pottery places where you get to paint bowls and mugs," I ramble. "Or those classes where you get to drink wine and paint. Those are always fun."

"I like the way you think, Carly." Jackson clamps a hand down on my shoulder.

"That's exactly what I was thinking," Sam agrees.

Jackson stands up. "Now, Carly, those pallets aren't going to unload themselves. I sure do love Monday deliveries!"

"Yes, sir," I say. "Me too."

Jackson gives us a nod and heads out the door. Sam and

I are alone again.

"Painting. That was good." Sam nods.

"It was the first thing that came to my mind."

"We should totally paint matching plates together."

I stand up. "Goodbye, Sam. I have palettes to unload."

"Sit with me at lunch at least?" Sam asks. "I'll give you my Doritos."

This guy sure is into the friend thing. "No."

He turns his attention back to the computer and scoffs. "I already know that means yes."

It's nice to have Sam. He gets me out of my head. In the last few years, there have been days when I haven't spoken to a soul. Days where I've just stared at the four walls of my apartment and prayed for something to happen. For something to change. Most days I talk to people because I have to. The people I work with, the customers, the cashier at the sandwich shop where I get my dinner sometimes, the guy who delivers Chinese food at two a.m.

The day goes on as usual. Sam and I have lunch together and make fun of the people cooking on the Food Network. He does, in fact, share his Doritos. I leave work a little early, because as much as I like hanging out with Sam, I'm not used to it and it feels exhausting. Besides, I'm going to Chicago on Friday for Annie's wedding and I still need to get my pants hemmed, buy a dress shirt, and figure out how to avoid Mollie Fae.

Although you'd think it should be, packing isn't on my list of things to do yet. I just can't trust people who are packed and ready for their vacation days before they're due to leave. Maybe those people have figured out something I haven't, but if I don't spend the night before I go somewhere packing, am I truly excited to go on the trip? Take on that unanswered question, Schrodinger.

5

Shrike
by Hozier

Annie's working on becoming a doctor, so she keeps weird hours, and the time difference ends up working in our favor. I tend to stay up late and let my brain get exhausted from dealing with a million and one existential thoughts. Annie's awake early, learning how to save lives. Incredible, really.

Cars is playing in the background on my DVD player. You know, the Disney movie about the washed-up race car that ends up in a tiny town Route 66 forgot. It's a cute movie, even if Rascal Flatts does butcher *Life Is a Highway*.

Anyway, because it's two a.m. and I'm bordering on delirious, I'm spewing out one of my favorite pop culture theories; that the cars in *Cars* actually became sentient and took over earth. I love conspiracy theories. Harmless ones. Not like the people who think those awful mass shootings in America are a stunt by the media. That's messed up. But cars from *Cars* becoming sentient and living out the history of earth as cars? Sign me up.

Annie always encourages me to rant about nonsense this early in the morning. She says it takes her mind off medicine when I sound like a crazy person. But listen. Why is there a school bus character in the third *Cars* movie? Why? It can't carry cars. Did it carry children in another life? If so, what happened to the children?

Tonight, or this morning, I'm attempting to do too many things at one time.

"What are you doing right now? You sound distracted." Annie cuts off my rambling.

"I'm trying to write a listicle," I say.

"A what? An icicle?"

"Annie, how would anyone even write an icicle?" I ask. "No, a listicle. Like a list article. Basically, what BuzzFeed built their brand on. I'm calling mine 25 Instagram Pugs You Need to Know About."

"Why are you doing this?"

"Everyone keeps getting on my case about writing something and I saw BuzzFeed's hiring, so here I am."

"It's after two a.m. and you're writing a weird list about dogs? I can't say this is what any of us meant when we suggested you write something."

"Maybe it'll get my juices flowing."

"Gross."

"Yeah, you're right, bad call," I agree. "But I think this is good. I've got 15 so far."

"Are you proud of it?" Annie asks carefully.

"They're dogs. With Instagram accounts."

"Well, as long as you're happy."

Am I happy? I mean, the slightest hesitation leads me to believe I'm not happy. But I've got a job and a roof over my head and food and some friends and family, so what excuse do I have? Am I just a whiny ass because some girl I dated millennia ago is getting married? I *should* be happy.

"Carly? You still there?" Annie asks.

I cough. "Yeah, sorry. Got distracted. This one's dressed as a firefighter and has two million followers. He's just a dog! He doesn't need that many."

"You're acting weird again," she says.

"No I'm not. I'm just getting wrapped up in these dogs. I'm sorry."

"If you say so." Annie moves on. "What time are you landing on Friday?"

"Two-thirty. You can still pick me up, yeah? Not too busy with bridal duties?"

"Never too busy to pick up my oldest and bestest friend," Annie gushes.

"Oh, stop." I blush just a little. "Do I need to bring anything?"

"It's a wedding, Carly. You bring yourself and your suit and that's it."

"Okay. I've never been to a wedding as an adult before."

"Not one?" Annie asks.

"Nope. You're the first."

"Well, isn't that something," Annie says absently.

"What?" I'm much more focused on trying to get this damn hyperlink to work.

Annie hesitates way too long. "I'm not sure how to tell you this."

"That sounds ominous."

"Mollie Fae's coming," she says evenly.

"No fucking way." The phone drops to the floor and I can't seem to do anything but stare at it. Annie's voice startles me, and I scramble to pick it up again.

"She just emailed me and said she wants to change her response," Annie says.

"No."

"She wasn't going to come because she and Jessie had to go to somewhere," Annie continues. "I guess plans changed. She says she's coming."

"No."

"Alone."

"No, no." Do I not know any other words?

"Carly, you'll be fine. You don't have to speak to her if you don't want to. You'll be busy taking care of me."

"No."

"I'm going to ask that you stop sounding like a skipping record. Please say something else."

"Hell, no."

"Carly Allen," Annie says sternly.

"I feel like my world just got flipped upside down." My head drops against the back of the couch.

"Just because she's coming alone doesn't mean she's not still getting married," Annie says a little nervously.

"I know, I know. I just...I haven't seen her in so long." I pick at the dried tomato soup stain on my shirt. "What if I forget what she looks like and I try to hit on her?"

"Carly, now you're just being ridiculous."

"I mean, probably, but you acknowledging it won't change that."

"Listen, if you guys do cross paths, just keep the conversation light. Tell her she looks nice, ask her if she liked the bouquet, and definitely don't mention your weird dog listicle."

"Hey, Annie, I think I'm gonna call it a night," I say abruptly, as I get up off the floor.

"Carly, don't be upset."

"No, I'm fine. I've gotta pack, y'know." My voice cracks only slightly. "I'll see you soon. Love you."

She sighs. "Love you too."

I hang up and fall into bed.

In the abstract, I think I handled the news of Mollie Fae's engagement rather well. It's easy when it's not right in front of me. I can put it in the back of my mind and yeah, it'll creep to the front of my thoughts on the rare occasion, but it's easy to forget again. The wedding, though. At the wedding she'll have a pretty ring on her finger and a fiancé she'll sneak away from the crowd to call. She'll tell her fiancé how much she misses her and that she wishes she could be here too.

6
Come Fly Away
by Frank Sinatra

I love flying. Everything about it. Airports, the flight attendants' outfits, the crowds, the whole floating metallic tube of recirculated farts and coughs we call a plane. All of it. I kind of wish I'd been alive back in the '50s at the heyday of commercial flight. Yes, there was rampant sexism and flight attendants were stewardesses and they were treated terribly. I know that. But there was something magical about it. People dressed to the nines, wore their Sunday best. Every trip was an adventure. Isn't it kinda sad how something that was so magical less than sixty years ago is a commonplace hassle today? Do all magic things eventually lose their sheen?

My bags are checked and I've got my laptop out while I wait here at the gate. The thing doesn't get much use except for when I watch Netflix in bed (because I don't have a decent TV in my room). However, it does have hundreds of wildly named Word documents I've decided to sort through. Some of them are papers from school about authors like Tennessee Williams and Virginia Woolf. Some are unidentifiable just from the name. For example, there are at least five documents with some iteration of Fuck This. I see a file that's named Novel Ideas. At the time it seemed like a clever play on words. Not only was it a collection of ideas for novels, but I deemed them novel. Get it? Let me know when you stop laughing. Another is just titled Sheep. What about sheep, Past Carly? What crackpot idea about sheep seemed so revolutionary that you were inspired to write it down? Lord, help me.

I hear the final boarding call for my flight and slip the laptop into my backpack. No one's left in line at the gate, so I quickly get my ticket scanned and make my way onto the plane. In case you were wondering, I'm an aisle girl. I feel like seat preference says a lot about who I am as a person, and I want to be one hundred percent transparent with you. After I'm settled, I take out my phone and shoot Annie a text with a whole lot of happy emojis. Annie loves emojis. I like them too, especially right now, because they let me pretend enthusiasm when in reality I'm beyond conflicted about this weekend. On the one hand, my oldest and bestest friend is getting married to a totally stellar dude who I adore. On the other hand, Mollie Fae is going to be there. The pendulum is swinging wildly between excitement and dread.

"Excuse me." There's a woman in the aisle looking at me. What's she doing here? I thought I was the last one to get on the plane. "I think we have the seats next to you."

"Oh, yeah, of course." I kick my backpack under the seat in front of me and stand up. So much for having a little extra room on this flight.

The woman smiles at me as she and her friend slide into the seats. Is it stereotyping if you're one of the group of people you're stereotyping about? Because on closer inspection I think I was wrong about them just bein' friends, if you catch my drift.

The one who's next to me leans over and says, "I like your shoes."

I look down as though I'd forgotten which shoes I had on. "Thank you. They're a little fancier than I'm used to. They're for a wedding, but I didn't want to pack them in my bag. You know how things can get scrunched." I trail off. "Sorry, that was way too much."

She laughs. "No worries. Whose wedding is it? That is, if you don't mind me asking."

I shake my head. "I don't mind at all. My best friend, Annie. We've been friends since forever."

"Aww, that's so sweet," the woman by the window says. She sticks her hand out to me. "I'm Alice and this is my fiancé, Martha, but you can call her Marty."

I shake both of their hands, smiling dumbly. "Carly. Wow, that's so exciting for you guys! When's the big day?"

"It will be in a few months," Alice says. "We don't have a date yet. I want to elope to France, but Marty over here keeps insisting that's not practical."

"I never said impractical," Marty says. "I'd just like some family to be there."

"Can you believe this girl? Family? At a wedding?" Alice smiles as she throws her arm around Marty. They lean into each other and suddenly my heart is very heavy.

"That seems like a reasonable request." I smile at the two of them.

"Thank you. I like you," Marty says.

We're quiet as the flight attendants go through the pre-flight safety instructions.

"Why are you guys heading to Chicago?" I break the comfortable silence.

"Dress fitting!" Alice squeals.

"You couldn't find a dress in L.A.?"

"We're not from L.A.," Alice says. "Well, I guess we are for the moment. We both work in the film industry, so we're from everywhere. In fact, we're going to be in Utah for the next few months for a movie."

"That's so cool." I don't want to be jealous, but if I'm honest, I am. Just a little. "But why Chicago?"

"Well," Alice sits up slowly.

"This is her favorite story," Marty laughs. "She thinks it's more fun to tell than the story of how we got engaged."

"Oh, hush," Alice says, placating Marty with a kiss on the cheek. "So it was three o'clock on a Tuesday morning. Marty was in Boston visiting her family. I was in L.A. because I was working on a movie. We were over budget and way past our deadline and we were working crazy hours every day. Anyway, I'd just gotten home and I was trying to wind down so I could get a little sleep before I had to be back at work for an early call. I had *House Hunters* on in the background and I was clicking through pages on the computer when I saw The Dress."

"THE DRESS," Marty emphasizes.

"It's perfect," Alice gushes. "I found it on Pinterest, which was terrible because most of the links on that website dead-end. I tried to reverse image search the picture and I wasn't getting anywhere. I was trying every possible search word combination. Finally, and I really do mean finally because by then it was almost six a.m., I found it. I found The Dress."

"THE DRESS," Marty adds again with a dramatic flourish, and I can't help but laugh.

"It's made by a little old lady who lives in Chicago. It seems she's something of a love guru. She only makes about ten dresses a year. But she has to interview you before she'll make a dress for you," Alice says.

"Interview you?" That sounds like a lot of work to me. And a little pretentious on the old lady's part.

"Yep," Alice continues. "I sent her all kinds of pictures of Marty and me through the years and told her how we met and fell in love. Then I heard nothing for weeks. Probably a month wouldn't you say, hon? It was incredibly stressful!"

Marty just nods in agreement.

"Then one day, out of the blue, I got an email from her. She included a phone number and asked me to call as soon as I could. We ended up talking for over two hours. She asked a million questions about Marty, me, and Marty and me together. Then, just when I was pretty sure I was going to run out of things to tell her, she asked when I wanted her to make the dress. Ta-da! Here we are!"

"Wow, all that just for a dress." This is so far from anything I would ever want to do. But Mollie Fae, I can see her asking for the lady's phone number. Maybe she already has it? That is not a road I should be going down. I push the thought out of my mind.

"That's what I said." Marty nods at me, like she knows I understand what she really thinks about all this.

Alice looks from me to Marty. "It's not *just* a dress."

"I know, I know, love," Marty says, and all signs of teasing instantly disappear. "It's going to be the best dress ever."

"Hell yeah it is," Alice says proudly.

"Well, we'll let you enjoy the rest of your flight," Marty says. "No one ever likes to be trapped on a plane next to strangers who won't stop talking to them."

"No, no," I say quickly. "I don't mind at all."

"Great," Alice says excitedly, and launches into another story.

I like them. A lot. They're sweet people and we spend the entire flight talking about anything and everything that comes to mind. They met in college and have been dating ever since. Marty walked into the wrong dorm room and Alice was there, lying on the floor listening to *Couldn't Get It Right* by Climax Blues Band. Marty said she knew she was going to marry her in that exact moment. Alice blushed a deep red and went on to say that she was sobbing about a test she was sure she'd just failed, but the second she saw Marty, she stopped crying.

"I was so embarrassed," Marty says, shuddering at the memory.

"You were embarrassed? I was crying on the floor of my dorm room to a song from the '70s," Alice says. "The '70s!"

"Okay, that might be worse," Marty agrees. "But I bought you pizza."

"You did," Alice says dreamily, then looks at me. "She said it was to apologize for walking in on me during a clearly turbulent time in my life, but I knew it was because she wanted to date me."

"If you knew, then why did you say no the first two times I asked you out? And why have you never told me this before?" Marty asks incredulously.

Alice shrugs. "You were so confident. I didn't want it to

be too easy for you."

"I can't believe I'm still dating you."

"You're marrying me," Alice corrects.

"You guys are cute," I say. I remember having this easy, comfortable feeling with Mollie Fae and that makes my stomach churn.

"What about you?" Marty finally asks the question I don't want to answer. Ever again. "Do you have a better half?"

"Is it, uh, too late to take you up on that no talking offer?"

"There's a story there!" Alice exclaims.

"Alice likes stories," Marty says with a sympathetic smile. "And you have nowhere to run."

"There's not much of a story." I try to act like that's the truth, but Alice looks at me, clearly not believing. "I'm serious! There's just an ex I haven't seen in forever coming to this wedding. It's not a story."

"Oh, no, that's a story if I've ever heard one." If the Fasten Seat Belts sign wasn't on, I believe Alice would be jumping up and down right now.

"Sorry, but I think she's right about this one," Marty says.

I sigh. "She's just this girl I dated for a long time. I thought I was going to marry her, but it didn't work out. She stayed friendly with Annie, my friend who's getting married, so that's why she'll be at the wedding. And she's not coming with her fiancé, she's coming solo."

"Tell me everything." Alice can barely contain herself, but in a nice way.

So I do. I tell her everything. I tell her the story of Mollie and me from the beginning to the bitter, bitter end. A story that even you guys don't know. Ha! Remember just pages ago when I said I was all for full transparency? Well, it turns out I'm a liar. Maybe later I'll fill you in. Maybe I won't. I am, what's the medical term for it? Ah, yes. Going Through It.

"And that's it," I say with a shrug. "She'll be there this weekend and it will be the first time we've seen each other since we broke up. It will also be the first time I'll see that stupid ring on her finger."

"Ladies and gentlemen, we are now beginning our final descent to Midway. Please fasten your seatbelts and return your tray tables to their upright and locked positions. Welcome to Chicago," the pilot says over the speaker.

"You should just get super drunk," Marty says. Alice slaps her arm. "Ow! What? I'm saying that's what I would do."

"That's my plan," I tell them. "And to avoid her. I don't know if I trust myself around her."

Alice narrows her eyes at me. "You're not over her."

I stammer a little, then give up without ever forming a full sentence.

"Maybe we should let Carly handle that on her own,"

45

Marty says quietly. She reaches over to hold Alice's hand and gives her a firm look.

"If you say so," Alice agrees.

"It's fine. I've accepted it." I haven't accepted it, but what else can I say?

We walk out of the plane together, and as we're about to go our separate ways in the terminal, Alice puts a hand on my arm.

"Wait," she says, and digs around for a moment in her large and messy purse. She pulls out a business card, flips it over, and scribbles on the back. "If you find yourself in Utah in the next few months, give us a call. If not, we'll find you when we're back in L.A."

I take the card with a smile. "Of course."

"It was nice to meet you." Marty offers her hand and I shake it.

"Likewise," I say. I extend my hand to Alice to say goodbye to her as well.

She looks at my hand and then at me. "What? No! Come here."

I'm pulled into a fierce hug that Marty finally has to pry me out of.

"Good luck," Marty says, picking up her bags. "With everything."

I nod. "Thanks. I think I'll need it."

7

Pony
by Ginuwine

Annie's loitering in the no parking zone. She's having a heated discussion with a parking enforcement person through her open passenger side window.

"Ha! See! I told you she'd be here." Annie points at me in triumph.

I smile faintly at the parking person and walk toward the trunk that Annie's popped open.

"Next time, you have to keep moving or park in the cell phone lot, ma'am," the parking person says.

"Oh, absolutely," Annie promises, smiling and pretending she means it.

I toss my bag into the trunk, throw my backpack on the back seat, and get in the front next to Annie.

"Carly, you're here!" Annie exclaims as she gives me a big hug. The side of my stomach presses firmly into the gear shift.

"You're here too!" I laugh into her shoulder.

There's a loud whistle just outside the car, and I turn to

see the parking enforcement person waving at us to get moving.

"Okay, okay!" Annie says, pulling away from me. "I get it, okay? I get it!"

"Come on, let's get out of here. I'm starving."

Annie shifts the car into drive. "Yes, let's get out of here and find some food."

I laugh as we pull away from the curb and head out of the airport. "Thank you for picking me up."

"Of course, you idiot," Annie says. "Tell me. How have you been?"

"It's only been a few days. Nothing has changed."

"I know, I'm just trying to gauge how you're doing." Annie sounds serious.

"Oh, I see, in terms of the Mollie Fae thing," I sigh.

"Yes, the Mollie Fae thing."

"I'm fine."

"You're fine?"

"I'm fine."

"Bullshit, Carly." Annie slaps her hand against the steering wheel. "Nothing in your life since the end of Mollie Fae has ever been fine."

"I don't know what you mean by that." I know exactly what she means by that.

"You guys were always at one hundred percent," she says. "There was no calm period. It was all in, all the time.

How it's supposed to be. And then she was gone."

"Well, it's all out now, so I don't know what to tell you." I shift a little in the seat. "Here's the thing, though. It's your wedding, so we should be talking about that. It's *your* time."

"You're avoiding talking about your feelings, but that's okay. I'll allow it since it is my freaking wedding weekend!" Annie says so, so happily. Seriously. It's the happiest I've heard anyone sound in a long time. Makes me want to bottle it up and sell it.

"So everything's good? No last-minute calamities?"

"No, but you'd better knock on wood because I don't want you to have just jinxed me. I'm not about to have a last-minute crisis," Annie says seriously.

I reach over and knock on her head. "I never understood why we knock on someone's head when we're supposed to be knocking on wood. Is it saying your head's hollow like wood? Wood isn't hollow though."

"I forgot how much fun you can be."

"Shut it." I shove Annie's shoulder.

"Do you have the bachelorette party all planned?" Annie raises an eyebrow.

"It's gonna be so great, you won't even know what to do with yourself. By the way, I'm really sorry I missed the rehearsal dinner."

She waves me off. "It's fine. You didn't miss anything important."

"No family fights?" I ask. "It all ran smoothly?"

"Well, I mean Todd's cousin Jason was drunk," Annie says.

"Belligerent?"

"Oh, god no. Todd's family isn't like that. You'd actually really like Jason."

"Why's that?"

"We found him drunk, crying in a bathroom about his college sweetheart. Seems he never confessed he was in love with her." Annie smiles sadly at me. "Seems on brand for you."

"Thank you very much. I'll be sure to steal a bottle of fine whiskey at your reception and hide in a bathroom after I get drunk to even things out. You know, someone from the groom's side, someone from the bride's side, crying in a bathroom about unrequited love."

"That would be the best wedding gift I could ask for," Annie laughs.

"Which reminds me," I say. I twist around to reach into the backpack on the back seat. "Boom. Happy wedding."

Annie looks at my outstretched hand. "You made me a mixtape, you total nerd?"

"You bet your ass I did. Did you think I was going to let my best friend in the whole entire world celebrate the most important day of her life without a bitchin' soundtrack?"

"First of all, 'bitchin'? Carly, your life is not *Clueless*. And second of all," Annie looks at me, a ridiculous smile spreading on her face, "did you make me a mixtape for my wedding night?"

"Oh, my god!" I exclaim, and frantically drop the CD. "Gross."

"You're gross," Annie giggles.

"Ugh, now you made something really nice into something sick."

"That's sweet," Annie says. "Put it in."

I reach down to pick up the CD. "You know, I could make a lovely joke about that in regard to your assumptions about this CD, but I'm a bigger person, so I'm willing to breeze past it."

"You are a martyr," Annie laughs.

"Anyway, I think you're really gonna dig it," I say, opening the case.

"Carly, if this is just a selection of Bruce Springsteen songs, I'm going to ask that you reconsider," Annie says.

"Just shush."

The one song from our childhood that was basically the anthem of our friendship was *Hey Juliet* by the one-hit wonder boy band LMNT. Guys, we even had a choreographed dance routine for this song. It was our song. So of course that's how I started the mix CD.

Annie makes us listen to *Hey Juliet* over and over, all the way into the city, because she hasn't heard it in forever.

We finally pull up to the hotel, music still blaring. As the valet approaches the car, I try to make sure Annie takes proper care of my gift to her.

"You'd better not leave the CD in your rental." I unclip my seatbelt and get out of the car.

"Oh, trust me, I'll guard this with my life," Annie says.

"Do I get to see Todd before the wedding?"

"Nope." Annie shakes her head. "You're in it with me. No Todd until tomorrow morning."

"How are you holding up without seeing him?" I ask, juggling my suitcase and backpack.

"It's not a big deal. We've been apart for longer. But," she fiddles with her keys, "it feels different this time."

I turn to look at her. "Like cold feet different?"

"No! Definitely not that," Annie says quickly. "I'm just anxious. No, I don't think that's the right word. What's the word for when you're just really excited for time to pass so you can get to the thing you really want to do?"

I smile at Annie. "That's called love."

"Stop being sappy." Annie blushes happily.

"It's called excited, stupid, youthful love." I throw my arms around her for a quick hug before we walk inside.

Annie waits in one of the comfy lobby chairs while I get checked in at the front desk. When I'm finished, I find Annie and we walk to the elevator.

"So," I say. "Are you ready for the bachelorette party?"

"Just tell me when and where," Annie says. "And what to dress for."

"Be in the lobby at six and wear something that goes with a life jacket." I walk out of the elevator when the door opens on my floor.

Annie sticks out her head and shouts at me. "A life jacket?"

"See ya later, Annie!"

****

I've never been to Chicago, Annie has never been to Chicago, and none of her bridesmaids have ever been to Chicago. No one could make any suggestions about where to go for the bachelorette party, so I felt pretty lost in this whole planning thing. There was talk of doing a bachelorette party before the wedding in Vegas, but we couldn't get schedules lined up. Annie took that pretty hard (we all know how much the girl loves *Magic Mike*). She was ready to see that show. *Magic Mike* is her rainy day movie. Her *Sleepless in Seattle*, if you will. But, alas, it just wasn't in the cards, so here we are. On a Duffy boat on the Chicago River.

"Carly, I just really wanna say thanks, y'know?" Annie slurs.

Everyone is drinking except me. Mostly because the place I rented this boat from allows alcohol on board as long as there's a designated driver. I decided to be the bigger person and act as the designated driver out of the goodness of my heart. Also, though, I bought a captain's hat on Amazon three months ago, and I look really good in hats, guys. This is my one chance to play captain dress-up while captaining a real boat, so I'm graciously taking one for the team.

"Aw, you're welcome, Annie. Are you having fun?"

"Oh my god. Just the best time. And I'm not seasick, but Todd's cousin is puking. Poor girl," Annie says.

I look around, and sure enough, there's Todd's cousin Rachel puking off the stern. The captain would call it the stern, you know.

"It's about time to turn around, but it looks like we might have trouble coming our way." I nod in the direction of a police boat heading toward us.

"The fuzz!" Annie shrieks.

I laugh. "The fuzz, Annie?"

"Be cool! Be cool!" Annie shouts to everyone.

I can't help but laugh as they all start frantically running around the boat. Honestly, drunk people trying to act calm and not drunk is one of my favorite things in the world. They look like ants when you put a stick in their nest.

I'm sure a lot of you are probably like, Carly, how can you act so chill when a police boat is coming your way?

Well, dear reader, that police boat is really just a regular boat with fake police lights I purchased on Amazon when I bought my captain's hat. And that fake police boat is really just a boat full of male strippers I hired. As the saying goes, if you can't take the girl to *Magic Mike Live* in Las Vegas, you take *Magic Mike Live* to the girl in Chicago.

"Prepare to be boarded!" As a man's voice booms over a megaphone, I press play on a boombox and the opening notes of *Pony* come over the boat's sound system.

****

I'll spare you the details of what transpired next, but I will say that I now believe Annie's okay we didn't end up going to Vegas. Judging by the amount of glitter that sparkles on her face as we walk into the hotel lobby hours later, I think she had a good time.

"Come on, kid, we've gotta shower that glitter off," I say, wrapping an arm around her waist to steady her as we wait for the elevator.

"I love you." She nuzzles her head into my neck.

"I love you, too, Annie. I don't love how much glitter you probably just got on my neck though."

She looks at me playfully. "You want more glitter?" Before I can react, she wipes her hands on her face and smears glitter onto mine.

"Annie!"

The elevator door opens and Todd steps out with his cousin Jason.

"Ah! My eyes!" Annie yells and slaps a hand over her face so she can't see Todd.

"I'm not supposed to see you yet!" Todd yells, closing his eyes quickly and throwing a hand over his face.

"Come here, Todd," I say, guiding him into a one-arm hug while Annie hangs onto the other side of me.

"Carly, it's been too long!" Todd hugs me tightly, eyes still squeezed shut.

I love Todd. He's like Captain America or Superman. He's unwavering in his beliefs and he's just very simple. Not like closed-minded simple, but if he was a color, he'd be a primary one. Do you know what I mean? He's just a *good* guy. All around, true-blue, great guy. If I found out his name was actually Clark Kent and Todd Glass was just an alter ego to his alter ego, I wouldn't be shocked at all.

"You guys are holding hands behind my back, aren't you?" I ask.

"Of course not." Todd.

"Yes." Annie.

"Alright, almost newlyweds, let's go." I push them apart. "Cousin Jason, please collect your responsibility."

Jason laughs and grabs Todd by the arm. "Got him."

"Where are you guys headed this late?" I ask them.

"Midnight Madness," Todd tells us, one hand still over

his eyes.

"Midnight Madness?" Annie repeats.

"I found an arthouse theatre downtown that's playing a double feature of *Frankenstein* and *The Bride of Frankenstein*," Jason says. "Todd here nearly peed himself with excitement."

"No I didn't!" Todd protests.

"Seems like something you'd almost pee yourself over," I say.

"We'll go with them!" Annie proclaims happily.

"You guys are covering your eyes because you don't want to see each other the night before your wedding, but you want to sit in a movie theatre for four hours together?" I raise an eyebrow.

"It'll be dark," Todd offers.

"Annie, you hate horror movies," Jason reminds her.

"Not super old ones," Todd says.

"That's true," Annie agrees. "Those aren't scary."

I look at Jason and we both know we've lost this one. He gives me a defeated shrug.

"Fine," I say, and Annie and Todd both smile widely. "But! But you guys can't sit next to each other."

The two of them start pouting at the exact same time.

"Good god, you two are like looking in a mirror," Jason says.

"We can sit next each other. We'll be in the dark. I won't

even be able to see him anyway," Annie says.

"Yeah, we won't be able to see each other." Todd starts nodding furiously.

"You're sure you want to include your wife in your bachelor party?" Jason asks.

"This is your bachelor party?" I guess I shouldn't be surprised.

Todd nods. "I didn't want to do anything too wild. What did you guys do?"

"Nothing." Me.

"Got drunk on the Chicago River with strippers." Annie.

"Just like *Magic Mike!*" Todd smiles. "That's what you wanted!"

I think there are a lot of ways to be sure two people are right for each other. Sometimes it's that person knowing your coffee order, or always picking you up at the airport with a cute sign, or the way they make you soup when you're sick before you even know you're sick. And I'm sure Todd and Annie can check all of those boxes, but I've never been more confident in their destiny than at this moment, when Todd is genuinely happy that his soon-to-be-wife-in-less-than-twelve-hours got to have her *Magic Mike* moment on a boat on the Chicago River.

Which is why Jason and I throw wedding tradition out the window and take those idiots to a cute artsy theatre in the heart of downtown Chicago at midnight to watch terrible horror movies from the thirties. It's why when we see them wrapped up in each other, sharing popcorn and Junior Mints, we don't say anything. Neither of us has the heart to tear them apart.

The Power of Love
by Huey Lewis & The News

"Let me look at you, superstar," I say, leaning against the wall of Annie's room.

"Is it okay? Do I look ridiculous? Is this all ridiculous?" Annie's excited, but not stressed out.

She turns around and my eyes tear up instantly. Annie looks beautiful, grown-up, and elegant, and it's all too much.

"Annie, when did you get to be an adult? You didn't even have the decency to warn me," I whisper.

"Speak for yourself." Annie walks over to me and straightens my tie, then grabs my elbows. "You look great."

I tug her around to face the mirror. "We've certainly come a long way." I bump her hip with mine. "And you've got a little bit longer to go today."

"I'm not scared. Am I supposed to be scared? My feet are so far from cold. It's like they're in an inferno."

I smile. "No, I think you're doing it right. I'm pretty sure you're feeling the way you're supposed to."

"Good." She lets out a deep, deep sigh.

"What's the plan now?" I ask.

"Um, I walk down the aisle." She turns to look at me. "Are you really this clueless about weddings?"

"Of course not. I meant, have you guys talked about kids?"

"Oh, yeah, there are some babies down at the baby farm we've been talking about harvesting," Annie replies.

I narrow my eyes at her. "That didn't sound jokey enough to entirely be a lie."

She moves toward me quickly and places a finger on my lips. "You can't tell anyone!"

"Annie!" I exclaim, my voice only slightly muffled by her finger still on my mouth. I swat it away. "Are you serious?"

She nods. "Serious."

"But you were drinking last night!" I say, eyes widening.

She shrugs. "I was pretending. Nobody knows yet, so all my screwdrivers were one hundred percent orange juice."

"That explains how quickly you sobered up in the hotel lobby."

She just smiles some more and shrugs bashfully.

"You're naming the kid after me, right?"

"Of course," Annie replies earnestly. "Even if the kid's a boy."

"Well, gender's fake, so don't worry about that," I tell her, "but how long have you known?"

"A couple of weeks. Not very long. It all just happened

so fast. I mean, we were trying, but y'know, you hear all these stories about people trying for *ages* and we both just assumed it would be like that and it was decidedly not like that at all."

"I can't believe I'm going to be an aunt," I say, wiping a tear away. "I've always wanted to be an aunt to a kid and confuse the shit out of it when it learns the true definition of an aunt."

"A godmother, if you'd like."

"Dude," I breathe out. "I'd be honored." I wrap her up in a hug. "I'm already picturing all the Bruce Springsteen onesies I'm gonna buy this kid."

Annie laughs and sniffles a little. "Do they even make Bruce Springsteen onesies?"

"Etsy," I say. "Everything's on Etsy."

The wedding planner peeks his head into the room and clears his throat. "Excuse me, Annie."

Annie pulls away from me and dabs at her eyes with a tissue. "Yes."

He points to his clipboard authoritatively. "We're two minutes behind schedule. Are you ready?"

Annie looks at him, then me, and says, "You bet your ass I'm ready."

"Annie!" I gasp. "We're in a church!"

"Worse things have been done in churches, Carly, let me tell you."

I roll my eyes and hold my hand out toward her. "Shall

we?"

Annie closes her eyes and lets out a deep breath. Then she moves forward with a smile and a small nod.

The ceremony's perfect. It's all just so perfect that I forget Mollie Fae is somewhere out there in a pew. That was nice, and probably the first time since we've broken up that I've been able to let my mind truly forget about her. It's been so easy because Annie and Todd are the absolute sweetest. Todd's sweaty, shaky hands make him drop the ring no less than three times, and Annie looks at him like he's the only person in the entire universe. They look at each other that way. My tissue is soaked through by the time they finally say I do, and the cheers are roaring when they finally kiss.

That's how it should be. Every single person who's ever known you should be that ecstatic when you get married. There shouldn't be a sliver of doubt in anyone's mind.

Yes, I'm talking about Mollie Fae's wedding in thinly veiled, broad, generalized statements.

No, I'm not ashamed.

****

I end up driving Annie's and Todd's grandparents to the reception in Annie's rental car. They're quite the chatty bunch. Apparently, *24* is very popular with the over seventy crowd and they're swapping plot theories and character development despite the fact that this show has been off the air for years. Color me one hundred percent surprised.

The reception is being held at this big venue just south of downtown. It's got the vibe of a country club, but I think it's just an event space. Annie told me what it's called, but I forgot. It's right along the shore and there's a deck that's covered with twinkling lights. From that deck, you can see all of Chicago, and let me tell you, it's one beautiful city all lit up at night.

The grandparents climb slowly out of the car when I park, giving me sloppy cheek kisses for being so kind as to drive them over. Their words, not mine. It's not like I had a choice. They just kind of started getting into my, technically Annie's, rental. I let them go ahead of me and take my time walking into the building. And no, it's not because a huge wave of people have just arrived and I want them to go in ahead of me in case Mollie's a part of it.

Okay, it's exactly that.

I enter through a door that's on the other side of the parking lot and meander down hallways and peek into empty rooms, trying to kill time and miss most of the appetizer hour. Thankfully, we took all the wedding party photos before the ceremony, so I don't have anywhere to be right now. However, Annie did pick terrible appetizers. I tried to tell her no one wants to eat escargot and frog legs, but she did not listen to me. You could argue that it's her wedding so she calls the shots, but also, she needs to listen to the opinion of her maid of honor.

"It's been a while, hasn't it?" I hear a voice say behind me. It's a voice I don't need to think about remembering. I know it. It's clear as day. I turn around to face the music.

Mollie Fae looks fabulous. Color me absolutely unsurprised. She's wearing a light purple dress, and the sleeves of her worn leather jacket are pushed up to her elbows. Her hair is down and lands just above her shoulders. She looks elegant and casual and beautiful. It's enough to take anyone's breath away, and here she is, standing right in front of me. There's no ignoring her even if I wanted to, and I certainly don't want to. If only she'd had the decency to look not so perfect. It might make this all a little easier on me.

"It has definitely been a while," I say, walking toward her.

Her smile is small. She reaches out, squeezes my forearm, and says, "It's so good to see you."

"Yeah, yeah, it is. It's good to see you, too. Last I heard you, uh, weren't going to make it."

"Plans changed. I wanted to be here for Annie and Todd. They've been good friends for a long time," she says.

"Annie really is a great friend. The best. A fantastic friend. We've known each other since forever. I love her." What am I even babbling about?

Mollie looks at me oddly. "Did you guys ever…y'know?"

65

"Oh my god! No! She's like my sister. Why would you even ask that?"

"Okay, okay," she says, holding her hands up. "I'm sorry, I had to ask."

"We dated for seven years. Why didn't you ever ask then?"

"I didn't want to know if you were secretly in love with your best friend while we were dating. That would've put a damper on things."

"That is such a terrible concept. I'll never get over it," I say, letting myself laugh a little. "I can't wait to tell Annie that for all these years you thought I was secretly in love with her. Did you think Annie was secretly in love with me too?"

"If she was, I wouldn't have blamed her," she answers quietly. I don't think I was supposed to hear those words, and judging by the look on her face, she wasn't planning on letting that runaway thought come tumbling out of her mouth either.

I swallow deeply, trying to get my brain to refocus. "So, ah, what about you? What have you been doing?"

She stands a little straighter. "Saving the world, of course."

"If anyone could do it, it would be you. I guess the Mollie Fae in the article I read about upholding the Clean Air Act was, in fact, you."

She shrugs. "That's me."

"You really are saving the world. My future children thank you."

She laughs. "Do these future children have names?"

"Of course. Like any good hypothetical children, they're named something completely insufferable."

"What? Like Mia and Sebastian?"

"Even worse. Mint and Julep."

"Oh my god," she giggles. "I'm going to call Child Protective Services. Those are horrendous names for kids."

I laugh with her. It's so easy to just be around her again. To be the Carly Allen she knew and once loved. "Could you imagine? I mean, Julep is kind of cute, but Mint is just a whole other level."

It should feel like something's changed, right? Like we shouldn't fall back into our old selves so quickly. We should be awkward around each other, stumbling, tripping over words. One of us should be making some flimsy excuse about why we have to leave this conversation. Instead, I feel like time hasn't moved since we last saw each other. That maybe our final fights never happened, and everything could go back to how it was. And then she brushes her hair out of her face and my eyes instantly focus on her engagement ring.

"Well, that's certainly new," I say.

She clears her throat and nervously twists the ring. "Oh, yeah. It is. We're getting married this Christmas."

"Congratulations." I try not to grimace.

"You don't have to say that."

"I did, though, so—" I trail off.

"Thank you."

"Of course," I say. "So, uh, what're they like?"

"Who?"

"Your fiancé."

"Oh, Jessie. She's a social worker. Right now she's working for a non-profit that works to open schools for girls around the world."

"Okay, but what's she like as a person? You know, does she eat crunchy or creamy peanut butter, does she eat pineapple on her pizza, what band is *her* band, who did she want Rory to end up with on *Gilmore Girls?* The essentials. The stuff you've got to know before you get hitched."

She shuffles, her eyes darting. "I'm not sure about the peanut butter or the pineapple and she doesn't listen to much music."

"Wait. Wait just a second. What do you mean she doesn't listen to a lot of music? What does she do on the subway or on airplanes?"

"She reads, mostly."

"Okay, yeah, so do I, but that's what you have a reading playlist for."

"I know what you're doing, Carly," she says, lowering her voice.

"I'm not doing anything."

"Not everyone listens to music all the time. That doesn't affect who they are as a person."

"I just figured you'd end up with someone who loves music as much as you do," I say, shrugging.

"Someone like you, you mean?" She squares her stance.

"That's not what I'm saying," I shoot back.

So much for feeling like our last fight never happened.

"What then? What are you saying?"

"I just want to know. You know I love talking about music. Are you guys even going to have music at your wedding?"

"We're having a string quartet," she says, bristling.

"What about your first dance?"

"A classical song."

I laugh.

"What?"

"It's just a shame. There are so many good songs and you're going to dance to some classical composition you probably don't even like."

"Do you have a better suggestion?"

"Okay, well, I mean, *Moon River* for starters. I've always pictured *Moon River* at my wedding. *Can't Help Falling in Love*, *Faithfully*, *(I've Had) The Time of My Life*, *Leather and Lace*, *If I Should Fall Behind*, *I Got You Babe*, *The Longest Time*," I say, ticking them off on my fingers. "There are so many and you're going to pick a classical song?"

"You've given this a lot of thought?" Mollie asks, her tone instantly sweeter, timid, unsure.

"Yes," I answer. My voice, for the first time I can ever remember, refuses to waver.

We hear footsteps, and then Todd and Annie round the corner, laughing, holding on tightly to each other.

"Oh, hey guys!" Annie calls.

"Hey!" I smile. "Great ceremony."

"And the party hasn't even started yet!" Annie exclaims. "Open bar!"

Mollie laughs at her unbridled enthusiasm. "I should probably go find my seat. Carly, it really was good to see you."

"Yeah," I say wistfully. "It truly was."

When Mollie disappears, Annie looks at me. "What was that about?"

"Later." I don't want to talk about it. "You guys just got married! Let's go celebrate!"

"I hope you're ready to dance," Todd says.

"No, but that's never stopped me before." I smile and turn to walk with them to the reception.

9

Dancing on My Own
by Robyn

I can see Mollie Fae clearly from where I'm sitting. She's tucking a strand of hair behind her ear and listening intently to something Annie's grandmother is saying. I miss that about Mollie. She would look at you, almost a little too intensely, when you told her a story. Even if you rambled on about something that disgusted or disinterested her, she listened like you were the universe spilling all of your secrets to her. Unwavering. It was unnerving to have someone look at you like that. I would always try to get her to crack, to take away some of the weight, but no luck. One time, I talked for ten minutes about topsoil and she still looked at me like what I was saying was going to change the world. No one has looked at me like that since.

Speaking of my impending spinsterdom, I don't think I'll ever be able to get over Mollie's engagement. Her hand is propping up her head when she nods, and the light catches her ring. It's a nice ring that suits her perfectly. Probably non-conflict diamonds or even cubic zirconia set in eco-friendly recycled metal, because that's just who she is.

You know, and I can't believe I'm about to tell you this because I've never told anyone, not even Annie, I bought her a ring once. I was very drunk. I had to put it on two credit cards, but it showed up in five to seven business days as promised. It was a behemoth. The kind of ring you see on the latest Hollywood celebrity's finger on the cover of *US Weekly* while you're checking out at the grocery store and gasp and think "Who in their right mind would buy that?" Well, as it turns out, drunk me is very much the type of person who would buy that. I kept it for 29 days, one day before the return policy ended. I didn't send it back because I'd changed my mind or anything like that. I just knew Mollie didn't need a massive ring.

Technically, I proposed back then. It was earlier on the night I drunkenly ordered the ring.

****

I was visiting Mollie in San Francisco during our senior year and we'd just been to an art gallery opening. Mollie's the kind of person who has friends who open art galleries. I have friends who play strip Settlers of Catan. Most of my time at the gallery was spent at the wine and cheese table, but every now and then Mollie would appear and pull me along to look at some of the paintings. I was in that drunken state where I was impressed by everything. I don't know if this is a normal drunken state for everyone, but it is for me. I get overwhelmed by the world. I was awestruck by the colors and the lights and the walls and just life itself.

"I mean, Mollie, oh my, can you believe we're standing in a building? Like someone built this and here we are, just standing inside it. Why isn't anyone impressed by this? We're looking at weird scribbles on a piece of canvas called Untitled #47, but why doesn't anyone care that we are inside of a *building?*" I knew I was a little over the top, but I couldn't help waving my arms (and my drink) around. I've been known to be a little hyperbolic in my day.

"People have been in buildings before, Carly. You included," she said, straightening the collar of my shirt, a smile tugging at her lips.

I exhaled dramatically. "This is just so far out."

She looked at me sweetly. "Wanna get out of here, superstar? Before your head explodes?"

"Mmmhmm," I said, and kissed her quickly. "Yes, please."

Mollie made the rounds and said goodbye to all her friends while I retrieved our coats.

"Ready?" I asked when she came back to me. She nodded. I helped her into her coat and we headed out the door.

I remember that it was cold, probably late in the fall. We

were bundled up, loosely holding onto each other and aimlessly letting our shoulders bump together as we walked. I also remember getting a déjà vu feeling about the whole night. It's such a weird thing, to feel like you're getting a glimpse of a chapter of the book of your life that's happening right now, yet maybe already happened, yet may not have happened yet. For a fleeting moment I saw future Carly Allen and future Mollie Fae walking down a city street, shoulders still amiably bumping along. Nothing changed. Just us, except a little older and a little wiser.

Yes, I know I'd had a lot to drink on a fairly empty stomach, but I still think I would've felt it stone cold sober.

I know I would've.

"Which one was your favorite?" Mollie asked.

"You," I said, staring at her, moonstruck.

"I meant the artwork." She laughed and gave me a little nudge.

"Hmm." I pretended to be deep in thought. "Still you."

She shook her head. "I forgot how sappy you get when you drink."

"You know you love it," I said in a sing-song voice.

"You should come with a high-fructose corn syrup warning," Mollie said, shaking her head with a smile.

"Good thing diabetes doesn't run in your family."

"And why is that?" she asked.

"Well, duh, I'm gonna marry you someday."

Mollie stopped dead in her tracks and looked at me. I'm sure I had the dopiest look on my face. Obviously, I hadn't given a lot of thought to the words I'd just said. I meant them though. That I'm sure of. I mean it, present tense. I'd mean it if I walked up to her today and dropped to my knees.

There was magic in that moment; in the simplicity of two fools in love taking a walk on a city sidewalk when the air is brisk and their breath dances like fog between them. Magic. I remember feeling it in my bones the way old people feel rain in their kneecaps. I could feel the certainty of a future with Mollie. There's something so beautiful about the beginning of the rest of your life when it's all wide and sprawling and laid out for the taking. The pile of kindling just waiting for the match. Long before you know whether the fire will keep you warm or burn you both to the ground.

"What did you just say?" Mollie whispered.

"I said I'd marry you. Someday. Soon, I hope. If you'll let me. Because I want to. If you'd want to," I ramble.

She pulled my beanie a little farther down on my head and caught her bottom lip between her teeth. No doubt she was weighing the heaviness of my drunken ramblings. "I think you should definitely ask me again. Later. When you're a little more sober." Then she kissed me quickly and tried to pull me along to continue our walk, but I wasn't budging.

"How about now?" I raised my voice and dropped to my knees. "Mollie Fae, I want to marry you someday! How's that sound?"

I could see her smile, brighter than the streetlights and the full moon and all of the stars. Both of us were beaming like fools. She walked back to me and dropped to her knees too. Two love-drunk idiots kneeling on a dirty San Francisco sidewalk.

"Come here, sweetheart," she said, and pulled me closer by the collar of my coat.

The few passersby not pissed off at having to maneuver around our little spectacle clapped a bit and went on their way. I rested my forehead against hers.

I looked at her, slightly cross-eyed because of the proximity and just from being in Mollie Fae's orbit. "Someday?"

She nodded earnestly. "Someday."

****

Sitting here now at Annie and Todd's wedding, I can't help but feel a terrible sadness that our someday will never come. If I'd proposed with the ring I'd bought that night, would we have broken up? Was a break-up the inevitable "someday" for us, not a wedding? Who's to say? All I can be certain of now is that Mollie Fae is going to get her someday wedding and I'm going to get to be all alone, thousands of miles away.

"Carly, hey, it's time for your speech."

My legs are woozy as I stand up and walk to the microphone. There's scattered applause, but it sounds muted in my ears. It's like the whole world is disappearing and all that's left, all that matters, all that my eyes can focus on, is Mollie Fae.

The microphone screeches a little as I stumble into it. "Um, hello, everyone. How're you doing tonight?" Everybody cheers and I smile a little. "First, I have to thank Annie and Todd for getting married here tonight. If they weren't, I'd be drinking whiskey alone in my apartment, but it's so much nicer to be drinking whiskey with all of you people."

My eyes focus on Mollie Fae again and I lose my train of thought. She's looking at me the way she used to, and the planned speech, carefully written on notecards, is quickly forgotten in my jacket pocket. I take a deep breath.

"Everything I know about love, I learned from '80s music. Yeah, you guys can laugh, but that's the most romantic musical era. You could be as sappy and saccharine as you wanted and you could still be a total rock star. No one saw love and romance as something dirty or weak. Take Aerosmith. No one thinks of Aerosmith and is like, that's some pop nonsense band. But have you guys ever actually listened to *I Don't Want to Miss a Thing?* Or The Police, *Every Little Thing She Does Is Magic?* Van Halen, *Why Can't This Be*

Love? That's pure romance. The unapologetic romance of hair bands." I laugh a little and run my hand through my hair. Annie and Todd are laughing and leaning into each other.

Now, I don't think of myself as a jealous person. I've got a roof over my head, a moderately well-paying job, good health. All the things that add up to what's generally considered a good life. As I look at Annie and Todd, though, I feel what I think might be jealousy. I feel jealous of their beginning, of their absolute comfort in each. They're teammates, and now they're going to have a built-in best friend forever.

You shouldn't be surprised at this point to know that my gaze has wandered back to Mollie Fae. My heart is pounding against my ribs and my breath catches in my throat. My arms are covered in goosebumps. I feel exhausted, like my heart has run a marathon. When I look at her, I still see my teammate. I still see her as the one for me, and I just wish there was a switch I could flip to turn off this feeling. To suddenly be able to forget her. But even thinking that I would maybe want to forget her, I know I never, ever could and I would never, ever want to. I look right at her and my heart takes over.

"The point is, I believe in love because I believe in '80s music. When you look at the one you love, you should feel like you're in an '80s music video. The world stops turning and the lights dim, except for a spotlight on that one special person. Your breath catches and they're all you know. The world doesn't exist beyond them. They're it. Forever, for now, for always. You can't fight it. You just can't. No outcome is possible other than the two of you spending the rest of your lives together."

And with that, my brain is gone. Catapulted back to every memory of Mollie Fae and me. The day we met again at Cameron's party, the cake, the mixtape that's stuck in my cassette player, the nights we spent cuddled on twin beds in dorm rooms, the days driving through forests and deserts, nights that ended with her, mornings that began with her, and it just doesn't seem fair. It doesn't seem fair at all. When a lead singer leaves a band, the replacement is never as good. The original magic is gone and you're left with a good backbone, but it's never really right again.

I can't help but feel like that's what's going on here. While I've never thought of Mollie and me as the equivalent of an '80s hair band, losing her to someone else feels a lot like all that's left are the D-list members of the band. That's where I am. I'm a D-list, bottom-of-the-barrel band replacement; a second-rate cover band without her.

"I don't have to ask Annie and Todd if that's the way they feel because it so clearly is. They look at each other the same way they did when we were eighteen in Mr. Hall's English class. Nothing's changed. Nothing will ever change. Annie has been my best friend since we were in kindergarten and she was still in diapers. You can't be mad at me, Annie. You knew that was coming. But here's to you guys, Annie and Todd. You're living the best real-life '80s music video ever. And here's to young love; yours, mine, and ours. I love you guys."

****

For a while, I get to lose track of Mollie Fae. I'm busy with the open bar, eating dinner, and helping Annie go to the bathroom in her ginormous dress. It's a good thing I have the distractions, too. The way things were progressing with Mollie, I'm sure I would've said something stupid.

"You and Mollie seemed quite chummy after all these years," Annie says from the bathroom stall.

"I told you, I'm not talking to you while you're peeing." I lean against the sink.

"Do you hear any peeing?" Annie shoots back.

"No, but I know you're about to," I answer.

"What if I was taking a shit? Does that change things?"

"You're a married woman still making poop jokes. You haven't grown up in the slightest."

I hear a blissful sigh. "I'm a married woman."

"You sure are. I honestly can't believe it."

"Me neither," she says.

"Are you actually going to pee or did you just make me

shove you into that stall for fun?"

"No, I'm going to pee. You're giving me stage fright."

"Fine, how can I give you less stage fright?"

"Tell me about Mollie."

"Your bladder does not give two shits about Mollie. Don't even pretend."

"Please," Annie drags out. "It's *my* day. Just turn on the tap and let the water run for a second."

I'm a couple drinks in and I just saw the love of my life for the first time in three years. My arm doesn't need to be twisted too hard. I turn on the faucet.

"She looked beautiful," I say. "I knew she would, because when doesn't she? It's not in her gene pool to look anything less than perfect. I honestly think my heart stopped beating when I saw her. I hope she's happy. Kind of. Not really, I guess. I mean, I want her to be happy, but I want her to be happy with me. Is that too much to ask?"

The sound of the toilet flushing snaps me out of my rambling. "Oh, my god, I said all of that out loud. I must sound insane to you."

The stall door slowly creaks open and Annie hobbles out, holding her massive sparkly skirt up to her chest. "You sound pretty damn hopeless."

"Annie!" I yell. I wet my hand under the faucet and flick some water in her face.

"Carly! My makeup!"

I turn off the water and shrug. "Oops."

She walks over to stand at the sink next to me. "Oops, my ass."

"Do you think I'm pathetic?" I ask.

"I wouldn't say pathetic," she begins, and I grimace. "Hey, I'm not done yet. Romantic, yes, but pathetic, I don't know. You have to know when to give in, though. I don't want you to tear yourself up about this until the day you die. You have to know when to move on."

"You think I should move on?"

"I don't want to say yes," she sighs. "But, Carly, she's getting married. Like really married. To a nice girl. She's happy, and I just want you to be happy too."

I nod, trying not to let the tears out of my eyes. "Yeah, yeah, you're totally right," I say meekly, then turn away from her. "You should head back out there. I'm just gonna finish up in here."

"Carly," she starts.

"No, no, I'm fine," I say. The last thing I want to do is put a damper on her day. "Go celebrate."

Annie looks at me sadly. "If you're not out in five minutes, I'll send my grandmother in here, and we both know you don't want that."

I watch her leave, and then I see the first tear hit the white ceramic. The tears keep coming and coming, a steady stream that seems like it could fill the sink. I don't know if

I've cried this much in a very long time.

Remember long ago when we started this journey together and I said I didn't think of myself as a sad person? The joke's on me because I *am* sad. God, even saying that sounds like a joke. Sad sounds like I'm a child who doesn't know how to process her emotions and just found out she's not getting dessert after dinner tonight. Sad doesn't even begin to cover what I'm feeling. I'm angry because I had this great girl in my life who gave a damn and was rooting for me. And I pissed that away because I'm selfish. Selfishly sad.

I look at myself in the mirror. There are bags under my eyes, a raggedness I can't shake that's been etched on my face for three years. Annie said I need to know when to give in. Is this the moment? Am I done for? Stick a fork in me, I'm burnt. A shell of the kid I used to be. I splash some water on my face. Unsurprisingly, it does next to nothing.

You know that movie, *The Adventures of Rocky and Bullwinkle?* With the blonde lady from that gay wedding movie and the animated Rocky and Bullwinkle show I can't remember the name of? There's that part where you see her younger self in her eyes, trying to cause enough of a ruckus to be remembered, to be heard. That's how I feel right now. Like there's a little eighteen-year-old version of me banging on my brain, trying to get me to give a damn.

And I want to hear her, I really do. It's just that everything else is so loud.

10

We've Got Tonight by Bob Seger and the Silver Bullet Band

The reception's winding down. Annie and Todd have already made their great escape and the hall is virtually empty. There are still a few kids whirling around, balanced on their parents' toes. Todd's grandparents sway with a walker between them. Out in the hallway, far away from my place at the wedding party table, I see Mollie pacing back and forth with a phone pressed to her ear. I know who's on the other end of the line. Todd's cousin takes a seat next to me.

"Hey, Carly," he says.

"Hey, Jason. Enjoy the wedding?"

"Yeah, it was a good time. Nice people," he says, whispering.

"Why are you whispering?" I ask.

He shrugs. "I don't want to disturb anyone."

"There are only fifteen people left. Annie and Todd aren't even here," I say.

"I know," he says, then looks at me. "You should ask her

to dance."

"Who?"

"My four-year-old cousin," he deadpans. "Who do you think?"

"You see her back there? On the phone?" I point to the hallway. "That's her fiancé she's talking to. I'll bet you anything."

"Ouch."

"Tell me about it," I sigh.

"Still, you should ask her to dance," he says. "No harm in a little dancing."

I look at Mollie again and she's pacing in a circle. When she twists around, her eyes meet mine, and for a second it feels like everything could be different. God, no, stop it, Carly. You lost. You fucked up and that's it. For real. There's no Hail Mary or anything else this time around. There's an engagement ring and the final bell's already been rung. You have no right anymore. Not a chance in hell.

"Think about it, kid." He slaps my shoulder as he stands up.

I get up a few minutes after Jason leaves. Before I can think about what I'm doing, I grab a bottle of Champagne and rush out of the reception hall to the deck, right past Mollie Fae and her phone fiancé.

It's gusty out here and more than a little chilly. I put my fingers just below the cork in the bottle. I'm about to pop it open when I hear someone shout behind me.

"Don't shoot!"

For a girl with a fiancé, Mollie's talking to me, her ex-girlfriend, a hell of a lot.

"I won't hit you. Don't worry," I say, lowering the bottle She's got her hands up and a smile on her face. Hair waving in the wind.

"Mind if I join you?"

I shrug. "It might give me a chance to apologize for earlier."

"It's fine. Weddings make everyone feel weird. We're good."

"Great, because I don't think I can drink all this alone. I mean, I can, but I really shouldn't," I say, turning my back to her.

I pop the cork and it lands somewhere off toward the end of the deck. The foam pours out and onto my hands and pants. I'm briefly concerned about whether or not Champagne will stain when Mollie reaches around me and grabs the bottle. She takes a long sip.

"Hey! That's not fair! And your mouth touched it."

She laughs and a little bit sputters out. "You know we've shared drinks before, right? You know we've kissed, too? I mean, we dated for seven years. That wasn't just some mutual fever dream. It happened."

"Yeah," I say, stealing the bottle back, "but it was

different. We were dating then."

"Semantics," she says, eyes glistening.

Mollie's looking at me in a way that makes me want to kiss her. And I'm feeling a little angry about the fact that I can't simply kiss her whenever I want to. You would think in the three years since we broke up, I would've moved on and gotten over the fact that I can't just kiss her. I mean, I have, and we all know that, but now, now is different. Now is proximity. Now is her windswept hair, her pretty eyes, and her Champagne lips. I feel like I don't know anything at all.

"So, are you flying out tomorrow morning?" I ask, then take a big drink.

"Evening," she says. "Why? Do you have big plans?"

"I do, actually, and if I tell you what they are, you're going to think I'm a nerd," I say, feeling just the tiniest bit foolish.

"I already think that." Mollie steals the bottle back. After a sip, she continues. "Have you forgotten I've seen your super-secret comic book collection?"

"Come on, don't expose me like that."

"I'll tell the whole world if I damn well please." All of a sudden, she runs to the end of the deck and leans over the railing toward the city. "Hey, Chicago! Carly Allen's a giant nerd!"

I run and stand right next to her. "Hey, Chicago! Mollie Fae's an even bigger nerd!"

"You've got no proof." She moves a little closer to me

and turns her back to the city, leaning against the guardrail. "So what's this big nerdy thing you're ashamed of?"

I sigh dramatically and lean down to let my head rest on the railing. "I'm going to a place called Hot Doug's to eat a hot dog named after Anna Kendrick."

"Shut your damn mouth, Carly Allen."

"I just…y'know, I just wish I was a better person," I mutter.

"Can I come with you?" she asks after a moment.

I stand up straight and take the bottle again. "You want to? The line can be two hours long."

"I've got time to kill before my flight. Might as well kill it with you," she says, a little louder now. Surer.

"That's the spirit," I say.

We're quiet for a little while, passing the Champagne bottle wordlessly back and forth to each other. The only sounds come from the water lapping against the shore and the occasional clink of the bottle against the railing we're leaning on. Our shoulders are almost touching, and I'm well aware that this is not the situation I should be in right now — more than a little tipsy and with the idea of *almost* hanging above the two of us.

Shoulders *almost* touching, feet *almost* brushing, and that ring on her finger *almost* being mine. I never told y'all this, but I bought Mollie a second ring. A cheap one this time that was definitely going to turn her finger green because that's all I could actually afford, but I knew she wouldn't have cared. Back then, I could've proposed with a plastic ring from a carnival and she would've said yes. There was a time when I could've asked her to spend the rest of her life with me, ring or no ring, and she would've said yes. Over the moon, walk-off home run in the ninth inning of the seventh game of the World Series, world peace-making, definitively, wholeheartedly YES.

I wonder if that's how it was when Jessie asked her. Or did they do the responsible thing and talk ad nauseam about the real-world repercussions and the tax advantages that come with being married before they went ring shopping together? I could ask Mollie how it happened, or I could get Annie to find out, but I don't want to know. I'm sure it's better this way, but right now, it feels so much worse. It makes that *almost* feel like it might've had a fighting chance if only I'd fought a little harder.

"Attention all you lovers out there! This is the last song we have for you tonight. It was selected by your one and only maid of honor, Carly Allen!" The DJ's voice booms over the speakers. "Carly says, and I quote, 'This one goes out to Todd and Annie and anyone else who's found the one they're meant for.' Thank you and goodnight, everybody!"

I forgot I did this.

It's Bruce Springsteen. Of course it's Bruce Springsteen. I mean, have you learned nothing about me? *If I Should Fall*

Behind to be exact. I hadn't anticipated hearing this song while standing next to a girl I did fall behind from. But all I want right now is to dance with her.

You can call me selfish, and I'd agree that would be a fair assessment. In a few months, Mollie's going to be married. My first love, the love I thought was going to withstand it all, the love I thought would change the world, will not be my love anymore. So yeah, I'm grown up enough to admit that I'm selfish and I'm tipsy and the lights of the city reflecting on the water are putting me in a kind of romantic trance. And this song certainly isn't helping.

Fuck it. My future famous last words, I'm sure of it.

"Do you wanna dance? A song like this shouldn't go to waste," I say, turning to her.

Mollie looks at me and a strand of hair falls into her face. It makes me feel like a teenager again. All of a sudden, I have all the hope in the world that this is going to be the beginning of a different story. A story where things go my way, where I do things right, for once.

She puts down the Champagne bottle and tucks that strand of hair back behind her ear. Mollie looks at me and nods, a nervous smile on her face.

Our hands fit together like they used to. So, so easily, just like we've done this a million times before. At prom, in the kitchen at 2:00 a.m. with no music, in the desert at sunrise with Top 40 music pouring out of the car stereo. I've held

Mollie's hand like this time and time again, and somehow every single time feels like it's the first. This time, though, this is finally the last time. And nothing could be more heartbreaking.

Mollie Fae this close to me again after all these years is terrifying. Not just because it's her, but because of who I was when I was with her. I had it all then. Potential, drive, happiness. I threw it away because, because why? Was I too proud to admit that failure was an option? Or too proud to admit that I'd already failed?

What scares me the most is that I don't know if I'll ever get to feel that way again. Does anyone ever find that much love twice in the same lifetime? As I look at this beautiful woman and listen to the most magical man singing in the background, the world gets a little hazy. We're slow dancing, swirling through the galaxy, and my feet will never touch the ground again.

That is, until that stupid phone of Mollie Fae's starts making noise.

She clears her throat. "I should answer that." She makes no move to pick it up.

"If you want to," I whisper, not moving an inch.

I know. I KNOW. I know I shouldn't be doing this. I know I shouldn't let this moment go on for one more second. For Christ's sake, that's probably her fiancé calling right now. There are three of us here, no matter how much

I try to pretend there are only two. And I am a grain of salt away from crossing a line that no one should ever cross. I'm dying to do it, but I can't. I have a few morals left in my life, but god, at this moment, I really, really wish I didn't.

Her phone stops ringing, and that's what finally breaks the magic spell.

"I think it's best if I go," she trails off.

"Yeah, of course," I say, still not moving.

"Carly?" she says quietly.

"Yeah?"

She swallows harshly. "I should probably call her back."

"Who?" Yes, I have the decency to be ashamed.

"J-Jessie. I told her I'd call her when I got to the hotel and I probably should've been there by now."

"Probably," I say.

"Yes," she says softly, then takes a step back. "Yes, I need to do that. I need to call her back."

"Right." I also take a step back. "Right. Go call. Say hi to her for me."

She gives me a look.

"I mean, you don't have to," I say.

"If it's okay with you, I probably won't." It's hard to be sure, but I think I see a hint of a smile on her face.

"That makes a lot more sense." I wipe my nervous hands on my pants. "I should probably head back to the hotel too. Not your hotel. Mine. But I think we're in the same hotel since there's a block of rooms for the wedding, but I'm gonna go to my room and you're gonna go to yours and you're gonna call Jessie and I'm gonna watch *House Hunters* until the sun comes up. Weddings are great, aren't they?"

"Did you just have an aneurysm?" Mollie asks.

"If I did, it was probably just a minor one. I'm sure everything's fine." I shrug. "I, uh, I'm going to say some goodbyes and head out."

"Yeah, you do that," she says, looking around. "I'm not sure I should go with you tomorrow."

"No?" Sure, maybe I do pout a little.

"Don't give me that look." She brushes her hair back again. "That pout doesn't work on me anymore."

"Fine," I say, and suddenly the weight of the finality of this moment slams into my chest. This is it. It's the last time I'm going to see Mollie Fae. For the possible future. Maybe even for all of eternity.

"I'll see you around?" she asks.

I shake my head. "Maybe not," I whisper, a few tears in my eyes. I let out a deep breath. "I'm rooting for you, Mollie Fae. I can't wait to tell my kids about how you saved the planet for them."

I see tears glistening in her eyes. "And I can't wait to read your second *New York Times* bestseller, Carly Allen."

She pulls me into a hug and I hold her tight. So, so tight, because this is it. This chapter of my life is officially over. Put it in the record books. This chapter that hurts more than I ever thought it possibly could, mostly because I don't think I ever really believed it could end.

Goodbye, love. It's been nice knowing ya.

11

Legendary
by The Summer Set

The TV's still quietly playing HGTV when I wake up. There's a half-eaten grilled cheese sandwich next to me and fries all over the bedspread. I sit up a little too quickly and my head feels like it's about to explode. My stomach, too. My stomach is definitely about to explode.

I throw off the blankets and walk as quickly as I can to the bathroom. I'll spare you the details, but know that it was not a glamorous experience. I'm wearing my fancy dress pants from yesterday and an old Bruce Springsteen tour shirt I paid too much money for on eBay. I flush the toilet and lie down on the cool tile, the memories of last night becoming less foggy. Honestly, I wish they'd stayed foggy.

My mouth is incredibly dry, so I pull myself up to the corner of the sink. I stick my head under the faucet for a drink, and that makes me feel moderately better; a little closer to being an actual human being. I sink back down to the floor and roll over so my forehead can rest against the tile.

What a morning this is shaping up to be.

After another ten minutes or so of self-loathing in the bathroom, I finally get up and order some room service. Coffee, bacon, more coffee. Since I have literally zero people to impress anymore, I don't even bother changing out of this outfit. I give my shirt a quick sniff and I can't detect any vomit, so I figure it's okay to wear when the room service person comes.

Guys, I know how repulsive this all sounds. You don't need to remind me. However, I'd like to say that I have just officially and finally lost the love of my life, so I think you can cut me a little slack. I'd like to see how functional you are after an experience like this one.

There's a knock on the door. "Room service."

"Just a second." I fish a couple bucks out of my wallet and open the door.

"Hey, how's it going?" I ask with a smile that I hope doesn't look too fake. It's a lot brighter in the hallway.

"I'm doing well. How are you?" the room service guy asks.

"Feeling like I just woke up in a sewer with a sledgehammer banging on my forehead, but I won't unload that onto you, kid," I say as I hand over the tip and pull the cart into my room.

He kind of stammers a reply, probably trying to figure out if my comment was a desperate cry for help.

I put him out of his misery. "Don't worry about it."

"Are you sure?" he asks.

"Dude, this isn't a conversation you want to have, okay? I promise, I'm fine. It was a joke."

"It didn't sound like one," he persists, clearly concerned.

"You'd be right, but you're also a room service guy and we're total strangers, so I'm not gonna tell you my sob story." Part of me really wants to tell him my sob story.

"Okay. Well, if there's anything else you need, my name's Brad." He nods and turns to leave.

"You're the nicest Brad I've ever met." I quickly pull the door closed.

A muffled, confused "thanks" comes through from the hall.

I push the cart next to the bed and turn up the volume on the TV. Hotels are great. When you eat food in bed hungover in your apartment, it's pretty dismal. But when you do it in a hotel, it's luxurious. Or at least that's what I'm telling myself.

Once the coffee and bacon run dry, I throw all my stuff into my suitcase. Whenever I travel, everything's packed so neatly for the journey there, and then it's all just thrown into my suitcase for the way back. I leave a tip for housekeeping and then, just as I'm about to leave, I drop a few extra dollars on the table. I'm sorry for what they have to walk into.

I give the room one last look, then drop my sunglasses from the top of my head onto the bridge of my nose and go down to the lobby.

"Hi there. Do you guys hold luggage?" I ask the woman at the front desk.

"Sure. Let me just grab a tag for you," she says, rummaging around in a drawer. "Is it just the one piece?"

I nod. "I'll keep my backpack."

She fills out my name and contact information, then rips the ticket at the perforation and hands me the smaller half.

"We'll hold it here for you, Ms. Allen," she smiles brightly.

"Thank you so much." I squint at her name tag. "Ashley."

"Of course."

I start to walk away, but then turn around quickly. "Oh, I almost forgot. What's the fastest way to get to Hot Doug's?"

"The old hotdog place?"

"That's the one," I say.

"It closed a while ago, I think. Let me check for you."

Ashley dose some quick typing on her keyboard and then nods slowly. "I thought so. Hot Doug's closed in 2014. It was good. My parents used to take me all the time."

"Thanks. I guess I should've looked that up before I got here."

"I hope that wasn't the only reason you came to Chicago," Ashley says.

"No. I'm here for my best friend's wedding. I just read about Hot Doug's years ago and decided that if I ever got to Chicago I'd try it."

"That's a shame. It was such a good place," Ashley says, almost wistfully.

"So, Ashley, if you suddenly had some free time and you were in Chicago for the first time," I ask, "where would you go?"

"How long do you have?"

I shrug. "Two, three, maybe four hours. It depends on how early I want to get to Midway."

"Navy Pier," she says. "For sure. Ride the Ferris wheel."

"Ferris wheel," I say. "Got it."

I hail the first cab I see when I step out of the hotel and ask the driver to take me to Navy Pier.

"You're not a local are you?" he asks.

"No." I shake my head. "I'm from L.A. Just in town for a wedding."

He snaps his fingers and smiles widely. "I knew it! I knew you looked like somebody. You're that girl from those vampire movies!"

I laugh. "I most certainly am not."

"You're somebody though," he says, looking at me closely in the rearview mirror.

"Can't say that I am." I look out the window at the people passing by. They're walking faster than the cab.

"Nah, I know you're somebody," he says. "You just don't want to tell me who."

"I promise you," I say, looking back at him. "I'm not anybody."

"I didn't say you were anybody. I said you were *somebody*," he replies.

"Well, I guess I technically wrote a novel." It feels strange to say that. "Not a novel, really, if you're splitting hairs. A short novel. A novella."

"See!" He slaps the steering wheel. "You're sitting back there trying to play it cool, but I see through you, kid. I see right through you!"

I blush a little. "That was a long time ago."

"A long time ago?" he exclaims. "Yesterday you were a baby. Look at your face! You don't know what it means to be a long time ago."

"Okay, fine." I shift uncomfortably in the back seat. "Not literally a long time ago. Just like, that was a different part of my life. It feels long ago."

"You're not old enough to have different parts yet. Me? I've got different parts."

"What kind of different parts?"

"I was born in the Philippines and spent half my life there. The boy I was there isn't the man I am in America," he says. "They can't be the same."

"Do you miss it?" I ask.

"For a while, it's impossible not to," he says. "Then one day you're in the Philippines and you say, 'I can't wait to go home,' and somehow America is home now. I don't know when it happened. I miss it. I still miss it, but it's a different kind of missing now."

"That makes sense," I say. "It makes a lot of sense."

"Enough about me," he says. "Tell me about this book of yours."

"It was just a day-in-the-life, stream-of-consciousness book," I tell him. "Nothing world-changing."

"See? Look how young you are, kid. So young you don't even know the world changes every day," he says.

"Yeah, I guess. But nothing really happens in the book."

"Everything happens day in and day out," he says. "You can't stop it."

"Do they give you a book of motivational phrases when they give you your cab license?" I ask.

"I'm like you, I make words matter. Have a purpose," he grins. "I just don't write them down."

"Writing's the hardest part." My voice sounds so small.

"It's very brave to write your truth and your stories. People often think of art as frivolous, but it's the entirety of the human experience. It's essential to everything. As essential as making money or breathing or having a roof over your head," he says earnestly. "You tell your truth to the world, so that others may find their own."

"What's your name?"

"Angelo." He beams at me in the rearview mirror. "My friends call me Lolo."

"My name's Carly."

"Carly." Angelo searches for something in the glovebox. "I have a notebook for people like you. I get people to sign it. Somebodies, you know? And then, when you get famous, I get to sell your autograph."

"You want my autograph?" I laugh so loudly. This is a first.

"I do." Angelo passes the notebook and a pen back to me. "Sign it wherever you want."

I take the notebook and pen from him and look at the other people who have signed this book. Every page is overflowing with warmth and love for this dude none of us even know. And none of us have spent more than like thirty minutes with him.

All of a sudden, it feels like we're friends. I scribble a note to Lolo and end it with my fancy signature. It's rusty and hasn't been used since that novella. Also, I know you're probably freaking out and flipping back through the pages of this book, trying to figure out if I've mentioned the novella prior to this moment and wondering how you could have forgotten something so important. I might've, but only briefly, so you can relax. I'm also not going to start talking about it now. Maybe soon. It's not the right time now, okay?

I just lost the love of my life, and you're supposed to be cutting me a little slack, remember?

When we stop at a traffic light, I pass the notebook to Lolo and lean back against the seat.

"Navy Pier," he says. "You planning on riding the Centennial Wheel?"

"Yeah," I say suspiciously. "Is that like a thing? The woman at the front desk of my hotel told me to do it."

"It is. I ride it once a year." Angelo pulls over to the curb.

"Only once a year?" I swipe my credit card to pay the fare.

"When I feel too much," he says. "When I feel heavy, I take the day off, come here to the pier, and ride it."

"And that only happens once a year?" I ask, with just a bit of sarcasm.

"Of course not." He turns to look at me.

"So then why only once a year?"

"I don't know. Sometimes I don't know why I do the things I do, but it's nice to have constants to hold onto," he says. "When you're up there, you can see all of America on a clear day. You see it all and you start to wonder how anything could possibly matter."

"Seems a little dark," I observe.

"Not like that," he corrects me. "How could anything matter when the world exists like this? So there's traffic and bills and all the things in life that we don't like, but there's also this. I just want to take people to the top of the world and say to them, 'Look. Look at this beautiful place and look how you're trying to destroy it.'"

"Thank you, Lolo," I say sincerely.

"Thank you, Carly."

I give him one last smile before I leave the cab.

The wind off Lake Michigan ruffles my hair. The pier itself is pretty empty. It's still early on a Sunday, so the place is almost entirely mine.

I like state fairs and carnivals. Mollie and I never missed one. Something about them feels very classic to me. I know the '50s are only truly idyllic to straight white dudes, but it's nice to get a glimpse of that time period. It's always remembered as simple and wholesome, and I think that's all I really want. I want things to be simple. I want to hold hands under strings of lights and kiss lips that taste like funnel cake, cotton candy, and milkshakes. I want to play carnival games and I want to not feel so alone.

There's a bored twenty-something probably college kid working at the Navy Pier Park box office. He seems genuinely shocked to see me.

Lolo was right. When I get to the top of the wheel, it's like I'm on top of the world and I can see everything. When I get back to the bottom, I ask if I can ride again and the guy lets me. When I reach the bottom for the second time, I hop off and buy some cotton candy. It's kind of nice to sit and look out at the lake while I eat it. I would tell you what's going through my brain right now if there was anything interesting, but it's uncharacteristically quiet. There are a million things I could be thinking about, but my mind is just kind of blank and empty. I don't know if I should be at peace or terrified.

12

I'm Not What You Need
by Joe Purdy

To say I fell into a funk when I got back to L.A. would be an understatement. It would also probably give me more credit than I deserve.

I didn't expect that coming home to my empty apartment would make me feel so starkly alone. After all, I haven't had a roommate or a long-term girlfriend or even a really close friend to come home to in a long while. This shouldn't feel new. Maybe it's all finally catching up to me. Being around Todd and Annie again makes this empty, drab apartment feel like the loneliest place on the planet.

It's weird being out of school, and I still don't know if it's a weird that I like. In college, you had the freedom to do whatever you wanted for the most part, but there were always vague guidelines to rein you in. Classes, assignments, due dates, that sort of thing. Now, though, there's just a whole lot of nothing. Time that I have to figure out how to spend. Work takes up some of it, but there are a whole bunch of other hours in the day that are mine and I can't figure out what to do with them.

I spend more time than I'd like to admit sitting on that navy IKEA couch in the corner of my living room, mindlessly watching shows I've seen before. I'm barely paying attention because there's this loud voice in my head yelling at me to do something else. What though? What do I do? What am I passionate about? Why isn't there something that can get me off this damn couch?

Do you know how much I want to not be sitting here? I would give anything to not be sitting here, but somehow that's not enough. Not long ago, I was so fed up with how I'm acting that I got fully dressed, went out the door, and sat in my car. The key was in the ignition, but I had no idea where to go. Miles and miles of road with a million places for me to visit, and I couldn't pick one. It was paralyzing.

I ended up at a psychic.

Yes, of course. You're probably shaking your head and wondering what the actual shit I'm doing with my life, but that's the answer. I'm doing shit with my life and now it seems I've hit the point where I truly believe that a 97-year-old woman in a glorified shack with a neon "Psychic" sign hanging in the window is going to somehow change things.

I didn't actually go in and talk to the psychic because I was too nervous. I sat in my car in the empty parking lot and stared at the blinking neon sign. I wanted to make my legs unstuck and I wanted to go inside, but I couldn't. I sat there for a good hour before I came to my senses and went home. I'm back now, though. I had a late shift at Target today and muscle memory kind of took over and here we are. That same neon sign brightly shining from the window and my same nervous heart beating overtime.

I step out onto the pavement of the parking lot and lock my car door. When I said it's a glorified shack, I was probably being too kind. The stairs creak and bend when I step on them and the screen door rattles in the light breeze. The obvious slant to the deck makes me a little nervous about its structural soundness, but I've come this far and I'm not chickening out now.

The little waiting room is exactly the way I pictured it would be. Tapestries cover the walls, candles and incense are burning, and a thin layer of dust is on everything. Not as many crystal balls as I expected.

There's one of those deli take-a-number things on a desk at the far side of the room. I pull the little tab and the number printed on it is "1." Now if I was thinking rationally, which I clearly am not, I'd probably be a little concerned that it was pushing eleven at night and I was the first customer, but, guys, I have not been rational for a long time.

"Number one," an airy voice calls out from kind of far away. I jump a little.

I clear my throat. "Hi, I'm number one."

"Enter," the voice says.

"Cool, cool, yeah. Enter where exactly?"

"Through the beads," the voice says hoarsely.

Great, I'm already testing this psychic's last nerve and she hasn't even started to look at my bleak future.

I see a glow of light past the doorway and gently push the beads out of the way so I can enter the back room. It's significantly darker in here and there are way more candles than the fire marshal would approve of. Seriously. It's a fire hazard and a Yankee Candle enthusiast's wet dream. Something tells me the shriveled old lady sitting on the floor on a massive pillow is not doing Yankee Candle unboxing videos on YouTube in her free time.

"Hi," I wave meekly. "I'm—"

"Carly. I know." She cuts me off and shocks me at the same time.

My jaw drops. "How did you? Did you just guess? Shit," I trail off. "Okay, I guess you're the really real deal."

"Sit, please," she says in a monotone.

I walk over and take a seat on the pillow directly facing her. "So, uh, what's your name? Is it Madame Zeroni? I feel like all psychics are named Madame Zeroni, probably because I watched that movie every single day for two years straight. Have you ever seen *Holes?* No? After your time? Sorry, I ramble when I'm nervous and I'm very nervous right now. A little about all the candles because these rugs seem extraordinarily flammable, but also about whatever it is you're about to tell me about my future, so if you could just spill it, that'd be fantastic."

She holds up her hand. "You're troubled."

I squint at her. "Yes. That much is very clear. Even to non-psychic people, I would think."

"You're missing someone."

"Aren't we all, Madame Zeroni?"

"That is not my name," she scolds.

"Okay, what is your name?" I ask.

"Not important, Carly," she replies.

"Right, sorry."

"What brought you in today? Of all days. Why today?"

"Oh. So you know about the other times I just sat in the parking lot," I say. "Cool. This is all very cool."

"Why today?" she presses.

"I don't know," I answer, exasperated. "I just got in my car and before I knew it, I ended up here. Since you're all-knowing or whatever, you can probably figure out what the hell it means."

"It's an important day," she says evenly.

"An important day? It's Tuesday. What's so important about Tuesday? Let's see, it's what, the middle of October? What's my phone say? Tuesday, Octo—oh. It's her birthday."

The psychic lady just looks at me.

I kind of thought that eventually I'd move on. You know, not think about Mollie Fae when I see some cute girl across the way in a coffee shop. I'm thinking a girl named something like Cathy or Beth. Let's call her Beth, for convenience. Start seeing our future together instead of Mollie's and mine. I'd be sitting on my couch with Beth, her head in my lap, fingers playing in her hair, and I'd get this weird feeling. A feeling like I forgot something, but I'd never be able to place what exactly it was. And Beth would ask me what I was thinking about and I'd say, "I feel like I forgot someone's birthday." Then I'd rack my brain, running through everyone's birthdays, trying to remember who I'd forgotten. Eventually, my brain would land on Mollie Fae. I'd try and remember when it was. Was it March? Or April? I always thought that'd be the day I finally moved on.

That day clearly isn't here yet.

October 18. It's there. It's always going to be there. I would give so much for the chance to just forget this. It's not for lack of trying, trust me. I feel like a lovesick teenager who keeps doodling her girlfriend's name in the margins of my brain. Just give it a rest already! When does it stop being romantic that I've been in love with my first love for this long? When does it just become desperate and sad and childish? Is it now? I'm 28 years old with a smattering of three-month-long relationships that amounted to nothing because there was always Mollie Fae out there on a golden pedestal. The voice in my ear that says this girl's cute, but she's no Mollie Fae, is not fading.

A long time ago, I thought I wasn't good enough for Mollie Fae. Even now I feel like that's the situation. She's a hot-shot lawyer and I'm earning just above minimum wage. I'm coasting is what I'm doing; hoping that chance and circumstance will drop her right in front of me one more time and just *one* more time. That's all I need. That'd be so easy. If only the stars would align in my favor. But stars are just stars that are probably long since dead. You know, I've always kind of fancied myself as Ryan Gosling. Unstoppable and unyielding, but here I am. The James Marsden of Mollie's story. I really didn't think it would end this way, and it fucking blows.

I look at the psychic through narrowed eyes. "How did you know that? I didn't even remember it was Mollie's birthday until just now."

"You can't forget about her," she says.

"Thank you for pointing out the obvious again."

"She hasn't forgotten about you either," the psychic says.

"What makes you say that?" I ask.

"You'll see. Not today or tomorrow, but soon." She finishes with a dramatic flourish, dangling bracelets clanging on her wrists.

"So, and stop me if I'm wrong," I say, scooting closer. "At some undetermined time in the future, Mollie is going to do something that proves she hasn't forgotten about me?"

The psychic nods.

I throw up my hands. "That's it? You can't even tell me where or what or why or how, just that she's going to do something? What if I miss it?"

"You won't be able to," she says coolly.

"I want to believe you because you somehow knew my name before I even said it, but I just need something more conclusive."

"When your white shirt turns brown," the psychic says.

"Right. That seems plausible and cryptic and entirely unrealistic," I groan.

"I can't make you believe it," she says. "You must take it into your heart. Let it burrow there until the moment arrives. When the time comes to make a journey, you must."

"A journey to where?"

"I'm not at liberty to say."

Little bits of disbelief are starting to creep in. "Any other cryptic pieces of information you'd like to send my way?"

"It's not over," she says, closing her eyes.

"What isn't? This session?" I look around for some sort of time-measuring device.

"It."

"The dude from *A Wrinkle in Time?*"

She makes a tut sound. "You're not ready."

I raise an eyebrow.

"You're not ready," she repeats. "When your white shirt turns brown, make sure you are ready."

"Okay, but which white shirt? I've got like ten," I say. "I bought a pack of them from The Gap."

"Our session is over," she says abruptly.

"Oh, okay." I awkwardly reach for my wallet. "How much do I owe you?"

She gestures for me to leave. "First readings are free."

"Wow, that's super generous of you," I say, but in my head I want to tell her that if she charged people from the get-go, she'd probably be able to make her shack look less dilapidated.

"Heed my warning," she says sternly. "Be ready when the opportunity for a journey arises. You *must* be ready."

I nod. "For sure."

On the surface, I'm not 100% sold, but there's still a part of me that feels like maybe I'm rounding a corner. Changing direction for the better. You know, maybe I'll be able to really throw myself into life and everything it has to offer. I mean, she did know my name right off the bat, which is still pretty spooky.

It isn't until I'm halfway home that I realize I'm wearing my name tag from work.

13

Badlands
by Bruce Springsteen

My New Psychic's Resolution, if you will, has been going pretty well. What resolution you ask? I guess just trying to be slightly more present in the world, y'know? Today, I even woke up early, did ten push-ups (which is ten more than I've done in the past year), cooked breakfast, and was fifteen minutes early to work. Of course, once I actually had to interact with a human, that resolution went to shit.

"Do you sell martini shakers here?" a lady asks. I'm unpacking boxes of mugs.

"You mean cocktail shakers?" I ask, and stand up a little straighter.

"No, that's different. Martini shakers." She enunciates dramatically, as if martini is an uncommon word only the cream of the wealthy crop would be expected to know.

"Okay. Well, no then," I say. "We've got some cocktail shakers over in aisle 18, though."

"No, that won't do," the woman turns her nose up. "It's no wonder you're working here. At your age."

Sometimes, when people are absolute dicks and my desire to keep my job just barely outweighs my anger, I'll push my glasses back up the bridge of my nose with my middle finger. It's my little act of rebellion. Everyone's got a trick to avoid customer service homicide. This woman didn't notice, but I feel better.

The rest of the day rolls on slowly. I get increasingly snippier with people. Five o'clock finally hits and I enter my team member number into the wall clock. 7-0-6-0-1-5-6-2. Cog in the corporate America machine.

Sam comes up behind me and slaps me on the back. "What're you doing tonight?"

"Well, it's Monday, so I'll be watching *The Bachelorette*. There will be whiskey involved, and I'll be tweeting jokes to my 62 Twitter followers. Busy evening."

"Christ, that's sad."

I nod in agreement. "It's even sadder that I'm genuinely looking forward to it."

"We're going out."

"I don't go out."

"Then I'm coming over and we're gonna watch the goddamn *Bachelorette* together," he says.

"Dude, you don't have to."

"I like hanging out with you. You make work here fun."

"Listen, you're new-ish here—"

"I've been here for two years," he says. "You know that,

right?"

"I get it. You want to be pals, but I'm not up to hanging out right now. It's not something I look forward to."

"Then I'm just going to show up unannounced," Sam says. He starts to walk away from me.

"You don't know where I live!" I call after him.

"I work in HR. You can't hide from me."

"Dammit," I mutter.

I spend some time after I get home half-heartedly cleaning my apartment. I put the wine I bought today in the fridge. Personally, I hate wine, but I feel like, as a begrudging host, I should have an option besides water and half-empty whiskey bottles. It's what Ina Garten would've wanted. The bare minimum.

Sam shows up at around the same time the pizza does. We settle onto the couch and it's only then that I realize how potentially awkward this evening could be.

He looks at me. "So you're gonna have to help me out here. I've never watched this show before."

"It's not that complex. One girl, a whole bunch of guys. She goes on dates with them, there are a lot of tears and fights, and at the end of the season she picks one of them to propose to her."

"Somehow that ends in marriage?"

"Hypothetically. As you can imagine, not every couple who gets together stays together. Forcing people to fall in love over the course of what's essentially a six-week competition shockingly doesn't have a high success rate."

"Wow, I didn't think this show was so ride or die."

"I doubt anyone has ever referred to *The Bachelorette* as ride or die."

The show starts and Sam is instantly invested. I get that *The Bachelor* is doing nothing for the feminist cause and there's not one good reason in the entire universe why I should watch it, but listen, the dudes on *The Bachelorette* come across as just as desperate and dramatic. Equality, y'know. Isn't that what feminism is all about?

"Are they just going to keep piling out of a limo for two hours?" Sam asks.

"Yep. Gotta get to know everyone," I say, grabbing another slice.

"Geez, it's like a clown car and everyone's blonde. Is everyone white? I have genuinely not seen someone who isn't white and from south of the Mason-Dixon line. Is this show racist?"

"Probably."

"I like your apartment." Sam looks around the room as the show goes to commercial.

"Very minimalist. Kind of a prison vibe, right?"

He laughs. "Definitely minimalist, but I'd drop the prison descriptor. It might put people off," he says, looking directly at me.

"Good. I don't want too many people around." I take another bite of pizza and meet his gaze.

Next thing I know, he's leaning in.

"Whoa!" I say, scooching back to the end of the couch.

"What? Was that wrong? I thought we were having a moment."

"A moment? First, I'm chewing pizza and talking about how my apartment looks like a prison cell, so I don't really feel like that constitutes a moment. And second, I'm totally gay."

"Oh, shit," he says.

"Yeah."

"I just thought maybe you liked me. And when you said you watched *The Bachelorette*, I thought it was pretty probable you were straight."

"Nope," I say. "I just like trash reality TV. Kind of a guilty pleasure of mine."

"Makes sense."

"Yeah."

Now it's just uncomfortable silence. I honestly don't even remember the last time a guy tried to kiss me. I sip my whiskey and fidget with the buttons on my shirt. On the TV, more girls pile out of the limo. My eyes glaze over. This is not how I planned on spending my evening.

Sam sighs dramatically. "God, remember that time I tried to kiss you? Fucking wild, right?"

I laugh out loud, the tension instantly gone. "Yeah, what on earth were you thinking?"

"Honestly, now that I look back on it, the evidence is pretty clear. Your DVD collection alone should've given it away."

"What? You don't have four copies of *Carol?*"

He laughs. "No. My sister might, though. She's gay."

"You've got a gay sister and your gaydar's that abysmal?"

"I didn't even know she was gay. And she had a massive *Xena: Warrior Princess* poster in her room right over her bed."

"Geez, Sam."

"I just thought she liked sci-fi. Didn't find out how wrong I was until I walked in on her and my girlfriend making out on her bed."

"Oh, you poor soul."

"Wouldn't be the last time either."

I can't help but laugh. "I hope she eventually learned how to find girls of her own."

He smiles. "Eventually, but my gaydar clearly still needs improvement."

"Maybe we should get you on *The Bachelorette.*"

"Yeah, I don't think that's for me. This is probably the first and last time I'll watch it."

"Come on. You've gotta get into it. Start shit talking it." I sit up and refill his glass. "That's the fun of it."

"You don't take this seriously?"

"God, no. The show is the definition of lunacy."

"Thank goodness. I thought you bought into all this crap."

"Nope." I shake my head. "Shit talk away."

Just like that, we're back to normal. Two friends messing around, making jokes at other people's expense. The show finally ends and Sam gets up to put on his jacket.

"Same time next week?" he asks when he gets to the door.

"Did I make you a *Bachelorette* believer?"

"Yeah, it's fun. I had a good time."

"You know I'm gonna stay gay, right?"

He nods. "Yeah, yeah. Stop flattering yourself. We're bros now. *Bachelorette* bros."

"That's it." I push him out the door. "Get out of my apartment. I don't need this kind of alliteration in my life."

"See you tomorrow, Carly." Sam is smiling as he turns the corner in the hallway.

14
Just Breathe
by Pearl Jam

Time has really flown by since the night Sam and I first watched *The Bachelorette*. It's December now and I finally gave in and turned on my heat. So much for growing up on the east coast and being used to the cold. Now I turn the heat on for sixty-degree weather. I'm an embarrassment to my family.

I know, you're probably saying, Carly, how are you just going to skip so much time like that? Did nothing important happen? Unfortunately, that's exactly it. Nothing important happened. Days started and days ended and before I knew it, December was here. Sam and I did go out for Halloween. That was a good time. If you've never been to a Halloween-themed amateur puppet show, then you're missing out.

We also went *out* out. Sam basically forced it on me and made me dress up as the Indiana Jones to his Shorty. We went to a young, hip, West Hollywood party. I kept getting asked if I was a safari driver, and people thought Sam was a real Yankees player. So I guess it was a success?

He's kind of great that way, in the whole pushing me out the door. Nine out of ten times, anyway. The tenth time is when we sit on my couch and watch *The Bachelorette*.

"It's already unlocked," I yell when I hear a knock at the door.

"You aren't worried about someone breaking into your apartment, Carly?" Sam kicks off his shoes and closes the door behind him.

"I'm surrounded by old people," I say. "Nobody's breaking into anything."

"Whatever you say." Sam drops a pizza box on the coffee table. "Pepperoni, onions, and mushrooms. I splurged tonight."

As he makes himself comfortable on the couch, the TV picture gets fuzzy. I play with the antenna and pretty soon it's clear again. Well, mostly clear.

"Carly, I will pay for you to get cable. This is ridiculous," Sam complains. "If you even breathe wrong, your damn bunny ears lose it."

"I don't need cable. This works just fine." I sit down next to Sam and open the box of pizza.

"It works fine because I got myself into this position."

I look at Sam, sort of lying half on the couch and half on the armrest. If I'm being honest, he doesn't look too comfortable, but it's the only way two people can sit on the couch and watch TV, even with the antenna.

"If you truly want to pay my cable bill, I will not stop you," I tell him.

He shushes me as the show starts. It's the finale, and kind of a big deal. Of course, the dude we were rooting for was kicked off during hometown week, so we're not too invested. Well, we're still very invested, but we already know she's making the wrong choice since she sent the right choice home two weeks ago. Like, come on, lady. If a straight dude and a lesbian think you sent the best, cutest boy home, then you gotta know you messed up.

She ends up picking our second choice, a nice guy with the tiniest gap between his teeth.

"You think they're happy?" Sam asks as the After the Rose part of the finale starts.

I mute the TV. "I've never thought about it."

"I think it's kind of nice," Sam says.

"After a whole season of drunk dudes being weird, you come to the conclusion that this is nice?" I ask. I'm kind of amazed.

"Come on." Sam sits up and the TV signal get scrambled again. "You can't be this much of a cynic."

"They're not in love!" I almost shout. "They barely know each other and he's ready to get down on one knee? That's insane."

"Yeah, but they're trying," Sam says. "They're putting themselves out there in a very weird and very public way, but they're trying. I have to respect that."

"Is some girl not texting you back?"

"Yes, okay," he says, pulling his phone out of his pocket. "We met at this used bookstore the other day and she was flipping through an ancient copy of *Moby Dick*. We struck up a conversation and I invited her to see this prog rock band that writes all their songs from the point of view of the whale from Moby Dick."

"God, L.A. is the absolute worst sometimes."

"And she seemed interested. I mean, she was the one to offer to give me her number," he says. "I didn't even ask. As soon as I mentioned the show, she offered."

"Are all their songs about swimming in the ocean?" I ask.

"A fair few, but focus, please," Sam says. "All I said was, 'Hey! Nice meeting you today. The concert's Monday at ten at the Resident. Can't wait!' Where did I go wrong?"

"When was this?" I ask.

"Three days ago. The concert's starting now, so it's pretty safe to say she's not going."

"Well, neither are you." I hit him on the leg. "You're not at the Resident, either. You're sitting on a couch eating pizza."

"Yeah, only because she never wrote back," he protests.

"Maybe she didn't feel the need to since you wrote it all there," I offer.

"See, this is why I hate modern dating," Sam says.

"Amen." I tilt my glass at him.

"Alright," he hops up. "I'm about to go on a tirade about technology and the downfall of love and romance, so don't even bother trying to stop me."

"Wouldn't dream of it," I say.

"I hate cell phones because everyone always has them on them. Honestly, when was the last time you left your house without it? Huh? Probably 2006. But now, now that's unheard of. We all use our phones for directions or to see what time that coffee shop closes or just to read the Wikipedia page of the new *90210* TV show. Which I read for like an hour yesterday. We should watch that together next. It seems insane," he says quickly. "Anyway, there's literally no excuse for not responding because I know she's at least looked at it.

"And, yeah, on the one hand, I wish there was a socially acceptable means of ignoring your phone because it sucks to be tethered to it all hours of the day. But there's not. There's just this." He points between me and him. "There's just overanalyzing every word you sent with your friend, who tries to make excuses for this person's behavior, because there's no nice way of telling your friend that maybe this person's just an ass."

"This is why I don't want to deal with dating anyone," I say.

"There are other reasons you're avoiding it too," Sam

says, lying down on the floor.

"What's that supposed to mean?" I ask.

"Uh, hello. I know about Mollie," he says.

"How?"

"You told me about her after Annie's wedding."

"Right."

"You've really never stopped thinking about her?" he asks quietly.

I rack my brain, trying to see if there has ever been a significant amount of time where I forgot about her.

"It's pathetic," is what I end up saying.

"Maybe it's romantic."

I laugh harshly. "That's what everyone says. I think it's the nice way of calling me pathetic without actually saying it outright. The same way we try to make excuses for text messages of people we don't know."

"So you were just deflecting about the text messages!"

"I don't know a soul on this planet who would want to go to a prog rock concert where the band plays songs from the point of view of the whale from Moby Dick. If it was Ahab, maybe you could get lit nerds, but the whale?" I ask incredulously.

"Whatever." Sam rolls his eyes. "They've got a couple good songs."

"Justin Bieber has a couple good songs. Those whale people do not."

"Regardless, where's the line?" Sam asks. "Where's the line between pathetic and true love?"

"Ain't that the million-dollar question?"

"Did you guys have a bad break-up? You didn't leave hating each other, right?"

"I mean, I wouldn't say it was a great break-up."

"Well, what break-up ever really is?"

"But no, we didn't hate each other. She was right," I say. "She was right and I was down on myself, pouting, and I couldn't admit it."

"See, that's the difference. That's where the line is drawn," he says excitedly. "If you guys broke up because one of you was an outright asshole to the other one, that'd be pathetic. Because who wants to get back together with an asshole?"

"People do it every day," I say. "Look at any Hollywood tabloid."

"I thought you were too highbrow for Hollywood tabloids. But it's decidedly not pathetic if things ended over a difference of opinion. Opinions are things you can get over."

"But I haven't, have I? I'm still the same kid who hasn't done anything to remedy the situation," I say. "That's where things get pathetic. Because at least those people on *The Bachelorette*, no matter how dumb or drunk they look, they're doing something. I can't even say that."

"So let's fix it." Sam is all of a sudden full of energy. "Where's your laptop?"

I point to the chair in the corner. "What are you going to do with it?"

Sam takes a seat on the floor and opens the laptop. "You don't even have a passcode on your computer?" He looks at me in astonishment.

I shrug. "I only use it to watch Netflix. I've got nothing to hide."

"Except your *Dawson's Creek* obsession, maybe?" Sam snickers, turning the computer around to show me where it's paused on a *Dawson's Creek* episode.

"Still not ashamed," I say.

Sam goes quiet, and I lie down on the couch and close my eyes. There's some shuffling on the floor where he's sitting and I can hear him tapping on the keys.

I'm not saying my bed's been empty since Mollie left. There have been some girls, but they never stuck around. Perfectly nice people who, in any other version of my life, could have been The One. You know, the one you gush about to your parents and friends until they're sick of hearing about her, but then they meet her and feel the same way you do. The One who sticks around forever.

But here we are in this world, this universe, this awful version, where I have no one. God, I've tried. I've tried so hard. I've kissed them earnestly and loved them as much as

I could. There have been moments when my brain would say "This is it! You've found a substitute. Now you can forget about her." A few times I was fooled into believing it, but it was always only for a moment. My head would tell my heart to race when I looked at her, but my heart stayed steady.

Mollie Fae. My breath would catch in my throat every time she looked my way. My palms would sweat and my fingers itched to touch her. Always reaching to be in her arms. It's funny how always doesn't seem to ever really mean always. But when she'd kiss me, there was nothing else. Together, we had *it*.

What is *it*, you ask? It's that thing where you just *get* somebody. It's the end of *Frances Ha* where Frances and Sophie can't stop looking at each other because they just inherently *know*. Mollie was the answer to everything. The world could be burning, but we wouldn't know. We were unstoppable. A force of nature. Knowing that I was the one to make her smile made me certain we were invincible. I'm sure winning the Nobel Peace Prize feels great, but I'm also pretty sure it pales in comparison to making Mollie Fae smile.

And I'm the reason it ended. We may have been a force of nature, but humans have no regard for nature. I mean, look out your window. Can you even see grass? I can't. We just pave everything we don't want to deal with. So, yeah, Mollie and I may have been a force of nature akin to the rainforest, but I was nothing short of a bulldozer.

That's why my bed is empty. Because I can't go from all of that to second-rate. Two-hundred-ninety-eighth rate. It couldn't have been youthful first love ignorance. That would've worn off by now. I can't accept that. No one has ever made me feel something close to what I felt with her. Sweet girls with shiny hair and even shinier smiles. Not all that glitters is gold, though. Once you have the real thing, it's kinda hard to take anything less.

"Done," Sam says, his fingers flying over the keys and then coming to rest in his lap.

"What exactly is done?" I ask, as I struggle to get back into a sitting position.

"I just cleared our work schedules for two weeks. *The Bachelorette* bros are taking this show on the road."

"Sam, I have to pay rent! You can't just clear my work schedule!"

"You're fine. I know you have to have some money stashed somewhere because your apartment looks virtually unlived in." He looks around at the lack of furniture, then points at the empty wall behind him. "You're not spending big bucks on interior decorating, or food that's not frozen pizza, or whiskey."

I grumble a little, but there's not much else I can do. He's not wrong.

"What's that? Begrudging enthusiasm?" Sam smiles.

"I'm going to begrudgingly and enthusiastically kick your

ass," I say.

"That's fine. How many miles are on your car?" He's distracted by something on the computer screen. "Mine's pushing 150,000 and not the most reliable."

"Where are you proposing we travel to?" I can't imagine where this road trip is going to take us.

"Not telling. That would ruin it. I cleared the browser history, too, so don't even bother. The journey is the destination."

I sigh. "I at least need to know what kind of clothes to pack. That's bare minimum information."

"Just like L.A. clothes. Maybe a jacket. It gets cold at night."

"Nice and vague. Fantastic."

"Just how I like my women. Nice, vague, and fantastic. Anyway," he stands and places the laptop back on the chair. "I'll be by tomorrow at 8:00 a.m. Don't be late."

"Tomorrow? I've got laundry to do. There are dishes in the sink. And work," I say, also standing up. "We're both supposed to work tomorrow."

"I already told you," he says, pulling on his shoes. "Cleared it off. Look, you don't want to be in a rut anymore? Fix it. Stop making excuses and get ready for the road trip of your young life."

I pause, ready to try to pick another fight. It feels like I should half-heartedly lob some feeble excuses, but the prospect of a road trip is the most exciting thing I've heard in years. The open road, junk food, shitty hotels. My very own, better, Kerouac moment. A feeling washes over me. It's something I haven't felt in years; the desire to write something. I can't remember the last time I felt the need to write, to tell a story. This story. The story of Sam and Carly, the runaways. My fingers are pleading for a pen and paper. Desperate for the thing I've been missing for so long.

"If you've suddenly gone mute, that will put a damper on our trip. I don't think I can learn sign language overnight," Sam says.

"Sorry, I was daydreaming."

He opens the door and smiles widely. "That's the spirit."

15

Sleep on the Floor
by The Lumineers

"One backpack? That's all you're bringing?" Sam asks as I lock the door to my apartment.

I turn around and see his two rolling suitcases. "Um, exactly how long do you expect us to be gone?"

"I told you I cleared our schedules for two weeks." He shrugs. "Who wants to do laundry on the road?"

"Two weeks is starting to sound like a really long time!" I yell a little too loudly for this early in the morning.

"Ten days might be enough, but probably two weeks."

"Sam!"

"What happened to the girl who was daydreaming yesterday? I liked her more," he says.

"Sam, come on. We can't possibly be gone that long. Think about the store."

"I have thought about the store, and I've also thought about you, and the best thing for both is if you take a break." He reaches for my backpack.

"Wait."

"You can't bail on me now, Allen." Sam narrows his eyes and tries to look very stern.

"I'm not." I fumble around with the pros and cons of everything in my brain. "Listen, if we're going to be gone for ten days, let me just pack a little more, okay? I don't want to wear the same three pairs of underwear and I don't want to do laundry either."

"Fine, but if you're not back out here in ten minutes, I will kick your door down. And remember, it could be two weeks."

I go back into my apartment and lean against the closed door. A part of me wants to throw the deadbolt and stay cooped up in here forever. Sam couldn't kick down the door. There's no way. I've watched him struggle to open a jar of peanut butter in the break room.

But then comes a voice in the back of my head that sounds sad and dejected and a little like it's channeling my mother. It's whispering, "You need to get out of here." I look around the apartment and I know that voice is right. Just from where I'm standing, there's too much. I see the faint stain on the floor where Mollie accidentally dropped a pot of chili. I see the chip in the hardwood where I dropped a knife because I was scared by Mollie's scream about a mouse in the bathroom. It was only a shadow. I see the nail in the wall where a framed photo of the two of us used to hang. I don't know where that photo is anymore. I don't know if she took it or if I threw it in the trash in a fit of anger, but I know I miss it. Everywhere I look, she's there. I'm living in a museum dedicated to our relationship and I'm not trying to forget about her. Sam's right about this vacation. I've been living here so long that I guess I just forgot how much of Mollie is still held here. And how much of myself I've lost along the way.

I grab extra shirts, socks, pants, and underwear, and pull on my jean jacket. It's soft, warm denim. I bought it my sophomore year of college in a secondhand store with my roommate, Hallie. She was looking for a Halloween costume and I was along for the ride. It was tucked away in the back of the coat rack, surrounded by windbreakers from the '80s. (If I'm being totally transparent, I did also purchase an '80s windbreaker that day.) I'd always wanted a denim jacket. They just embody America to me, and while I'm not the biggest fan of the way this country is going (no thanks at all, Trump), I do have a soft spot in my heart for the ideals America is supposed to stand for.

The American Dream is a lie, but it's the most beautifully packaged lie in human history. This country presents itself as a place for dreamers. For people who want to make their lives better and do the thing they've always wanted to do. Los Angeles is a great example. When you're stuck in mind-numbingly long traffic standstills on the five, you're surrounded by aspiring everybodies.

I used to know someone who thought L.A. was sad and, don't get me wrong, it is. As someone who's spent a lot of time being sad in L.A., I feel like I have the authority to support that notion, but this person thought it was sad because of the qualifying "aspiring." That's my favorite part of L.A. and of all America. The aspiring.

Of course there are people who aren't serious. They come out here to give it a half-hearted shot before heading back home with stories to tell at dinner parties about the time they ran into Kim Kardashian at a Starbucks. I guess I have the possibility of falling into that category, but I haven't left yet.

The other people, the actual aspiring ones, I love them. I don't even know who they are, but I love that they have this thing in their lives they're so utterly sure of that they leave everything behind just to take a shot at it. It's never a guarantee they'll make it or even get a taste of it, but just the chance is enough for them to uproot everything and fight like hell to make it so. Those are the people who have kept me in L.A. If they're pursuing something that passionately, maybe I could too.

With that America in mind, I bought the jean jacket and wore it right out of the store. Hallie made fun of me because I was already wearing jeans, so I was now wearing what she called a Canadian tuxedo, once she finally stopped laughing. I didn't care. I felt like I'd just bought into the American

Dream. Why do I equate denim jackets with the American Dream? No idea.

I head back outside in just under ten minutes, and as I swing the apartment door open, I'm faced with Sam's foot getting ready to kick the door in.

"Hey! Were you really going to kick in my door?" I push him away and lock the door.

"I just wanted to see if it was possible."

"And then what was your plan?" I unlock the car and toss my backpack in the trunk. Sam puts his suitcases in too. "We'd have to go buy a new door and your precious road trip would be cancelled."

"Lucky you opened it when you did then, isn't it?"

We get into the car and I look at Sam. "So where are we going?"

He shakes his head. "I'm still not telling you."

"How exactly do you expect me to drive when I don't know where to go?"

"Nobody knows where they're going anymore," he says, punching something into Google Maps on his phone. "That's the beauty of cell phones."

"Come on, give me a hint." That sounded a little like a whine. Maybe it was, but I'm entitled.

"No way." Sam's voice stays firm. "This is for your own good. It's going to be great. I promise you."

I give up. There's nothing left to do but turn the key in

the ignition and let the engine roar to life. Well, roar probably isn't the right word because I drive a Prius. Yes, I know.

"Ready?" Sam looks at me.

Ready for what, exactly? To leave L.A. behind for a while and see America? Yes. When I moved out here, I flew from Maryland because I didn't have a car yet. Flying out to California doesn't have the same feeling as making that drive across America. And as someone who grew up idealizing Bruce Springsteen, a guy who made his entire career writing about love and America, yeah, I've always wanted to do a road trip. I don't know how far Sam plans on having us drive, but there's a tangible excitement buzzing in my bones.

"As ready as I'll ever be."

****

After about the four-hour mark, we stop for gas and switch drivers. Since Sam gave me no notice on this adventure, I had to stay up obscenely late last night doing laundry, washing dishes, and just making sure my apartment won't look like a shit show when I get back. As soon as Sam pulled onto the highway, I reclined my seat and fell asleep.

I want to sleep for another few hours, but I feel hands on my shoulders shaking me awake.

"We made it!" Sam exclaims.

I open my eyes and I can see we're in a parking lot. I wipe

away the sleep and sit up in my seat.

"Where exactly are we?" I ask suspiciously.

"The Grand Canyon!" Sam unbuckles his seatbelt and jumps out of the car. I hear the trunk open.

"This is a parking lot." I'm a little slow getting out of the car, and when I get to the back I see Sam's suitcases on the ground.

"I guess that proves you're awake," Sam says. "If you want to get technical, this is the parking lot of our hotel. We're not actually in the national park yet. I figured we'd unpack and then go see the canyon."

"Is it covered in snow like this parking lot?" I ask, pulling my backpack on.

"Probably, but that will make it look even cooler," Sam says. "You ever been here before?"

"Nope."

As we walk across the pavement and into the hotel, it occurs to me that there's nothing here to make me believe we're almost within walking distance of one of the Seven Wonders of the Natural World.

"Hi, checking in. The reservation is under Chavez," Sam says to the front desk person.

"One moment," a young man named Don tells us.

"How did I not know your last name until this moment?" I ask Sam.

"I'm mildly insulted," Sam responds, although I believe

he's more focused on getting his wallet out of his back pocket.

"Okay, here you are. One night, two queen beds?" Don asks, looking at us.

"Sounds right to me." Sam puts his credit card and driver's license on the desk. "And can you tell us how to get to the park and the canyon views?"

"I'll be happy to tell you, but the roads are closed. The last word we had is that they won't be open before morning," Don says.

"So there's no way to see the canyon?" Sam asks.

"Unfortunately." Don seems genuinely sad for us. "The cleanup crews are having a tougher time than they expected removing all the snow."

"So we can't see the canyon?" I repeat. Ten minutes ago I didn't even know I was going to be here, and now it feels like a disaster that the roads are closed.

"Not tonight," Don says. "But there is good news. You should have no problem for sunrise tomorrow morning. So long as you know how to drive in snow. The crews will get most of the roads clear, but there are spots where snow blows back over the pavement."

"We'll figure it out," Sam says confidently.

"I will definitely be driving tomorrow," I tell him.

"Great," Don says. "I'm glad you won't have to miss seeing the Grand Canyon. It's spectacular." He goes back to the computer. "Does everything else sound okay?"

"Yes, it's all good," Sam says. "Wait. One more thing. Is there a restaurant in this hotel, Don?"

"We have a great bar and restaurant. Oh, and you guys picked the best night to stay with us! It's karaoke night." Don points toward a doorway across the lobby.

I turn around to look, and I can just see a few empty tables past a big Karaoke Tonight sign.

"Tell me, Don, just how popular is karaoke night in the middle of the week in almost the middle of December at a hotel whose main attraction is inaccessible?" I ask.

He gives me a serious look. "You'd be surprised."

"Can't wait," Sam grins.

"Okay," Don says, shuffling some papers together. "Here are your key cards, a brochure for the park tomorrow when it opens, and our entertainment schedule. Let us know if you need anything else."

"Thanks, Don!" Sam and I say at the same time.

"Just to be clear," I say as we get into the elevator, "we're not going to karaoke, right? We're going to get takeout and go back to our room and watch *House Hunters.*"

"What is it with you and *House Hunters?*" Sam asks.

"It's just soothing," I shrug.

"Well," he says, gathering his bags as the elevator reaches our floor, "I am definitely going to see what Grand Canyon karaoke looks like."

16
Why Can't This Be Love?
by Van Halen

As it turns out, Grand Canyon karaoke is not the saddest karaoke I've ever been to. In case you were wondering, the saddest karaoke I've ever been to was at an Applebee's on New Year's Eve. I'm sorry if you got secondhand depression just from reading that sentence. But yes, to answer your question, it was as tragic as you're imagining it was, and four people sang *Walking in Memphis*.

We've been here for about an hour, and now it's a lonely-looking boy's turn. His white dress shirt is still half tucked into his black pants and he looks like he's about to cry.

"He's gonna sing an Ed Sheeran song," Sam whispers in my ear. "Somebody just annihilated his heart."

I snort. "Nuh-uh. Classic rock. *Careless Whisper* or *Alone* or something like that," I whisper back, watching the boy talk quietly to the man in charge of the karaoke machine.

"Five bucks and you're on," Sam says, sticking out his hand.

"Deal." We shake, just as the DJ takes the microphone.

"Ladies and gentlemen, put your hands together for Chase, who will be singing *Every Rose Has Its Thorn.*"

"No way," I say as the canned saxophone comes out of the speakers.

"Is this a coping mechanism do you think?" Sam asks.

"No idea, but you owe me five bucks."

I wince as the kid on stage accidentally bumps the microphone and makes it squeal.

"You think he's actually going to sing?" Sam slaps a five-dollar bill on the table.

"I just want to know how he got here." I put the money into my wallet. "Like who hurt him so badly that he's singing *Every Rose Has Its Thorn* in a hotel bar?"

"I'm saying left at the altar," Sam says.

"The kid's twelve! Look at his baby face."

"Look who's talking Miss I-Got-Mistaken-For-A-High-Schooler-Yesterday." Sam laughs, like my constantly being mistaken for a child is the funniest thing he's ever seen.

"Yeah, well, at least I don't have any gray hairs coming in yet," I say, ruffling his hair.

"Listen! He's finally started singing."

I look at the stage and the poor kid's staring down at his shoes, mumbling what we can only guess are the song lyrics. He's so quiet we can hardly hear him and he looks like he's about to bolt.

"I genuinely have so many questions," Sam says.

"Do you think we should buy him a drink when he's done?" I ask.

"Do you think he's old enough to drink?"

"Stop it, Sam. Have a little sympathy. Somebody hurt him really badly."

"Gotta give him props for getting up there and oh, no." Sam stops and leans forward for a better look. "Is he crying a little bit?"

Sure enough, the poor kid is crying over a thirty-plus-year-old '80s power ballad, and he's doing it in public. I've never felt more empathy in my entire life. Mostly because I know I'm a drink and a half away from being that kid.

"I don't care what you say, I'm buying him a drink," Sam says as the song ends.

We clap the loudest when the song's done. The kid, Chase, I think the DJ said his name was, nods once and walks off the stage.

"Let's have another hand for this kid!" The DJ takes over the microphone again. "Next up is Mike singing *Walking in Memphis!*"

I have a theory that at any given time, on any given day, there's someone, somewhere in the world, singing *Walking in Memphis* at karaoke.

"Hey! Poison boy!" Sam calls out.

"His name's Chase," I remind him.

The kid turns around, tears still wet on his cheeks, with

a look of confusion. He gestures to himself, checking that he's the person Sam is talking to. Sam nods enthusiastically and waves him over.

"Five bucks says he can't drink," I whisper quickly.

"You're on," Sam whispers back.

The kid comes up to our table cautiously. "Um, hi."

"Hey, dude, take a seat." Sam pulls out a chair.

"Thanks." He says it more like a question than a statement.

"You were really good up there," I offer.

"Yeah, lemme buy you a drink. What can I get you?" Sam asks.

Chase shifts awkwardly on the chair. "I actually just turned 19."

I smirk at Sam. "He'll still buy you a Coke."

"Oh, yeah, a Coke would be nice," the kid says, and Sam nods before walking to the bar.

Now it's just me and the sad karaoke boy.

"So, you like '80s music?"

He nods. "I do. Poison's not my favorite though."

"Hey, I'm not judging. I think '80s music is the best. Springsteen, Tom Petty. I love hair bands too. Like Starship. And Madonna's great.

He smiles at that. "I love Madonna."

"Yes! Nobody appreciates '80s Madonna anymore. *Like a Prayer* is such a good time." I smile back at him, hoping it will help him relax a little.

"I like *Papa Don't Preach*," Chase says almost sheepishly.

"You're the first person in the world I've ever met who likes *Papa Don't Preach!*"

"What're you kids talking about?" Sam asks as he puts our drinks on the table.

"Madonna," I say.

"Doesn't surprise me."

"Do you have a favorite Madonna song?" Chase asks, looking at me.

"Glad you asked, kid," Sam says. "I'll be right back."

He slides off the stool again and walks over to the DJ. Sam whispers something in the guy's ear and he nods, smiling wildly.

"What did he just do?" Chase asks.

"I don't know, but that look on his face is scaring me," I tell him as Sam walks back to us.

"What did they say your name was again? Chase?" Sam asks as he sits down.

"Yeah," Chase says. "What did you tell the announcer dude?"

"Unimportant," Sam says dismissively. "So tell us a little about your life."

"Is this Oprah?" I ask.

"I'd prefer not to," Chase says, sipping his Coke. "You guys are strangers. Basically."

"We did just see you cry while singing an '80s power ballad, so I feel like we're at least acquaintances," Sam says.

I give Chase a half smile. "I mean, he's not wrong."

"That was nothing," Chase says. "Just blowing off steam from work."

Sam gives Chase a look and I shake my head.

"Listen. This kid," I say, jerking my thumb in Sam's direction, "is really bad at making friends. He does it in weird ways. He's just looking out for you."

"By buying me a Coke?" Chase asks.

I shrug. "He gave me Starbursts, so I'd say it's his thing."

"Okay." Chase plays with the straw in his Coke for a second. "Whatever. I'm never going to see you guys again. You seem like you're from out of town."

"Los Angeles," I nod.

Sam tugs on the sleeve of my denim jacket. "It's her jacket, isn't it?"

Chase laughs a little. "Yeah, that didn't help."

"What?" I yelp. "Half the people in here are wearing denim jackets!"

"None that have patches sewn on them. And anyway, everyone in here's a tourist," Chase says with some authority.

"Touché," I grumble.

"So my money was on you being left at the altar, but now that I know you're basically twelve, I'm probably wrong," Sam says.

"There was definitely no altar," Chase agrees.

"Knew it!" I say.

"What is it?" Sam asks. "Girlfriend troubles? Boyfriend troubles?"

"The latter," Chase says, not looking up.

Sam and I proceed to have a nonverbal conversation that involves a lot of gesticulation without actually getting either of our points across. I'm pretty sure Sam wants me to say something because I'm gay, but I want him to say something because he's a dude.

I end up losing.

"That sucks," I say, and Sam smacks me. "Ow! What? It sucks, okay? We've all been there."

"Except not with dudes," Sam says.

"True, no dude issues, but I've got more girl troubles than you could fathom," I tell Chase.

"Yeah?" Chase asks, finally looking up.

"What happened?" Sam asks. "Some douchebag broke your heart?"

Chase can't even get the words out, so he just nods.

"Forget that dude. You don't need him," I say, throwing an arm around his shoulders.

"Yeah, there will be better dudes out there. Don't worry," Sam says.

Chase snorts. "Here? In Arizona? Right."

Sam and I are silent because neither of us knows what to

say to that. I can't imagine growing up in a place that wasn't Towson. Yeah, it wasn't perfect, but I wasn't alone and I wasn't afraid. That makes all the difference in the world.

"It just sucks," Chase says after a couple of minutes. "All of a sudden my life has changed, flipped entirely upside down, and I have no one. Sure, my parents, who are kind of supportive sometimes, but who the hell wants to talk about getting dumped to their parents?

"I've got friends, but I feel like they get weird when I talk about it. It's fine when we just hang out and talk nonsense, but whenever I try to talk about him, they clam up. Maybe nod a few times, but then they'll try to change the subject as quickly as they can." Chase slumps in his chair. "I just want someone to talk to, and the dumbest, most ironic thing is that the only person in my life who would understand what I'm going through is the guy who dumped me."

"Hey," I say, putting my hand on his. "You've got us."

"For what? One night? Then you guys go back to L.A., where things are easier," Chase says.

"Give us your phone," I say.

"Why?" Chase sniffles a little, but he still pulls out his phone.

"We've got your back." Sam grabs Chase's phone and puts his number in it.

"You've got less than a year until you graduate," I say. "I know that feels far away, but it's around the corner. Trust me. And then the world's yours. As far as I'm concerned, anyone who can do karaoke can change the world."

Chase lets out a shaky breath. "I just miss him, y'know? I know I shouldn't, but he was my first boyfriend and the first gay guy I ever knew. I've lost my boyfriend and the only connection to gay people I had."

"That's not true." I look up from putting my number into Chase's phone. "You've got me. And Sam, who's not gay, but he's one of the good straight dudes."

"One of the proud few," Sam says.

"You call, we answer," I say. "I know it's not ideal, but we're what you've got right now. And we want you to know you're not alone."

"It's perfect." Chase cuts me off. "You're the first lesbian I've ever met."

"What an honor," I say, laughing.

"And you are definitely not the first straight guy I've ever met," Chase tells Sam.

"If I was, I'd be shocked," Sam says.

"I don't know why you guys called me over, but thank you," Chase says.

"Dude," Sam deadpans, "you were crying to *Every Rose Has Its Thorn*."

Chase laughs loudly. "Yeah, that was pretty dramatic, wasn't it?"

"Super dramatic," I agree.

Chase is a good kid. He's going to study journalism and he wants to write something that's going to change the world. We spend the next hour or so talking about anything and everything. I give him a list of all the quintessential gay movies he hasn't seen. My exact words were, "What do you mean *Brokeback Mountain* is the only gay movie you've ever seen? Get me a pen and a napkin."

Karaoke continues. Another dude sings *Walking in Memphis* and I consider that proof of my theory. A lot of people sing country, then a classic rock song will start and I'll hum under my breath. I'll even admit that I stood on my chair and sang along to *Jukebox Hero*.

"And last up for the night," the announcer says, looking right at our table, "The Three Musketeers!"

There's light applause from the few people left in the bar.

"Please tell me we're not The Three Musketeers." Chase looks like he wants to run out the door as fast as he can.

"I have a bad feeling we are," I say.

Sam throws back the rest of his drink and makes a face at us. "Let's go, kids."

Chase and I hesitate, so Sam grabs our hands and pulls us off our chairs. Chase is putting up a little bit of a fight.

"I don't even know what we're singing," he protests.

"Madonna," Sam answers.

That gets me to stop fighting. What can I say? I really can't resist Madonna.

And that, dear reader, is the story of how I sang *Like a Prayer* at karaoke in a hotel bar near the Grand Canyon with a literal stranger and a work acquaintance to a grand total of fifteen people. Maybe I'll never hear from Chase again. Maybe he'll find his path just fine on his own and he'll never call Sam or me. If I was where he is, I would've wanted to feel a little less alone, too, even if I never called. I think that's the big secret of life. We all do the things we do so we feel a little less lonely. Sometimes it works and sometimes it doesn't, but the most human thing in the world is to try.

I stopped trying and turned into someone unrecognizable. Never let me stop believing in '80s music ever again. My world is the same, yes. My circumstances haven't changed, but I feel like I'm waking up. I may be groggy, but I'm waking up. There's nothing like a good old-fashioned karaoke therapy session to dust off the cobwebs of your soul.

17

Back in My Body
by Maggie Rogers

Sam starts trying to wake me up at some ungodly hour. I don't even have to open my eyes to know it's way too early for anyone to be out of bed. I try to burrow deeper into the mattress and pull the covers over my head.

"Wake up, Carly!" he shouts. "I called the front desk and they said we can make it to the canyon. Don't you wanna see it at sunrise?"

"It's a hole in the ground," I reply, my voice muffled by the pillow I've pressed my face into. "How much do I really need to see a hole in the ground at this hour? It'll look the same later. Lord knows it isn't going anywhere."

"What kind of nonsense are you spouting? Fine. I'm not going to force you to come with me, but if you want your car to come back in one piece, I suggest you get out of bed now. Remember, I've never driven in snow."

I grumble. "Sam, that's not fair."

"Life's not fair," he reminds me.

As I listen to him jingle the car keys, I do a quick

calculation to determine if it's worth risking my car to stay in the cozy warmth of the bed. Ultimately, I decide it's not, but I want you to know it was close.

I roll over and pull the blankets down so just my face is peeking out. "Fine. But I'm going in my pajamas and I'm one hundred percent getting coffee from that free machine in the lobby."

"God, I love your constant, unbridled enthusiasm. Two minutes!" Sam dances a little jig and I throw a pillow at his face.

It's too early to respond to Sam's remark, so I just climb out of bed and pull on a sweatshirt and a beanie. Sam's got a beanie pulled down tight over his hair too. If I was more awake, it would probably cross my mind that it's December at the Grand Canyon and there's literally so much snow outside that roads were closed, meaning our California sweatshirts and beanies aren't going to do us much good. However, I am not more awake because it's way too early. It's a miracle I'm even upright.

We stop briefly in the lobby for my cup of complimentary coffee. Sadly, no matter how much sugar I put into it, I just can't mask the burnt taste. Sam's tapping his foot impatiently because he's worried we're going to miss the sunrise and then what even was the point of us being up this early.

The car radio quietly plays Cat Stevens as we drive along

the road near the edge of the canyon. So I'll come clean here. My only knowledge of the Grand Canyon revolves around the episode of *Parks and Recreation* where this weird cult group predicts the world is about to end. April and Andy take this as an opportunity to knock things off Andy's bucket list. It all culminates in them driving overnight to see the Grand Canyon at sunrise. They drive right up close to the edge of the canyon and, because Andy's a lovable fool, he asks where the presidents' heads are.

And yes, I know television shows are filled with inaccuracies and lies, but I truly didn't expect to have to drive for so long on frozen, snow-covered roads just to reach a parking lot. Not even the damn edge of the canyon. On the one hand, I'm kind of glad we're not driving up to the canyon edge because I'm sure I would slip on ice and tumble all the way to the bottom. On the other hand, though, I'm feeling that sense of emptiness that comes from being disillusioned. I get that being disillusioned by a TV show is a little dramatic, even for me, but let me remind you – IT'S STILL DARK OUTSIDE. CUT ME SOME SLACK.

"Shall we?" Sam asks, his hand on the door.

"I'm bringing my coffee."

"Wow!" he yells as he leaves the shelter of the car.

I roll my eyes, thinking he's being overly dramatic, but as I open my door I realize that, if anything, he's being underdramatic.

"Oh my god," I say. "This was a mistake. We came far enough. Oh, this was such a mistake. We're going to die if we go five more steps. Let's just lie and say we saw it, okay?"

"We are going to look at this damn hole in the ground even if we turn into icicles before we get there," Sam says.

"Look at us." I can't help but laugh as we struggle across the ice-covered parking lot. "Two idiot Californians who thought sweatshirts would be enough to keep them warm when it's below freezing and the wind is blowing at 175 miles an hour."

"This was a mistake," Sam proclaims.

"Glad we agree," I nod, taking a sip of my coffee. "My coffee's ice cold and we've only been here for two minutes."

"This is worse than the fucking tundra," he says through chattering teeth. "Where even is this stupid canyon? Shouldn't we be able to see it by now? It's a massive hole. How can it be hiding?"

Those were the last words Sam said before he bit it. Hard. I'm doubled over laughing as he struggles to find traction.

"Stop laughing and help me."

"I can't. I don't want to fall," I gasp between laughs.

"I will push you into the canyon when we get there," he complains, finally getting up slowly, kind of like a baby giraffe standing for the first time.

"Come on," I say, feeling pretty good because I haven't

fallen yet. "I'll let you pick the music when we get back to the car."

"If we make it back to the car."

"You're fine. Only your ego's bruised." I pull him down the walkway.

"And my coccyx," he wails.

"Your coccyx is fine. You just wanted me to say coccyx."

"Somebody's wide awake now," he says, hugging me for warmth as we walk.

"Yeah, if you'd fallen on your coccyx earlier, maybe I would've been more receptive to being awake this early."

"I think the view over there might just change your attitude." Sam nods in the direction of what I assume is the canyon.

And you know what? He's absolutely right. This view is pretty damn incredible. Well worth freezing to death for. It looks like it goes on forever. It's something that's been here for so many, many years before me and all the other people freezing their asses off this early in the morning. And it's something that's going to be here for a long time after we're gone. It's so deep I can't even see the bottom, but I have to trust there's ground down there and it's not just a straight shot to the center of the earth. I feel very small, like when I was on the Ferris wheel on Navy Pier back in Chicago. I think a lot of the world's problems could be solved if we all felt small every once in a while.

Standing here, looking out over this grand, expansive canyon, watching the sun rise and the day begin, I know I've lost myself. That's not something that's as easy to know as losing your wallet or your keys. It's subtle. You spend your time bumbling around, knowing something's off, but you can't identify what or why or how to fix it.

It's like watching your favorite movie, the one you know by heart and love every time you see it. Then all of a sudden, you feel like it's bland and you start to wonder if it's always been bland and you're only just now seeing that. So instead of giving the movie your full attention, you start surfing the web and you miss the part where their eyes meet across the room for the first time. It's your favorite part. So you rewind, but you go too far and then you miss it again when it finally comes back around. This time you don't rewind it though. You just let the movie play and keep surfing the web, getting lost in your cousin's best friend's sister's boyfriend's dog's Instagram page. Somehow, when you look up again, the credits have already rolled, the TV's stuck on a black screen that flashes No Signal, and you have no idea how you got here.

That's how it starts, but you don't know it's started. And then it spreads. It spreads slowly to all the things you love, and before you realize it, your record player's dusty and your pens have all run dry, even though you've never even used them. That's how you lose yourself. What I don't know is how to find yourself again. Honestly, I don't know what leads people to losing themselves either. Standing here, though, on the edge of this beautiful canyon with Sam's hand in mine, the rays of the sun slowly stretching before us, helps put things in perspective.

Sam squeezes my hand. "You ready?"

I shake my head. "Almost. Just a little bit longer, okay?"

"Says the girl who didn't even want to get out of bed this morning." He acts a little grumpy, but I know he doesn't mean it.

I feel like I can breathe again. I didn't even know I'd stopped breathing all this time. I feel like there's a new beginning for me that's rising with the sun. And, yeah, the forecast today is calling for rain, but I think I've forgotten what it's like to dance in a downpour. Maybe it's time to try to remember. No more messing around. No more excuses. It's time to start facing things head-on again.

I don't know how long we actually stayed there, gazing out at the canyon, but I think I could have looked at it all day...if the tour group hadn't arrived. Nothing ruins a peaceful and enlightening moment like a hundred noisy strangers pushing past you to take selfies on the canyon edge.

"So what's the plan?" I ask, when we're back in the car.

"Well, I know we were originally booked for two nights here, but I canceled tonight," Sam answers.

"Why?"

"Poor planning. How was I supposed to know it snows in Arizona and there's nothing to do at the Grand Canyon except nature stuff that's all closed because of the snow?"

"Nature stuff is the entire point of visiting national parks. They're literally there to preserve nature." Does he really need me to tell him this?

"That's fine. Besides, I had a brain blast last night." Sam smiles in a way that makes me very nervous.

"And what would that brain blast be?"

"Vegas, baby," he says, doing a horrendous Elvis impersonation.

"We're backtracking already?"

"Listen, just because it's on the way back to L.A. doesn't mean we're going back to L.A.," he explains. "You've got to trust me."

"Why didn't we just go to Vegas first?" I'm wondering if I should have trusted him with planning this adventure.

"I feel like it doesn't pack the same emotional punch, y'know? You needed a good punch."

"Thank you, I think."

"You didn't need to see Vegas because Vegas is filled with sad, desperate, lonely people, and you're a sad, desperate, lonely person."

"Hey!" I protest.

"You are, Carly," he shrugs. "I don't make the rules."

"You don't have to be rude about it."

"I'm not. All I'm saying is that you needed to believe the world is still grand and huge and beautiful," he says seriously. "That's what the Grand Canyon was for. Vegas is to show you that you can still have fun."

"Fun? In Vegas? What could we possibly do in Vegas that would be considered fun?"

"Just you wait and see," he promises.

****

We take our time leaving the Grand Canyon and make a stop to see the London Bridge. Who knew Arizona had so much to offer? I only knew the London Bridge existed because my mom tried to teach me piano using that lame song. Sam whistled it incessantly the whole time we were there. That detour gets us into the city just after dark and we head directly for the Paris Las Vegas, where Sam has made us a reservation. You know, the one with the Eiffel Tower. It's the closest I've ever been to the real tower.

"I need you to stop looking for parking," I say, kicking my feet on the dash. "This is insane. You think you're going to find a place to park that's free, close to our hotel, and safe?"

"Yes, hence why we're looking," Sam says.

"I'm paying for valet," I say. "Just go to the hotel."

"Valet is a scam. I know how to park my own car." Sam

sounds like he's ready for a fight.

"First of all, this is my car," I remind him. "Second, I feel like not wanting to valet is a dude thing because my dad hates it too. And third, since you're so insistent about paying for the hotel rooms, the least I can do is throw a couple bucks at the valet."

"Fine," Sam groans. "But only because I'm sick of sitting in traffic. It's starting to remind me too much of home."

He whips a U-turn and we've dropped off the keys to the valet in no time. We walk up to the front desk and Sam starts checking us in.

"I see you've requested two queen beds," the front desk lady says.

"Yep," Sam replies.

The woman's brow furrows. "It seems we're out of double rooms. Let me see what I can find for you."

"Oh," Sam says, turning to look at me and see how I react to this news.

"Are you sure there are no more rooms available with two beds?" I ask the front desk person.

"What? You're worried about sharing a bed with me and giving in to my undeniable charm?" Sam asks.

"No." I glare at him. "You snore. Loudly. It was bad enough just being in same room with you."

"You guys are so cute," the front desk woman says.

"I barely know him." Me.

163

"Thank you, we're married." Sam.

He drapes his arm around my shoulders and I try to shrug my way out of it.

The woman clicks around on her computer for a few more minutes. "It looks like we definitely don't have any two-bed rooms left."

"Please tell me you at least have a room with a king bed," I beg, only half kidding.

Sam starts humming *Let's Get It On* by Marvin Gaye and I elbow him in the stomach.

I sigh deeply. "Alright. Whatever you can do is great."

"That's the spirit," Sam says cheerily.

I wait impatiently while the woman swipes Sam's card and encodes our room keys. We give her a little wave and take the elevator up to our floor.

When we get to the room, Sam flops face first onto the bed and inhales deeply. "Ah, you can almost smell the bed bugs and STDs."

I drop my bag onto the floor. "I swear, if you turn out to be a cuddler, I will push you onto the floor and roll you out to the balcony."

"We have a balcony?" Sam asks excitedly and hops off the bed.

He slides the glass door open and steps out into the Vegas night. I walk out with him. A whole, wide city of lights is sprawled out below us. People walking on the sidewalks look like ants, and the sounds of at least five different over-produced pop songs drift up to our window.

"Look at this place," Sam whispers, a hint of awe in his voice.

"I like the lights," I say.

Sam snorts.

"I'm serious. They're beautiful. They let you forget for a moment that this city is built on alcoholism, extramarital affairs, prostitution, and gambling."

"Okay, okay. I know what you mean. There's something about big-city lights that's intoxicating. They make you want to believe in your dreams. Which, in my humble opinion, is far more dangerous than gambling, affairs, prostitution, and alcohol combined."

"They make you believe in love and art and music and hell, maybe even poetry."

We smile at each other and look back at the cityscape. I've always loved city lights. It doesn't matter how big or small the city. Manhattan is my favorite, though. When you look at it from New Jersey, it sits across a river that's black as bats, seemingly untouchable. So far beyond the reach of any mere mortal. Twinkling skyscrapers reflect their immensity on the water. It's easy to forget there are 1.665 million people endlessly bustling on sidewalks and blaring horns in traffic jams and sitting at desks and making dinner in those tiny skyscraper windows.

When I was a kid visiting my grandparents on the Upper East Side, it was inconceivable to me that people were allowed to live in that gleaming metropolis. It's so real and rare and magical. You feel it. I know you feel it. That excitement bubbling in your chest when you get your first glimpse of the skyline. The feeling that there's still magic in this world. Remarkable, possible magic. There's still a place for dreamers.

Vegas doesn't feel like that. No place in the world feels exactly like that.

"Well," Sam says, clapping his hands together. "That fills my sappiness quota for the day. Let's go."

"Where are we going?"

"Did you think we were going to spend our only night in Las Vegas in our hotel room? Oh, sweet, naïve, Carly Allen," he says, putting his hands on my shoulders. "Hell, no. We're going to get drunk and kiss some pretty girls if we're lucky."

"I was voted Most Likely to Accidentally Get Married in Vegas my senior year at Oberlin. I'd prefer to not make that a prophetic statement."

"You should probably wear white just in case."

18

Pour Some Sugar on Me
by Def Leppard

Sam's wearing a shit-eating grin as he pulls me along the Strip. It makes me insanely nervous.

"You're going to love this place," he says.

"Are we going to a strip club? I always feel so uncomfortable in those places. I never know what to say."

"I feel like if you're talking at a strip club, you're doing something wrong," Sam laughs.

He keeps weaving us in and out of groups of people, like a dog following a scent. Finally, we end up in front of a building covered with so much neon it's probably singlehandedly keeping the neon industry afloat. Not to mention the electric company.

"Ta-da!" Sam drops my hand and gestures grandly at the facade.

"I don't know what this place is," I say, squinting at the name. "Heaven? Is that the name of this place?"

"Yes."

"Sounds like a strip club."

He winks at me, that smile growing bigger and bigger. "Not a strip club."

We open the door and step inside. Def Leppard's *Pour Some Sugar on Me* is playing and we're face to face with more neon. There's a big pink neon sign that says Heaven and then, smaller and below it, a green one that reads 'A Place on Earth.' Safe to say, my jaw is on the floor.

"Is this an '80s club?" I shout to Sam.

"All '80s, all day, every day," he says proudly.

"I think I'm finally home." You can't imagine the huge smile on my face…or maybe you can.

Despite the fact that I moved to L.A. when I was young, I never went through a club/party girl phase. Before you start praising my mature choices, let me tell you that I never went through that phase because I could never find a place that exclusively played '80s music. Had this place, Heaven, existed in L.A., know that my liver would be in very bad shape right now.

Pretty soon I'm singing along to song after song, drink in my hand, dancing with Sam until he says he needs to take a rest, and then I'm dancing alone. But it's like being at a concert alone. You don't feel alone because you're surrounded by people listening and singing and dancing with you. The music makes them all your friends. At least while you're in the club. As a wise woman once said, "In the club, we all fam."

Finally, even though I'm in my element, I have to take a break. I walk over to the bar and order a drink. While I'm waiting, a loud and tipsy bachelorette party comes up and stands next to me.

"Give the bride a shot!" one of them squeals.

"Last night of freedom!" another one yells.

The bartender looks less than enthused that he now has to deal with this rambunctious gaggle of girls. I can't blame him. One of them keeps bumping my elbow and I just want to get my drink and escape from them.

"Guys, guys, give him a second to finish what he's doing," a girl says from behind me. The voice sounds so familiar. I can't immediately place it, but it's tugging at something in the back of my mind. "Can you *believe* how much neon there is in this place?"

There it is! The lightbulb clicks on in my brain. I'd recognize that voice filled with disdain anywhere.

I turn my head. "Claire?"

Her face pokes through the group of girls. She's wearing a tiara and a sash. She looks exactly the same, but her eyes are a little kinder. It looks like the years have worn down her tough exterior just a bit.

"Holy shit! Carly Allen. Of all the gin joints in all the world." She pulls me into a big hug. When she moves away, she tugs on the collar of my shirt. "I barely recognized you without the Hawaiian shirt."

169

"I barely recognized you wearing whatever the hell this is," I say, flicking her tiara.

"You swear now?" she teases.

"I am definitely not your tutor anymore, so I think I'm allowed to."

"What are you doing here?" she asks.

"Soul searching," I say. "When's your big day?"

"Tomorrow."

Everyone I know is getting married. Literally everyone. Annie, Todd, Mollie, her fiancé, the lesbians from the plane, and now even Claire.

"I can't believe you're getting married. Who's the lucky guy?"

"Isaac," she says. "We met in bio class in college."

"College sweethearts. In biology class, too." I whistle. "Would you look at that?"

"Where's your sweetheart?" She punches my arm.

"Ah, yes. Her. Getting married."

"And you didn't invite me?" she asks.

"You didn't invite me to your wedding," I point out. "No, but, uh, I didn't get invited either. She's marrying someone else. We didn't make it."

"No, way," Claire says, color draining from her face. "Shit, I am so sorry. I didn't know."

I nod, swallowing the tears as best I can. "Hence the soul searching."

"I can't believe it." She runs a hand through her hair, barely missing the tiara. "I was rooting for you guys."

"Join the club."

"Claireeeee," one of the girls in the group calls out. "Come on! Why aren't you dancing?"

"I will. Carly's an old friend. Let me catch up for a second," Claire yells, and the girl flounces away.

I study Claire. She's changed. It seems like it's for the better. Not as tough, but still hopefully as headstrong as she was back in the day.

"You look good," I say. "Growing up looks good on you."

She rolls her eyes. "I see you're still stupidly cheesy."

"Nobody ever really changes all the way."

Another bridesmaid comes up to us. "Claire, please come dance! You're being a wallflower!"

"One more minute. I promise." Claire shoos her away.

"Go," I say, nodding toward the dance floor. "Have fun. It's your night. Go get married, superstar."

She looks at me for a moment. There's so much to tell each other. So much unknown about how each of us ended up here on this exact day and time. So much to fill in, but now isn't the time. She seems hesitant to leave me. I see a look that's not far from pity and I certainly don't want that.

"Go," I say a little more forcefully, but still with a smile.

"Okay." She nods and hugs me again. Then she whispers

in my ear. "You should go get the girl."

The universe is weird like this. When I hear someone like Claire tell me to go for it, I feel like it's less of a fool's journey. Claire, who's so sarcastic. Claire, who's rooting for me. My, oh my. The tables sure are turning.

I pick up my drink and scan the crowd, trying to find Sam. I see him in a booth with a pretty girl and they're chatting up a storm. The ounce of sober in me says to leave them alone, but drunk me wants to sit for a while and damn the consequences to poor Sam.

"Sup, bro," I say, taking a seat beside him. Apparently, drinking in my old age turns my lexicon into that of a frat boy's.

"Hey," Sam says. "I was just talking about you."

The mystery girl nods. "He was. He says you guys are on some soul-searching road trip."

"*Bachelorette* bros!" Sam and I shout, cheersing our drinks. Had I been soberer, I would've realized how much soberer Sam's new friend was.

"Carly's in love with a girl who's getting married and I wanna take her mind off it," Sam says. "Aren't I a good friend?"

"The best," I concur.

"Y'know," Sam says, turning his attention to me. "You know, we can get to New York in time for her wedding."

"Whose wedding?" I slur.

"Duh, Mollie's."

"Who's Mollie?" the new girl asks.

"The girl Carly's in love with who we were just talking about." Sam says this like it's a fact everyone in the world should be aware of.

"But not to you?" the girl asks me. I nod.

"No!" Sam shouts, slamming his hand onto the table. "And we should fix that. We gotta fix that."

"She must be really cute if you're gonna stop a wedding," she says.

"Totally," Sam whistles. "Wait. I've never actually seen a picture of her."

"Oh, well, I can fix that," I say, reaching for my phone.

I flip through my photos and find the one I took of Mollie the day she graduated from Stanford. She's pulling a face, her tongue peeking out at me because she complained I took too many pictures, outstretched arms, sunny California shining like a halo around her. I smile as Sam snatches the phone out of my hands.

"Talk about a babe!" Sam cries as he shows the picture to the girl sitting next to him.

"I didn't know you liked boats," she says, looking at me in an odd way.

"I don't," I say, brow furrowed.

"Then why do you have a picture of a dreamboat on your phone?" she asks, and Sam cackles.

"Dear lord." That sounds like one of my dad's jokes.

"C'mon, Carly. Road trip across America with your best friend for true love," Sam urges.

"We could just fly. It'd be easier," I point out.

"True love's not supposed to be easy," he says.

"It's never easy," the girl adds.

"Yeah. No fun, no leg room, no nothing," Sam continues, and I must look pretty unconvinced. "I'll let you pick the music."

All of a sudden I'm interested. "The whole way?"

He nods, smile spreading. "The whole way. Las Vegas to New York City, baby."

"Never call me baby again," I warn him. I'm trying to convince him that I'm super serious about this, but I don't think it's working.

Sam looks at the girl he's certainly enamored with. "I think I wanna call *you* baby."

She blushes.

A ridiculous thought pops into my head. "You should totally come with us."

Clearly, drunk me forgets the concept of Stranger Danger.

"Really?" she asks, looking at me in surprise.

"Yeah," Sam and I say together.

"But you guys could be serial killers."

I grab Sam's face. "Look at these cheeks. You really think

he could kill someone?"

"Yeah! And you think a girl driving thousands of miles to stop a wedding could kill someone?" Sam asks.

She looks back and forth at us for a little while before a smile creeps across her face and she squeals, "Road trip!"

The three of us stand up and yell "road trip" like the sorority girls I'm sure none of us ever were.

That's the last thing I remember.

19

Ready to Run
by One Direction

I wake up with a cold In-N-Out burger on my chest, and I have to say that even though this feels weird, it's not the strangest situation I've ever been in. I examine the burger, and since it still looks good, I take a bite. As I start to chew, someone stirs next to me. I look over, expecting to see Sam's curly hair, but instead, there's a messy bun of black hair on the pillow. The body attached to the hair is sleeping soundly. I have never leapt out of a bed so fast.

"You don't remember her either?" Sam whispers frantically from behind me.

I jump and turn to look at him. "Dude, I am so fragile right now. Don't scare me like that again!"

"I remember a girl last night, but I don't remember her coming home with us."

I take another bite of my burger. "Clearly she did and it sure looks like we all spent the night cuddled on that goddamn queen bed."

"She's breathing, right? We didn't *Jawbreaker* her, did

we?" Sam asks.

"Hold this." I pass my burger to him and he immediately takes a bite.

As quietly as I can, I lean down and put my ear as close to the girl's mouth as possible. The only thing I can hear is Sam chewing, and I'm about to pronounce her dead and start planning our escape to Tijuana when she speaks.

"Good morning to you, too."

"Shit!" I jump back.

"You're alive!" Sam says.

She smiles brightly. "You two are the worst serial killers ever." She hops out of bed, kisses Sam's cheek, and steals the burger. Looks like I'm not getting that back.

"So when are we leaving?" she asks through a mouthful.

"Leaving?" Me.

"We?" Sam.

"Yeah. Are you already chickening out?" Her.

"Oh my god," I murmur, as memories start hazily coming back.

"How do you remember anything that happened last night?" Sam asks her.

She shrugs. "I grew up here. This ain't my first rodeo."

"We invited you to road trip to Mollie's wedding," I say.

"Yeah," she says, taking another bite. "So how about it?"

"We can't stop a wedding," I groan. "I'm sorry, but we just can't."

"No one ever said anything about we. That's all you, kid," Sam says.

"Okay, look, I'm all for your big dramatic road trip, but just because I drunkenly agreed to stop a wedding, that doesn't mean we should actually stop a wedding," I ramble.

"Again with the we. It's all you," Sam reiterates.

"What if we just start driving and see where it takes us? Do you really wanna give up on a road trip before it even starts?" the mystery girl asks.

Sam and I look at each other, telepathically running through the pros and cons of this scenario. Pro, we think we all had fun together last night, but Sam and I were drunk, so who really knows. Con, she could be a murderer. Pro, we'd have another person to drive when Sam and I get tired. Con, we did just meet her and we'd be confined to a car for a minimum of 5,000 miles if we went all the way to Mollie's wedding and back. Pro, she's cute. Neither of us can think of a con to go with that pro. Sam and I reach our telepathic conclusion.

"Let's do it," Sam says, breaking the silence.

"Let's road trip across America," I join in, still somewhat in disbelief. "Why not?"

"And crash a wedding," the stranger says, winking at me.

"Keep that on the back burner," I warn her. "We'll have to wait and see."

"Well, you've got 2,500 miles to think about it."

I sigh. "Listen, if I'm going to do it, and I'm still deciding whether or not I want to, I need to do it right," I say. "You know, should the time come when I decide I want to do it. I don't have a tux or even a suit. I'm not going to run through the church doors wearing a t-shirt that says What Happens in Vegas, Stays in Vegas."

The girl laughs. "Okay, fair point. We'll get you a suit. I know a place."

I look closely at her and cannot remember if I ever learned her name last night. Y'all know I'm not good with faces and names.

"So I'm just going to get this awkwardness out of the way now," I say. "I was super drunk last night and I have no idea what your name is."

She laughs out loud. "I'm so glad you said something because I don't know what your names are either. I'm Sam."

What are the odds? Ha! A Vegas joke. "No fucking way." I point to Sam. "That's Sam too. I'm going to have to refer to you guys as Boy Sam and Girl Sam."

"Why can't I just be Sam? You've known me longer," Boy Sam complains.

Girl Sam ignores him and looks at me. "I'm not the biggest fan of gendered things like that. I kind of prefer the whole they/them thing."

"No problem. What about Old Sam and New Sam?"

"Now I'm Old Sam?"

New Sam smiles. "I like it," then they pause. "Wait, your name isn't Sam, too, is it?"

"Can you imagine? Old Sam, New Sam, and Gay Sam traveling across America. No. I'm Carly."

They nod. "Well, nice to meet you, Carly and Old Sam. Remind me again whose wedding we're stopping?"

"That'd be Mollie Fae," Old Sam pipes up. "Carly's long-lost lover."

"Ew, never say lover," I cry. "It sounds weird. And it's not a definite thing that anyone is stopping the wedding."

New Sam looks at my current outfit. "You're right about the suit, though. Your shirt's got a few too many holes in it."

"I keep telling her to throw that shirt away," Old Sam agrees.

"And I keep telling you it's an original from Bruce Springsteen's 1975 Born to Run tour and that you can throw it away over my dead body." I cross my arms in front of my chest, ready to defend this piece of history.

"You kids can settle this later. We'd better get moving if we're going to find you an emergency suit," New Sam says. "Pack your stuff and let's get this show on the road."

****

In record time, we're packed, checked out, and have purchased a suit. I'll save you the fashion montage, mainly because it's boring. To recap, I tried on a black suit, then a brown one, then a slightly darker black one, then finally bought a nice navy one. God, I even got bored just from writing that.

We're finally on the road out of Vegas, me driving, New Sam riding shotgun, and Old Sam lounging in the back seat.

"Are we there yet?" Old Sam asks.

"We haven't even been driving for five minutes," New Sam says.

"Yeah, and we don't have a real destination. We're just heading east. Searching for the rising sun and all that poetic stuff. So get comfortable." I smile at Old Sam in the rearview mirror.

"I like this," New Sam says, gesturing to the highway in front of us, kicking their feet up on the dashboard.

"Let me get my playlist going," I say, pressing a few buttons on my phone.

"You made a playlist for this? Already?" New Sam asks.

"Did you just expect me to listen to the radio?" I counter.

"Is the radio really that bad?"

"It's terrible," I say.

"Carly loves music. She has a playlist for all things driving. Driving when it's raining, driving when it's sunny, driving when it feels like fall, driving when it's sunny but she feels sad. And the list goes on and on and on," Old Sam explains.

"I just put my library on shuffle," New Sam says.

I'm sure there's a pained expression on my face. "I don't think I could do that."

I finally find the right playlist and Elvis' *Viva Las Vegas* comes through the car speakers.

"I'm going to assume it's not a coincidence that *Viva Las Vegas* is the first song that's playing as we're leaving Las Vegas," New Sam says.

Old Sam pats their shoulder. "Now you're catching on."

I smile. "I made songs for every state, just in case I ever got the chance to drive across the country."

"Y'know, I was confident you guys couldn't possibly be serial killers, but now I'm not so sure. Your attention to detail about these playlists frightens me," New Sam says warily.

I laugh, then continue my Elvis impersonation as he guides us through the dusty, rambling desert.

They say the sky is bigger out west. I never really understood that. How could the sky in one place be bigger than the sky in another? We're all on the same planet, right? And I still don't get it, but it's true. The sky is massive out here. There's no end in sight. It just goes on and on for forever. The sun is behind us and mixing with the day. Somehow the sunset's different out here, too. More colors, brighter, bolder. The desert is a weird place, but my god, if it isn't the prettiest place ever.

****

The thing about road trips is that not a lot happens for long stretches of time. Don't get me wrong, I like road trips. I like that it's basically doing nothing while still actually doing something. You know what I mean? Like I'm just sitting in a car, letting it do all the work, but no one's gonna call me lazy or anything because I'm technically en route to something. It's great. I just get to eat junk food and sing songs. Thankfully, New Sam and I have similar tastes in music. Old Sam is the only one complaining.

"Should we start thinking about where we're going to stay tonight?" New Sam asks.

"According to the GPS," Old Sam says, "the next city we're going to pass through is Crescent Junction, Utah. Junction is such a great word. I wish people said it more."

"It's fairly limited in its uses," New Sam says.

"You said Utah, though, right?" All of a sudden I have an inspiration.

"Yes. Why?" Old Sam asks.

"I know people who live in Utah," I say, pulling Alice's business card out of my shirt pocket.

"Utah's a pretty big state," New Sam offers.

I ignore them and tell the car to dial Alice's number. She picks up on the second ring.

"This is Alice."

"Hey, Alice. It's Carly. Carly Allen."

"Oh my god, Carly! How are you?" she exclaims.

"I'm good. How're you and Marty? How'd the dress turn out?"

"The dress is insane, Carly," she says. "Marty is good too. We're looking for cakes now, so if you've got any cake tips, you let me know."

I laugh. "I will. Definitely. Listen, though, I remember you guys saying you were in Utah for the time being, right?"

"That sure is right," Alice says.

"Well, here's the thing, I'm currently in Utah."

"What part? It's a pretty big state, you know," Alice says.

Does everyone think I failed geography? "Yes, I know that. We're in Crescent Junction. Or, well, we're about to be."

"Crescent Junction! That's right near us," Alice exclaims. I hear her yell away from the receiver. "Marty, get some pillows and sheets, Carly's staying the night."

"Oh, that's so nice of you," I say.

"Of course. It's no trouble at all," Alice says.

"I don't want to impose, and if it's too much, we can find another place to stay, but I'm not alone."

"You're not alone? Oh!" she gasps. "Is it the girl you told us about?"

"No, no, no," I say quickly. "It's two friends of mine, but the reason we're in Utah is kind of related to that girl. It's a long story."

"Say no more," Alice tells me. "Save it for when you get here. I'll text you the address and don't you three dare think of eating before you get here. Marty is going to cook for you."

"Thank you, Alice. This is all too nice."

"We're looking forward to it," she says. "See you soon!"

I hang up the phone and look at the Sams. "We've got dinner and a room tonight. You're welcome."

"How do you know these people again?" Old Sam asks.

"I met them on my flight to Annie's wedding," I say.

"Cool," New Sam says. "Listen, I like that you made friends on an airplane, but how do we know they're not going to murder us. They're total strangers."

"Technically, so are you," I reply. "And look at us all now. Bonded by sharing the same In-N-Out burger for breakfast."

"That bond's unbreakable," Old Sam nods.

20

She Lit a Fire
by Lord Huron

We get in around nine and Alice is out front, smiling and waving from the porch.

"That woman looks too enthusiastic to be safe," New Sam says. "I'm terrified. I don't think I've ever had that much enthusiasm in my entire life."

"She's waving like one of those good luck cats in Chinatown on speed," Old Sam says.

"Be nice," I say, unclipping my seatbelt. "She's sweet."

As soon as I'm out of the car, Alice has sprinted down the stairs and launched herself into my arms.

"Hey," I laugh into her hair. "It's so good to see you!"

"You too!" she squeals in my ear.

"Let the poor kid breathe," I hear Marty say.

"Fine." Alice slowly lets go of me.

"It's good to see you, Carly," Marty says, pulling me into a softer, less intense hug.

"You too," I say.

"And who might you two be?" Marty and I turn to see

Alice talking to the Sams.

"Sam," they say at the same time.

"Well that's not confusing," Marty laughs.

"Sam," Old Sam says. "He/him."

"Sam also," New Sam smiles. "They/them."

"I'm so excited to meet friends of Carly's!" Alice swallows them up in a joint hug.

"Should I rescue them?" Marty asks as we watch the Sams struggle under Alice's impressive hold.

"Nah, they'll be fine." I give the Sams a thumbs up.

"Come on." Marty claps a hand on my shoulder and turns toward the house. "You can help me with dinner."

Their home is very simple and a little empty. Marty tells me they're only here while Alice works on a film, and they couldn't bring themselves to waste money decorating it for such a short period of time. They did bring some photos of the two of them. They're stuck to the fridge with magnets and they're from all over the world. Marty catches me staring.

"You're lucky," I say, pointing at the photos.

"Luck's only part of it." Marty is next to me.

"What do you mean?"

"I mean, yeah, you have to be lucky enough to be in the same place at the same time so you can meet. But after that, luck's got nothing to do with it."

"Luck's got everything to do with it," I counter.

"Ah," Marty sighs. "You are so young."

"I don't think that has anything to do with it either."

"That wasn't an insult. Everyone feels that way. They think love is this big grand cosmic thing that happens to us. I was like that." Marty turns back to the stove.

I look closer at the photographs. "What changes?"

"You realize love doesn't happen to you, that it's more of a conscious choice," Marty explains.

"Are you trying to tell me that being gay is a choice?"

"Shut up," Marty laughs. "Okay, so you don't have a choice there. Not in who you're attracted to or anything like that, but after you start dating someone, you have to make a choice about whether the relationship is what you want. The world and the universe don't just *happen*. The course of true love never did run smooth, or something like that."

"I never thought about it that way," I murmur.

"Nobody does when they're young," Marty offers. "It's probably because of all those romantic comedies that make it feel so inevitable, you know? Like there's no other outcome, but there is. There are a million outcomes. Maybe more when it comes to love, but eventually you have to make a conscious decision to fight for what you want. Love's very easy to lose, but I guess I don't have to tell you that."

"You definitely do not," I say.

"All I know is that most of the world has it wrong," Marty repeats. "Love is a choice. Always. You have to choose to stay in the thick of it and fight for it. It's not always easy, but it's also not just going to fall into your lap."

"Are you a closet hopeless romantic?" I tease Marty.

She looks away. "I have no idea what you're talking about."

Just then, Alice comes into the kitchen with the two Sams.

"Alice!" I exclaim. "Is Marty a romantic?"

"Are you kidding me?" Alice takes a seat on a stool at the island. "Is she telling you about the time she played a boombox under my dorm window?"

"Alice!" Marty squeaks.

"No? Maybe about the time she stood on a chair in our cafeteria and asked me on a date?"

"I want to hear both of those stories," New Sam says. "Now.

It's infectious the way Marty and Alice are around each other. I can see what Marty means about a choice. It'd be easy to turn and run when things get hard. Hi, I'm the poster child for that. But I guess real strength comes from knowing whether to stay or go. Staying isn't always the best choice, because not all relationships work and not all relationships should work. But in that same vein, not every relationship is doomed to crash and burn. Fight or flight. The hard part is figuring out how to tell the difference.

Alice loves stories. It's obvious if you spend five minutes with her. She'll already have told you three stories in that amount of time. Marty knows that, so she does all these things to give Alice stories to tell. And it's not the fact that she's standing on a chair in a cafeteria proclaiming her love that proves she loves Alice, it's the fact that she knows Alice well enough to know that this is what makes her happy.

Isn't that all love is? When wanting to make somebody happy makes you happy? And when you know they'll do the same for you? It's so painfully simple that it's easy to forget.

****

After dinner, we all go to bed. Alice and Marty have an early morning, and driving takes a toll on the body, even if you are just sitting there. I let the Sams take the big bed in the guest room and I'm on the pull-out couch in the living room. I'm probably the only one in the house still awake. I can just make out the clock on the wall, and it's well past one a.m.

Marty's words about love not being fate keep knocking around in my head. I've kind of always taken solace in the fact that whatever's supposed to happen will happen. Like no matter what happens, my future's mapped out. Of course, that would mean I have no free will and I'm basically just a glorified Sims character. And if we don't have free will, then what are we even doing here?

Do I truly want free will, or am I happy being a pawn as

long as my life pretty much goes the way I want it to go? But I guess there's no reason to believe my life will be what I want it to be just because it's going down the path it's supposed to. People don't necessarily want their lives to go the way they go, and so many people feel like they're in a trap they can't get out of, but that's the thing about life. It just keeps going.

I can't think about this anymore, so I get out of bed and tiptoe into the kitchen to get a glass of water. I take a seat at the table and start playing with the ends of the placemats.

"What are you doing up so late, Carly?" I hear Alice ask.

"Oh, shoot, I'm sorry if I woke you," I say as I turn around in my chair. "I just couldn't sleep, and sometimes a glass of water helps."

"You didn't wake me up. Don't worry." She puts a hand on my shoulder before she sits down next to me. "Do you often have trouble sleeping?"

"Not really. Mostly just when I'm in new cities or new people's houses."

Alice laughs. "I couldn't sleep the entire first night we moved here. I think I stayed up for two days straight before I finally crashed."

I laugh. "I hope it won't be that bad. There's just a lot on my mind."

"It's that girl again, isn't it?" Alice asks.

I shrug. "Part of the reason the Sams brought me out

here is to go to her wedding. We're talking about total movie moment, barge in through the church doors, and ask her to pick me. I don't know. I just don't know if it's what I want, or what I *should* do even if it is what I want. My brain won't shut up."

"You know what I think?" Alice asks, leaning back in her chair.

"What?"

"I think everyone has one person they'd stop a wedding for." Alice says this as if it's a simple fact everyone in the world knows.

I look over at her. "What exactly do you mean?"

Alice considers for a moment. "Every single person has that someone in their life they'd fly across the country for, knock down church doors for. Their could've been, should've been, would've been."

"What would you say to that person though?" I take a deep breath. "Like, okay, how would you feel if someone just burst through the doors of your wedding like that? Wouldn't it ruin everything?"

"No one would burst through my doors."

"I'm speaking in the hypothetical."

"Okay, but I'm talking about the real world," she says. "There's no one in my past who would do that."

Now I'm really confused. "Alice, you literally just said that everyone has someone they'd ruin a wedding for."

"Yes," she nods. "Sometimes, though, that's the person you get to marry. If anyone on the planet would burst through the doors to stop my wedding, it'd be Marty."

"Oh."

"I stand by what I said." She sits up a little straighter. "We all have that person. Everyone has that person and that relationship lodged so deeply in their heart. I'm just lucky enough to be marrying that person. Some people have to fight a little harder."

"So you think this is reasonable?" I ask quietly.

"Carly, I'm going to be honest with you because I like you." Alice's eyes drop to the engagement ring on her finger, and she twists it around a few times. "I don't know much about you. All I really know is that for some reason, after all these years, you can't get this girl out of your head. That has to mean something."

"Yeah. It could mean I'm obsessed with one of the first girls I ever dated and I can't move on," I say wearily.

"Do you believe that?"

"That I'm pathetically obsessed?" I ask. "Yes."

"Then why are you here?" she asks, gesturing around. "Why are you in Utah?"

I shift uncomfortably. "I don't know."

"People don't just start driving across the country for no reason, Carly," Alice says softly.

"First time for everything, right?" I sigh.

"If you still love her, you have to tell her." Alice is insistent.

"Why?"

"It's the right thing to do. What if she still loves you?"

"She doesn't. She can't." I raise my voice. "She's the one who gave up on us. She's the one getting married."

"But maybe only because she thinks you aren't an option anymore! This is a two-way street, remember. You didn't call her because you thought she'd moved on and that's the same reason she probably didn't call you. Unless you sent out a fucking bat signal telling her you were still interested, she had no reason to believe you were."

"I guess," I mutter.

"I'm right and you know it. Listen, I can't tell you what to do or force you to go to that church, but I can tell you that if you don't, you're going to think about it every single day for the rest of your life. I can't guarantee she'll say yes or that it won't be the most nerve-racking moment of your life, but I can guarantee that it's something you *need* to do."

"I just want a sign," I say. "A sign from the universe that there's a part of her that wants this too. Because maybe we all do have that person we'd stop a wedding for, but maybe I'm not that person for her. Maybe she's marrying the right girl."

Alice puts her hand on mine and gives it a squeeze. "Maybe you're right," she says with a sweet smile. "But it also sounds like you're hiding behind maybes."

I grimace. "I just want a sign. That's not too much to ask, is it?"

"I guess not." Alice pats my hand and sits back in her chair. "Just promise me that when you do finally get the sign you're looking for, you follow it. It may not lead you to Mollie, but when you do find the girl, whoever she is, never let her go."

I nod once. "I won't."

21

I Fought the Law
by The Clash

Alice and Marty left a note saying they had to head into work super early, so they wouldn't be able to send us off. We spend the day driving through Colorado to North Platte, Nebraska. Aside from a brief near-death experience for Old Sam due to altitude sickness, it's an uneventful day. We're all kind of tired, so we make it an early night.

The next morning, we leave our sketchy motel and head to the nearest McDonald's. After everyone's satisfied with their food and caffeine purchases, we walk back to the car. I go to the driver's door, but Old Sam beats me to it.

"Yes?" I look at him threateningly.

"I was thinking I could drive."

"And why is that?" I ask.

"Can you guys open the door? It's cold and I'm going to drop something," New Sam says.

Old Sam clicks the doors open, but doesn't get out of my way.

"You drove yesterday," he says.

"It is my car," I reply.

"I've got a plan for today," he says.

"I don't like the sound of that." I narrow my eyes, trying to figure out what he's up to now.

"Yeah, well, I'm thinking a little detour would be fun."

He's not wrong, but I also don't want to give him the satisfaction of being right. However, napping in the back of the car does sound like a really nice time.

"Fine," I say. "One detour."

"Not to add to your guys' weird power struggle thing, but can there really be a detour if we haven't figured out a route?" New Sam spouts wisdom from the passenger seat.

Old Sam opens the driver's door and pokes his head inside the car. "Have I told you yet that I like you?"

New Sam blushes a little. "Not yet."

"Okay!" I know when to give in. "I'm getting into the back seat. Old Sam, please wake me up whenever we get to whatever weird detour you've chosen for us. New Sam, please stop encouraging him."

And then, after I drink my coffee and eat my egg sandwich, I fall right asleep.

****

I don't know how much time passes, but eventually I feel a hand on my leg lightly shaking me awake.

"Carly. Hey, Carly, wake up. We're here," Old Sam says.

"Where is here exactly?" I keep my eyes closed because I was in the middle of a really nice nap. If wherever here is doesn't sound great, I'm going to continue with that nap.

"Boys Town, Nebraska?" New Sam guesses.

"Oh, no, no, no. Boys Town, Nebraska, does not sound like a good place for a lesbian." I sit up, suddenly wide awake.

"Listen, we're not going to be here long," Old Sam says, unbuckling his seatbelt and opening the car door. "Real quick, I promise. I've always wanted to come here."

"Boys Town?" Me.

"Nebraska?" New Sam.

"The World's Largest Ball of Stamps," Old Sam announces to the world, his arms open wide.

"Yeah, this is where I die. At the World's Largest Ball of Stamps in Boys Town, Nebraska." I begrudgingly follow New Sam out of the car. "I guess I've had a good life, all things considered."

"Logistically, how did they make this stamp ball? Like, is there one crumpled stamp in the middle they made it around, or is it a big ball they glued stamps on and therefore a massive lie?" New Sam asks.

"Wow, okay. Clearly, you and Old Sam are more invested in this than I will ever be," I say.

"Get in the spirit, Carly," Old Sam urges. "Welcome to the Middle of America."

"Fine, but I reserve the right to choose a detour at some point during this trip."

"Done deal," Old Sam says. "You name it."

"Oh! We should go to Disneyland!" New Sam shouts.

"Love the enthusiasm," Old Sam says. "Kinda the wrong direction though."

The last time I went to Disneyland, I was still dating Mollie Fae.

****

"Carly, I really think you're not heading the right way," Mollie said, neck craning to try and read the name of the exit we just blew past.

"What? Oh, that's fine. I know this back way. Avoids the highway and all the traffic." I looked over at her. "You know, Southern California traffic's just the worst."

"We're literally on a highway right now." Mollie gestured at the cars surrounding us and the four lanes stretching in front of us.

"I meant it avoids the busiest highways."

"I don't trust you." She fake glared at me.

"I am so offended. All these years and you don't trust me?" I pretended to tear up. "I really thought our relationship was built on a firm foundation."

"If it was, you'd tell me where we're going."

"Oh my god." I sighed dramatically. "It's a surprise! Humor me please, love." I gave her my best smile.

"Fine," she said. It was the nickname. Something about it just made her soften instantly every time.

I laughed. "When we get there, you're going to feel like such a fool for pouting."

She closed her eyes and quickly fell asleep. I didn't wake her until we were parked in the lot.

"Hey, Mollie," I said gently. "Wake up, please."

She stirred. "Five more minutes."

"No, no, let's go. Day's starting," I said.

She finally opened her eyes and looked around blearily. "We're in a parking lot."

"Nothing gets by you, huh?" I said, slapping her thigh. "Hop out. C'mon."

She mumbled incoherently before opening her door and getting out. "Why are so many people wearing Disney shirts?"

I laughed. "I'm gonna let you mull that one over for like five more seconds," I said, walking ahead of her.

"Wait," I heard her whisper, and then she ran up next to me. "Are we at Disneyland?"

I nodded and she squealed with excitement, jumping onto my back. I hiked her higher to give her a proper piggyback ride. "It took you long enough."

She leaned down and kissed my cheek, leaving a bright

red lipstick stain. I remember it stayed on my cheek all day and even left a mark on my pillowcase that night.

It was one of my favorite days. Mollie bought a pair of Minnie ears and we got matching t-shirts. The whole nine yards. Our fingers were sticky from cotton candy. My stomach felt queasy from all the sugar and the rides, and maybe the feeling that this was it. Maybe this was how it was going to be for the rest of my life. Mollie's hand in mine, taking on the world, laughing. How naïve.

We closed the park down. It was past eleven when we headed out to the car, and here's a piece of advice for all you young lovers out there. If you've spent all day together in a weird environment when it's 90+ degrees outside, don't talk. You're both exhausted. Mentally and physically. You're not in a good headspace, even if you just had the best day ever. Trust me. It's not going to end well. Also, thank you for ignoring the fact that I used the phrase "young lovers." No, I don't know when I aged 97 years.

"You really should let me pay you back for the ticket," Mollie said, head lolling back on the headrest, her eyes fighting to stay open. Every sign in the goddamn world to not push this.

"You really should stop offering," I said, more harshly than I should have. "I've wanted to do this for a long time, okay? Would it make you feel better if I said I got a good discount?"

"Moderately," she said. "But you need to be saving your money."

"And I am. Even without you constantly reminding me," I snap. "Almost like a real adult."

"That's not what I'm saying, Carly."

"No, no, I get it. You're going to be a big lawyer and make lots of money. Having to tell all your law school friends that your girlfriend works at Target bums you out. I get it. We can't all get what we want right out of college."

"You've been out of college a couple of years now," she said quietly.

"Sorry my career path isn't going the way you want it to," I shot back.

"I don't care that you work at Target!"

"Then why are you acting so weird about the fact that I bought tickets to Disneyland? Why? What is this about then? I didn't throw a fit when you took us to that insanely expensive restaurant when I visited you in San Francisco!" I said loudly. Too loudly for my small car.

"Clearly it bothered you, since you still remember it enough to bring it up!"

"No! God, I trusted that you could afford it because I trust that you know what you can and can't afford. Clearly that doesn't go both ways," I said.

"You're right. I'm sorry," Mollie said. She probably said it sincerely, too.

And that should've been the end of it. But I couldn't stop. Every shitty feeling of self-doubt I had about where my life was at this point was coming out.

"You know you could dump me, right?" I said in the worst, most biting tone I could muster. "Like, if I'm such an embarrassment to you, nothing's making you stay here."

She shook her head and looked out the window. "I'm not going to participate in this."

"Participate in what?"

"This! This self-deprecating soliloquy and defensive tactic where you take your feelings and try to force them into my mouth and...and I just can't handle it," Mollie trailed off.

I didn't have much to add to that. She pretty much called me out in a 100% factual way. That was *exactly* what I was trying to do.

"Look, it's been a long day. My feet are killing me, your face is beet red, and I think we should both just cool off. I'm sorry if you feel like I belittled you. That's not what I intended. I'd never do that." She reached over and put her hand on my thigh.

They say hindsight is 20/20, but I still don't know what made me act like that. I mean, when the person you love is getting everything they want, you should be happy for them. And I thought I was happy for her. In retrospect, I shouldn't have lost my mind when she asked if I could afford it because I was making $12 an hour. Hell, even now I only make $15 an hour. Side note, can we please make the minimum wage a living wage?

I think it was probably jealousy that made me act that way. Anger dissipates. You can only be angry for so long before it gives out. Something about it makes it unsustainable, but jealousy lives forever. It's not the anger of someone cheating that ruins the relationship, it's the jealousy of that mysterious other person. Before you freak out, no, nobody cheated on anybody. But that jealousy never left. Instead, it took up a post at the forefront of my feelings about Mollie. A chasm had opened up and I didn't know how much longer I'd be able to hold on.

I remember seeing the highway exit for Disneyland in my rearview mirror and thinking it felt a lot like a last hurrah.

The last good day.

****

"Come in, Carly Allen. Carly Allen. Earth to Carly Allen," Old Sam's voice echoes.

I put on a fake smile. "Hey."

"Where'd you go?" New Sam asks.

I don't like that they're this perceptive.

"This place just reminded me of something," I say.

"What kind of fucked up–" New Sam starts.

"Let's go inside, shall we?" Old Sam says, saving me

from going back down memory lane.

There's an entire visitor's center dedicated to this ball. I thought we'd have to go into someone's garage that had a distinct urine smell. That's just how I picture any weird roadside attraction. In someone's garage that smells overwhelmingly like urine. Oh, and probably a homeless cat or two roaming around.

"It's smaller than I expected," New Sam says as we make our way into the room with the stamp ball.

"I've never been told that before." Old Sam gives us a wink.

I shove him. "Yeah, I second that. It's not even taller than me."

"I will say that I, too, thought it would be bigger," Old Sam adds.

"You've been dreaming of coming here and you never once looked at a picture of it?" I ask, poking the ball and trying to see how sturdy it is.

He shrugs. "I wanted it to be a surprise."

"So how long are we gonna look at this thing?" I ask.

"Do you think spit or glue is the adhesive?" New Sam asks.

"I hope it's glue, because otherwise I'm going to pour a whole bottle of hand sanitizer on myself." I move the hand I touched the ball with as far away from my body as I can.

"Don't be dramatic," Old Sam says. He hands me his

phone. "I'm going to climb on top of it real fast. Take a picture before we get thrown out."

"Please do not make me go to the police station in Boys Town, Nebraska," I beg as I open the camera app.

"New Sam, make sure the coast is clear," Old Sam says, then walks casually to the ball.

"There's one old dude in here, and he's reading the newspaper. He could also be asleep. Or dead. We should check his pulse," New Sam whispers.

"How are you going to pose?" I ask.

"I'm just gonna jump up and sit on top of the stamp ball and then we're gonna haul ass out of here." Old Sam bounces on his toes a little to get himself prepared. "Ready?"

"Yeah, I'm just gonna shutter the hell out of this." I get Old Sam and the stamp ball in frame.

"Now!" Old Sam jumps.

I don't know if the old dude reading the newspaper is magically connected to the World's Largest Ball of Stamps, but the second Old Sam jumps on top of it, he shoots up out of his chair like he's protecting the gold in Fort Knox.

"Get down from there, you heathen!"

Man, I love that he just casually calls Old Sam a heathen. I start laughing, and then I hear the sound of a shotgun being cocked. I yank Old Sam off the World's Largest Ball of Stamps and he lands with a thud.

"Old dude with a shotgun coming this way!" New Sam

shouts.

"Let's go!" I grab both of them and run back to where I remember seeing a fire door.

The three of us stumble through other stamp things and end up in a hallway where the old dude is casually standing, his shotgun pointed right at us.

"You meddling kids!"

Until this moment, I didn't know Boys Town, Nebraska, existed in the Scooby Doo universe. We all scream and head back the way we came.

"Make a right at that display case!" New Sam yells.

We get through another section of the visitor's center and there it is; the emergency fire exit. Old Sam bursts through the door and the fire alarm wails.

"Who has the keys?" New Sam asks as we run to the car.

"Old Sam, if you lost the keys while you were climbing on top of that idiotic ball of stamps, I will leave you here to be murdered," I say.

Old Sam's patting every pocket he has and coming up empty.

"OLD SAM, I SWEAR TO GOD YOU'D BETTER FIND THOSE KEYS!" I yell.

"Aha!" he exclaims, pulling the keys out of one of the pockets of his flannel.

"Open the doors!" New Sam cries.

We throw ourselves into the car and slam the doors shut.

Old Sam's trying to make my Prius burn rubber, but it's a Prius, so at best we're only lightly toasting.

The old dude comes out of the fire door as we're pulling onto the main road, one hand holding the shotgun, the other shaking a fist in the air.

"He looks like the Scooby Doo villain version of Clint Eastwood," I say, staring out the back window as we speed away.

"I thought so, too!" New Sam laughs. "It was the meddling kids thing."

I face forward again. "Old Sam, I would've never forgiven you if you'd made us die at The World's Largest Ball of Stamps in Boys Town, Nebraska."

"What a story!" he says, slapping the wheel. "We could've been shot!"

"Yeah," New Sam says flatly. "Not an experience I need to ever have again."

"Oh my god," Old Sam says, his tone more solemn now. "We could've been shot."

"Yeah, you idiot," I agree, laughing weakly.

"Nothing like near death to give me a jolt," Old Sam says, his enthusiasm resurging.

New Sam kicks their feet up on the dashboard. "Next time, let's just stop for some damn coffee."

"So." I clear my throat. "Where to now?"

"Anyone else have any detours they're dying to take?"

Old Sam nudges New Sam's arm. "Get it? Dying? Because we just almost got shot by a Scooby Doo villain."

22

Jack and Diane
by John Mellencamp

"What do you think these people do?" I ask.

We're in The Heartland. Tornado Alley. Middle of America, USA. A whole lot of nothing stretching as far as the eye can see.

"Like for fun?" New Sam asks from the back seat.

"Yeah, or even for work," I reply. "There's literally nothing out here."

"How are you sure there are even people out here?" Old Sam asks.

"People have to live out here. No way there's this massive expanse of nothingness without some sort of human colonization," I tell him. "Especially in America. We pave everything."

"Look! Smoke!" New Sam points ahead of us.

Sure enough, there's a small house with smoke coming out of the chimney. One car is parked out front, but it doesn't look like it's driven often.

"Where do you think they get groceries?" I wonder.

"Maybe they're self-sustainable," New Sam suggests.

"No way," Old Sam says. "Think about what people need. We can't live like pilgrims anymore. Just take toilet paper. No one's making their own toilet paper at home. Food, maybe, but I guarantee you no one is at home making toilet paper."

"Maybe they don't use toilet paper," New Sam offers.

"No way. They have to use toilet paper. We need toilet paper." Old Sam thinks for a moment. "Unless our need for toilet paper is just something created by corporations, and there's no actual reason for us to use it. Oh my god, what if it's all a lie?"

"Sam! Chill," I say. "People need toilet paper. You've explained to me in excruciating detail what happens after you eat at Taco Bell. You need toilet paper after that."

"What if Taco Bell's in on it?" Old Sam exclaims.

"Everyone please just relax," New Sam says.

"Old Sam really likes conspiracy theories." I offer this as a half-hearted explanation for whatever mental breakdown he just had.

"It's true," Old Sam nods.

"So you think the moon landing was directed by Stanley Kubrick and he left clues in *The Shining?*" New Sam asks.

Old Sam gasps ever so softly. "You watched that documentary too?"

"Sure did," New Sam nods. "I thought it started pretty

strong, but it became convoluted and repetitive by the end."

"Oh my god, I think I love you," Old Sam whispers. I slap his arm.

"Hey! Don't mess with the driver!" he cries.

"Do you think these people are happy out here?" New Sam asks.

"I don't know," Old Sam says.

"I'd like to think so," I join in. "I mean, somebody's gotta like this. People like being away from the hustle and bustle, y'know? People like simplicity."

"Isn't this less simple, though?" New Sam asks. "Have you seen a hospital lately? I haven't. What if there's an emergency? Do you just hope your neighbor, who probably lives ten miles away, can help?"

"Hell, what if you just wanna date somebody?" Old Sam wonders.

I give him a weird look.

"I'm serious! How do you find anybody?" he continues. "Are you just stuck with whoever ends up at your high school? Do you go to tractor pulls and hope for the best?"

"Are there even tractor pulls to go to?" New Sam asks. "Where would they have them? And what is a tractor pull?"

"People get together and literally pull things with tractors. They'd probably have them in some of these massive fields." I gesture out the window. "They've got a lot to pick from."

"Those aren't just empty fields, though. They're people's farms," New Sam says.

"This is making my brain hurt," Old Sam groans.

"All I know is that I'm never complaining about sitting in L.A. traffic again when this is a possible alternative," I say.

"The no traffic thing is quite nice," Old Sam says.

"Yeah, because no one has anywhere to go." New Sam laughs. "Ergo, no traffic."

"Still, I'd take L.A. with L.A. traffic any day over Middle of Nowhere, USA, with no traffic," I say. "But I'm still choosing to believe these people are happy."

"Me too," New Sam agrees.

"You guys are ridiculous. I couldn't live out here. They probably don't even have WiFi," Old Sam says.

New Sam shrugs. "I dunno. In the same way people can be unhappy anywhere, I think people can be happy anywhere."

"I live in L.A. and I've been unhappy for years," I remind them.

"I've lived in Vegas my whole life, and on paper that sounds great," New Sam says. "All the neon, people from all over the world, the music, the shows, everything. But I spent most of my life confused about who I was because I couldn't fit into the picture of who society thought I should be. And that sucks. It doesn't matter that there's a whole world outside; feeling alone in Vegas is the same as feeling alone in the middle of nowhere."

"Ergo, feeling happy in Vegas is the same as feeling happy in the Middle of Nowhere." I nod in agreement.

"Stop with this ergo nonsense. You guys aren't smarter than me," Old Sam complains.

I laugh. "I'm just saying, there are probably people out here who are unhappy because they live here, but there are probably just as many people who are happy that of all the places in the world, they ended up here."

"You guys ever watch that Disney Channel movie about the pop star who goes to a small town and loses his phone and two girls help him learn how to be happy?" Old Sam asks.

"Yeah, yeah!" I shout. "It's the guy who's married to Robin from *How I Met Your Mother!*"

"That's him," Old Sam agrees. "But yeah, I guess it's the same thing. You can be happy or sad wherever you are."

"That movie messed me up as a kid," New Sam says. "You had that mega-famous dude who was deeply unhappy, and these girls who had everything going for them who were also wildly unhappy. Disney wasn't messing around."

"So basically, the conclusion we've come to is that anyone can be sad, no matter who or where they are?" I ask.

Old Sam nods. "Well, ain't that dismal."

"But anybody can be happy no matter who or where they are too. You can't forget that part," New Sam reminds us.

"This is getting too deep for me," I say. "Let's change the subject."

"What was your favorite Disney Channel movie?" Old Sam asks instantly. It's like he's been waiting this whole time to talk about the things that really matter.

"Easy," I answer quickly. "*Eddie's Million Dollar Cook-Off.* Hands down."

"What? You hate sports," he scoffs.

"Yes," I say. "But do you remember the blond girl?"

"There it is," New Sam snickers.

"Stop it, I'm being serious," I say. "I mean, if I'm being honest, I probably did think she was cute. However, she also just wanted to play baseball and didn't want to be girly, but she was still a girl. Changed my life. Oh, shit, or *Motocrossed.* I forgot about that movie. It's a toss-up."

Old Sam is unmoved by my choices. "Color me completely unsurprised. New Sam? What Disney Channel movie shaped your childhood?"

"*Cheetah Girls,*" New Sam says, in a voice just above a whisper.

"I'm sorry, what was that?" I ask. How can I resist a little teasing?

"Yeah, speak up for those in front," Old Sam joins in.

"*Cheetah Girls,* okay? I loved *Cheetah Girls.* I had a *Cheetah Girls* party for each new movie," she says defensively. "Carly just liked the gay ones!"

"Hey! I'll have you know I didn't know I was gay when I watched those movies," I retort.

"Not helping yourself, kid," Old Sam laughs.

"No, you know what?" New Sam leans between the two front seats. "I will not be ashamed about liking *Cheetah Girls*. *Strut* is one of the greatest songs that ever existed and yeah, the third one wasn't that great, but what third movie is?"

"*High School Musical*," I say immediately. "*High School Musical 3* is the best."

"Carly Allen, if you didn't have to convince a woman to love you instead of her fiancé in a few days, I would slap you so hard across your face just for saying that," New Sam says sternly.

"Which one could possibly be better?" I ask incredulously.

"The second one," they say matter-of-factly. "It had every iconic moment from the franchise. *Bet On It*. Troy's weird Mufasa moment in the pond. When Troy gets jealous over Gabriella and Ryan hanging out, even though Ryan is so obviously gay. *Gotta Go My Own Way*, the most heartbreaking duet of our generation. That Hawaiian song that got cut. I could go on and on."

"Dunno why that song got cut. It probably would've made it a better movie," I say.

"Okay, here's where you're both wrong," Old Sam interrupts. "The first one is the best one."

"Shut up, Old Sam," New Sam and I say at the same time.

"I'm willing to humor New Sam because they're not painfully wrong like you are," I tell him.

"First of all, you guys wouldn't have your precious sequels if it weren't for the first movie," Old Sam continues. "And besides, are you telling me there's a song in that franchise that's better than *Breaking Free?*"

I sigh. "You do have a point, but the third one has *Scream.*"

"I don't even know what *Scream* is," New Sam says.

"It's the pouty song Troy sings during the thunderstorm. He's in the school and just throws himself against lockers," I say. "It's incredible, and also proof Zac Efron can't dance."

"Don't insult my boy like that," Old Sam says.

"You and my dad would get along great," I laugh.

"So was *High School Musical* your favorite, Old Sam?" New Sam asks.

"Nah, *Alley Cats Strike*," he answers.

"Get out of my car," I tell him. "The stupid bowling movie?"

"That's the one. I wanted to be a pro bowler for a brief period of time. Sue me."

"And now you work HR at Target," I remind him.

"Hey, not everyone's dreams come true," he says.

"Not with that attitude," New Sam says. "If you could

have any job in the world, what would it be?"

"I like my job," Old Sam protests.

"Nuh-uh," New Sam cuts him off. "Any job in the world and you pick HR at Target after you grew up wanting to be a pro bowler? That's a lie."

"We're not shitting on your job," I offer. "Just go along with it. Completely hypothetical."

"Okay, if we're being hypothetical, I guess I've always kind of wanted to be a teacher, like Robin Williams in *Dead Poets Society*. Change lives. Get kids passionate about something."

"A teacher? Dude, that's totally doable!" I say.

"I don't know. It's a lot of school and maybe I don't have the patience," Old Sam says.

"Those sound like easy things to overcome," New Sam says. "Maybe they're just excuses."

"Easy for you to say!" Old Sam exclaims.

"Why's that?"

"Well, um, because you–" Old Sam falters. "What exactly do you do as a job?"

New Sam smiles. "Look at you making assumptions that I just fell into my dream job."

"I'm curious, too, though. What do you do?" I ask. "I feel like you know so much about us and we know nothing about you."

"That's because you guys never stop talking about each

other," New Sam laughs. "I run a restaurant on the Strip."

"And you just abandoned it to go on a road trip with two strangers? What kind of business are you running? Who's running it now?" Old Sam is very concerned.

"The executive chef is running it," New Sam says. "I'm just the owner now. We've been open a while, so it's kind of hands off unless tragedy strikes."

"Did you always want to do that?" Old Sam asks.

New Sam nods. "I've loved cooking ever since I was a kid. I worked any kitchen job I could to get through culinary school, became a sous chef at a nice place in Vegas, went on *Chopped*, won, and opened my own place."

"Holy shit." I whip around in my seat. "You were on *Chopped*? Was Alex Guarnaschelli one of your judges? Why didn't you tell us this earlier?"

"Settle down," New Sam laughs. "Yes, I was on *Chopped*. Yes, Alex was there."

"Oh my god, we have a celebrity in the car." I have to do some deep breathing.

New Sam shrugs. "I'm pretty happy with where I am."

"See." I smack Old Sam on the arm again. "Follow your dreams, kid. Dreams do come true."

"You gotta go for it," New Sam agrees.

Those words throw me back in time.

****

"You gotta go for it," I said, looking up from the letter.

"I don't know," Mollie began. "New York is so far away from you, and everyone says it's an impossible city. I'm a West Coaster. I'm not cut out to make it over there."

"I'm pretty sure Jay-Z and Alicia Keys say that it *is* possible. Like that was the whole point of the song."

She rolled her eyes. "It's just a lot, okay? This law firm is so big."

"Okay, but you always say how you want to do something that will change the world. You need a big law firm to help you do that," I remind her, reading the contents of the letter again.

"Yeah, but I don't know if it's too big a jump. So fast." Mollie bit her nails.

"Shit, you didn't say they wrote to you unsolicited," I said, wide-eyed.

"Um, yeah." Mollie shuffled nervously.

"Mollie! That's incredible!" I smiled widely. "They already have so much faith in you. That's the dream. A job handed to you on a silver platter."

"Carly, slow down," Mollie said, eyes darting around.

"What's wrong?" I asked softly.

She took a deep breath and closed her eyes. "What if they made a mistake. What if I screw up? What if I mess up a case file? Or lose evidence?" Mollie rambled.

"Mollie, look at me. You're going to mess up."

"Carly!"

I laughed. "Let me finish," I said, taking her hands in mine. "Everybody messes up, but they want you. They wrote to you and chose you. They probably had people apply for this job and they were like fuck 'em, we want Mollie Fae. Can't blame them. You're graduating at the top of your class, you're smart, you're passionate, you give a damn, and you work so insanely hard. If the only reason you're worried about taking this job is because you might make a mistake, then you're being ridiculous."

She sniffled. "You're getting good at pep talks. It's almost like you're a writer."

"Used to be a writer," I corrected.

"Carly."

"This day isn't about me. Let's talk about you."

"I just don't understand how you can stand there preaching to me about following my dreams, but you refuse to take your own advice," she said.

"We don't have to talk about this, okay? Today's for celebrating. A law firm in New York fuckin' City wants to hire you! Mollie, can't you see how great this is?"

"I guess so," she said, and a smile started to creep over her face. "New York City, baby!"

I picked her up and twirled her around.

"Aaaah! Put me down! Put me down!" she giggled.

I set her back on the ground and pulled her close.

"Come with me," she whispered. "Come live with me in New York."

"With you?"

"Don't you want to?" she asked.

"So you're for sure taking it?"

"I thought you wanted me to," she said, pulling back a little.

"No, I do. I just didn't know you'd want me to come with you," I said.

"What? You thought we'd just do this thing long distance for the foreseeable future?" she asked.

"When you put it that way, no, but, I don't know. I just hadn't pictured moving to New York. I mean, I have a job here."

"I'm sure you could get transferred if you wanted to," Mollie said. "Besides, I thought you were going to get back into writing. New York's full of publishing houses. You'll be so much closer to them when you do write something. You can just bang on all their doors."

"That's not exactly how publishing works," I said.

"I thought you were excited for me."

"I am! I one hundred percent am. I guess I just didn't consider what it would mean for me."

"Carly, is there something you want to tell me?" Mollie asks, her voice small. "Like, did something change for you? With us?"

"What do you mean?"

She stepped away from me. "I mean, whenever I think about big decisions, you're always right there. The first thought I had when I opened that letter wasn't about my job or my office or anything. It was about you. And me. In New York City. Ice skating at Rockefeller Center at Christmas and going to Shake Shack in Bryant Park in the summer and seeing shows on Broadway. It was a life together. Do you not think that way?"

"Of course I do!" I said. "It's just...this, come on, Mollie, you have to know this is a huge decision."

"Which is why we're talking about it," she said. "Just tell me if you want to go."

"Two minutes ago you didn't even know if you wanted to go!" I raised my voice.

"Are you saying no?" Mollie asked sharply.

"I'm not saying that! I just don't know about New York. It'd be fucking scary to pick up and move our entire lives across the country again, but I know I want to be with you. That's the only thing I've ever known. The only thing I've never doubted. It's just a lot to think about, okay? But I know I want a life with you in it. I'm always going to want that."

"Okay," she nodded slowly. "I'm going to want you in mine too. Always."

I kissed her softly. "Good."

"I think that's as much as I need to figure out today,"

Mollie whispered.

"You wanna celebrate?" Excitement was coming back to my voice.

She nodded, biting her lip.

"What do you have in mind?" I asked, pulling her closer.

She kissed me again, ever so softly. "I'm sure we'll think of something."

****

"You should go to teaching school."

"You think?" Old Sam asks nervously.

"You'd be an idiot to let go of your dreams," I say.

"Maybe I will," he says, almost wistfully.

Why is it so easy to tell other people to follow their dreams? Why can't I turn the mirror on myself and say those things to me? The things I need to hear. What makes their dreams different from mine? Maybe I see other people's dreams as more attainable because they aren't mine; because the hard work that goes with them isn't mine to complete. It's easy to believe in anything when you don't have to do any of the doing.

There's something I've been avoiding telling you guys because it's something I try not to dwell on. Here goes, though. I wrote a novella. Whew, feels kinda good to come clean about that. We've been together for this long, I doubt you'll abandon me now. Not after all we've been through. I'm sure you want to know how this is all going to end as much as I do.

Oh, man, this is *not* fun to talk about.

So, the novella. You probably saw it flutter by on your newsfeed on some form of social media. You might even remember that I made a brief reference to it earlier in this book. Part of it was published in *The Atlantic.* I didn't go on a book tour or anything, but I did have a feature done on me on NPR. Not as glamorous as Rockefeller Plaza, but I was over the moon. I'd done it. I was an author.

It's still floating around places. The bargain section of Barnes and Noble, for starters. You can find it in droves at used bookstores all across the country. I buy it every single time I see it.

There's a box chockful of copies sitting in my closet. Taunting me. Everything about it is a slap in the face. From its mere existence to my stupid acknowledgements in the back to the dedication page in the front. Eight words seared into me.

"For Mollie. Here's to the first of many."

The first of many. What an overconfident ass. There'd be no more. That was the first and last thing I wrote that mattered. Someone once told me never to Google myself. Every single day, I wish I'd listened.

Ten people utterly annihilated my book. Tack their

names onto the list of things I'd give anything to forget. There are probably more than those ten who hated it, but their comments were the first ones I read.

Those reviews threw me off the tracks. It didn't matter that I was on NPR or featured in *The Atlantic* or any of the other cool things being offered to me, because those ten faceless reviews rattled me. Broke all the self-confidence I'd managed to build up over the years.

Here's what fucks me up the most; they probably don't even remember. They probably couldn't even tell you anything about my book. Barely a blip in their lives.

I feel like it's different when it comes to creative things. Like, if you're a mathematician and you say hey dudes and dudettes, look at this new formula for space travel I just figured out. And then someone's like, right on, but you forgot to carry the negative exponent or whatever math thing, so sorry, but it's actually super wrong. That's lucky. There's objective proof that determines something's worth.

When it comes to creative stuff, it's all subjective. There's no rhyme or reason to any of it. Why does some of it matter and some of it get laughed at? Like that dude who sent all his worldly possessions through a wood chipper to make a statement about consumerism. First of all, what kind of privileged nonsense was that? Second of all, when my mom throws my stuff out, it's called spring cleaning, and no one gives a damn.

Writing is just glorified scribbles. Words that mean something to one person could mean absolutely nothing to someone else, and there doesn't have to be a reason behind it. Just a shrug and an "I didn't like it." Talk about gut-wrenching. As you can see, I've been bottling up these feelings for years.

I got emails back then from people asking me to write all sorts of things, but I ignored them. I haven't logged into that inbox in years. I can't. Not with the sea of doubt I've been drowning in.

I've always been envious of one-hit wonders. Songs like *867-5309/Jenny*. Everyone knows that song, and Tommy Tutone is probably living quite nicely off those royalty checks, but he can still go grocery shopping. He can go to movies and museums and Target without causing a scene. But he's also got a boatload of money too.

That'd be nice, right? Put your art out there and get remembered before drifting off into well-loved obscurity. As I'm getting older and further from that novella, I'd give anything to write something again. I'd be a two-hit wonder. I desperately want to write something that matters, but it all sounds so hollow now. Like an alien who studied earth and English and is trying its hand at writing for the first time.

I sound like I don't know a damn thing. Which, ironically, might not have been something I realized until just now.

23

I've Got Dreams to Remember
by Otis Redding

It's late afternoon and we're an hour past Kansas City, Missouri, when I get a text from Annie.

> Listen, I know you're not into writing anymore or whatever, but I think this could be good for you.

There's a link that follows and I click on it. It's some online magazine blog thing. They're taking submissions on the subject of loss just in time for the new year. I roll my eyes and text Annie back.

> Ballpark it for me. On a scale of 1-10, how dismal do you think my life is?

> I don't think you're dismal. I
> just think you know about loss
> and I think you could write
> something really good.

I read the text, then shut off my phone. I know what she's trying to do and I appreciate it, but I've been numb to our end destination. The three of us are in this car, driving across the country, because there's a girl getting married. A girl I never stopped being in love with. It all seems so foolish. So juvenile.

On the other hand, it feels inescapable. Like maybe Mollie getting almost married to someone else wasn't originally in the cards, but the end result stays the same. The Us of it stays the same. It's the next song that comes on the radio that does me in.

I'm not going to tell you the name of the song. It matters too much and I've told you guys too much about it. And I don't want you listening to it and thinking *this?* This is the song? Because it is. It's the song that finally gets through to me, and for the first time since I heard about Mollie and her wedding, I cry.

I cry loud, thick tears that make it from my cheeks to the collar of my shirt in record time. I can't stop. They're like a tidal wave pouring out of me. Finally, my brain catches up to what my heart's been screaming all this time. "You're still in love with her and you let her go all those years ago! You! You! You!"

"Jesus, Carly!" Old Sam says, looking in the rearview mirror. "What's happening back there?"

I gulp a few times. "Oh, nothing. I'm fine. I'm just going through some stuff."

"What the hell does that mean? Should I pull over?" Old Sam sounds a little panicked.

"Yeah, yeah. Maybe just for a second."

We're on a little dusty two-lane road in Middle of Nowhere, Missouri. Old Sam steers the car to the shoulder and slows down. I open the door and shakily get out and stand up.

This whole trip has been proving to me that anything is possible. I know that's cheesy and a stupid thing to say because of course anything is possible, but sometimes we take that for granted. We don't think about how amazing it is. Anything can happen every single day. Why should we get worked up about things when they can literally change at the drop of a hat? Why did I care so much back then about what other people thought of me? For every ten people who hated me, I could find ten who liked me, but of course my brain focused on those ten people who despised every word in that novella. Those ten people were louder than everything else.

"Fuck you, Alice Regan!" I yell to no one from the roof

of the car.

"Who's Alice Regan?" I hear New Sam ask Old Sam. I imagine he shrugs in response because he doesn't know.

"Fuck you, Alice Regan and Michael Jonson and Tanya Young and Earl Harp and Olivia Smith and Eric Williams and Kris Anderson and Mary Hernandez and Ray Patel and Henry O'Toole! Screw all of you!" I shout, climbing onto the roof of my car. "You guys can go to hell!"

Who am I trying to curse with eternal damnation, you ask? Those ten assholes I couldn't let go of. The ten names I might as well have tattooed on my forearm because there's no way I'm forgetting them. They're the ones who sent me spiraling all those years ago. The ten people who have made it impossible for me to write anything.

Well, I'm done with them. They can die out here in the middle of Missouri because I'm done. Not literally die, of course. They don't deserve that, but I'm letting them go. I'm sick of holding on to them.

I look down at the Sams. They look at me like I've officially gone off my rocker.

I smile at them. "What's up, guys?"

New Sam looks between me and Old Sam. "Are we not going to talk about your meltdown?"

Old Sam just smiles at me in a weird, knowing way. "You're alright, aren't you?"

I look out into the dark fields. "I am."

"Eastward ho?" he asks.

"No one's going to explain to me what this is about?" New Sam asks. "Who were those people?"

"Irrelevant," I say.

They narrow their eyes at me. "I'm worried again that you're a serial killer."

"They're just people I gave too much credit to before," I say. "Fuck 'em."

"I like this you," Old Sam says. "You're spunky."

"No one has called anyone spunky since 1958," I reply.

"You gonna get down from there?" New Sam asks.

"Oh, yeah," I say, looking around. "I forgot I was up here. Kinda blacked out for a second. Should I just jump?"

"Slide," Old Sam suggests. "I feel like you'd twist your ankle if you jumped."

I nod and take a seat on the roof of the car. I swing my legs over the side before pushing off. It's a good thing I didn't jump, because my coordination has never been great. Which is how I end up in a puddle of mud.

"I'm not letting you into your own car like that," Old Sam tells me, once he stops laughing.

"If nothing else, it's an accurate depiction of my life." I stand up and pull at my shirt, which is stuck to my stomach. "This was one of my favorite shirts, too." I'm starting to notice how cold it is.

"It's a white t-shirt," New Sam deadpans.

"It's worn out just the right amount so it's not stiff anymore, but there aren't any holes yet," I say. "God, I can't believe I'm like this."

"What's your game plan?" Old Sam asks, holding his nose. "I think there was manure in that puddle."

"Stop overreacting. Can you just grab some new clothes from my bag? And that plastic bag from the gas station? I'll wash these tonight at the hotel."

"It's cute how you think there'll be a washer and dryer in the hotel," New Sam snorts as Old Sam grabs some clothes. "We've been staying in glorified Bates Motels."

I wipe my arms and face on the already ruined shirt. "I'll wash them in the shower then."

"Yeah, then you're showering last," Old Sam says, holding new clothes out to me.

After I change and tie my clothes up in the plastic bag, we're on the road again. We keep driving until we hit Cape Girardeau, Missouri. Since this road trip is lasting longer than we anticipated, we can't afford to stay in an actually nice hotel in Cape Girardeau. Instead, we find a Motel 6 just outside the city limits.

We're at the front desk checking in and I take a minute to look around the lobby. Between the static on the TV that absolutely no one is watching and the indiscernible stains all over the carpet, I see what New Sam meant about the whole Bates Motel thing. Someone was probably murdered here.

"Quick question," New Sam says, taking the room keys from the front desk person. "Which way is the laundry room?"

"Oh, there's no laundry room here," the front desk person tells him, "but there is a coin-operated laundromat about a mile down the road."

"Thanks so much," New Sam says, smirking at me.

24

Time After Time
by Cyndi Lauper

After we checked in and mindlessly watched some television, we ventured out to get dinner to take back to the hotel. I don't know if you've ever driven across the country, but let me tell you—America loves Subway a lot more than I thought it did. As someone who hasn't set foot inside a Subway since I was a child, you can imagine my surprise when literally every exit on every highway in America advertised Subway as the only dining option. This is why the country is broken. Because people in the Middle of America only eat at Subway. This is the first time we've seen a McDonald's in like three states.

"I honestly think I'd vomit if I had to eat another Subway sandwich," New Sam says when we pile into the room with our take-out bags. "This isn't leagues better, but the last Subway we stopped at gave me the runs."

"Not me," Old Sam says. "But I guess I don't have the sensitive palate and digestive tract you have."

"I don't know if anyone in the history of the world has

ever been this excited to eat McDonald's food," I say, taking a bite out of the cheeseburger from my Happy Meal.

"Don't get me wrong. I like fast food as much as the next person. Just because I'm a chef, it doesn't mean I eat good food all the time. I can cook," New Sam says. "But I hate doing dishes. I just eat scraps at my restaurant and never have to clean a thing."

"Your restaurant," Old Sam repeats in wonder. "I only have my own office and you've got your own restaurant. Carly over here barely even has her own box cutter."

"Hey!" I yelp with a mouthful of food. "Listen, I do have my own box cutter. I just keep losing it, okay?"

"Carly's also got her own novel," New Sam says.

"Novella," I correct.

"Stop trying to sell yourself short," Old Sam says. "I don't care if it's trash, you still wrote a novel. That's cool. Cooler than having my own office. On par with having your own restaurant."

I shift uncomfortably. I'm not the best at taking compliments; I kind of always sit there waiting for the "but." Also for the other shoe to drop and the truth to come out. Some part of me just can't trust compliments.

"Can we change the subject?" I ask.

"Sure," New Sam says.

"I've got a fun new topic," Old Sam says. "Who would you stop a wedding for?"

"Sam," I groan.

"Oh, I'm sorry. Hit a little too close to home?"

I flip him off.

"You know," New Sam begins, "I thought about it once. The whole running into a wedding thing."

"What?" Old Sam and I exclaim.

"I mean, not to the extent you have," New Sam says, gesturing at me. "It was this boy from college who I really loved. At least I thought I really loved him, but we were terrible together. We dated for almost two years, and I think we fought every single day of those two years."

"And that justified you wanting to stop his wedding?" Old Sam raises an eyebrow.

"Only for a minute. He was the first guy I dated who was getting married. So for a minute, I pictured running through the church doors," New Sam says. "It was only a fantasy. I was never going to do it. I think I just got swept up in the what-might-have-been of it all. That's a dark, dark road to go down."

"I always wonder what happened to Kara Jean," Old Sam says wistfully.

"Kara Jean sounds like the fakest name in the world," New Sam says.

"What part of Canada is she from?" I ask.

"Hilarious," Old Sam says. "She was from Sedona originally, but we met at a bar in L.A. She was very, very into the hippie spiritual mojo stuff, and like a year and a half into the relationship, she got into tarot card reading. She believed it would tell her about us as a couple, and apparently we were not in the cards, so to speak. That was it."

"What?" I ask. "She broke up with you for that?"

He shrugs. "Yep. Haven't heard from her since."

"That blows," I say.

"Look her up on Facebook or Instagram," New Sam encourages.

"She's not on Facebook, but I've never tried Instagram." Old Sam reaches for his phone.

"Do it! Do it!" I chant.

He wipes his hands on his pants. "Okay, hold on."

Old Sam's quiet for a couple minutes, then tosses his phone onto the bed behind him.

"Nada," he says.

"I don't believe that," I say.

"I'm not surprised." Old Sam turns his attention back to his food. "She's real of-the-earth crunchy."

"If Shailene Woodley has an Instagram, Kara Jean has an Instagram," New Sam asserts.

I turn to New Sam. "You should look up your college boy."

"I should?" New Sam will need some convincing.

"Have you since he got engaged?" Old Sam asks.

They shake their head no.

"Now's the time," Old Sam says in a singsong voice.

"Fine." New Sam pulls out their phone. "But know that I am against this."

"What's his name?" Old Sam asks, picking up his phone again. "I want to look at him too."

"Jackson Rhodes," New Sam says.

"You gave me shit for Kara Jean and here you are, still in love with Jackson Rhodes?" Old Sam asks.

"Hey, I never said I was still in love," New Sam says quickly. "This was years ago."

"Looks like you dodged a bullet though." I lean closer to see Old Sam's phone screen. "Unless matching family vacation t-shirts are your thing."

"Jackson Rhodes, Dad of the Year," Old Sam scoffs. "He looks ridiculous."

"Oh my god, I never thought he would turn into the dad who wears matching shirts at Disneyland," New Sam murmurs, scrolling through his account.

"That seems like the type of person Carly was born to be," Old Sam suggests.

I blush. "Shut it."

"You totally would!" New Sam exclaims. "I can picture it clear as day. You with a little kid on your shoulders, walking into Disneyland with that girl. What's her name?"

"Mollie Fae," Old Sam answers for me.

"We should look her up on Instagram," New Sam says.

"We definitely should not," I protest.

"You wanted us to look up our old loves and leave you out? Where's the fun in that?" Old Sam asks.

"Fine," I grumble. "You won't be able to find anything. Her account's private."

"It's only fun if you look too." Old Sam tosses my phone onto my lap.

I put down my fries and unlock my phone. As soon as I open the Instagram app and search on Mollie's name, I recognize her face in that tiny little circle of a profile picture. My thumb hovers over her account before selecting it, fully expecting to see nothing since she's been private for as long as I can remember.

"Holy shit."

"What did you find? Is it public?" Old Sam asks.

"It wasn't public before," I whisper to myself.

"Well, it is now," New Sam says, engrossed in their phone.

"So what's got your panties in a twist?" Old Sam asks.

My mouth is flapping, but nothing is coming out.

"It's just a picture of a church." New Sam shows their phone to Old Sam.

"Probably where she's getting married," Old Sam suggests.

"That's my song," I say slowly. Each word feels brand new in my mouth.

"You have a song?" Old Sam asks.

I sigh dramatically. "I was in a One Direction cover band in high school, and I may have written a song for Mollie."

"We're gonna come back to the song you wrote for Mollie, but at the moment I'd really like to focus on the fact that you were in a One Direction cover band," Old Sam says in amazement. "Did you guys have matching outfits? Or synchronized dances? Please tell me you have videos of this."

"I do have videos, and I promise I'll show them to you someday. But look at the church post again," I say quickly. "Read the caption."

"Oh, darling, won't you run away with me?" New Sam reads slowly.

I leap dramatically to my feet. "I wrote that! I wrote that for her when we were in high school!"

"No way," Old Sam says.

I nod enthusiastically. "Yeah, way. One hundred percent way."

"It's such a common phrase," New Sam says. "You don't know she's referring to your song."

"Fair point," Old Sam starts. "But she did put quotes around it."

"Somebody Google it before I lose my mind." I start pacing.

"Ahh, okay, okay, on it," New Sam says. After a few moments, I hear amazing words. "Um, good sign so far."

"What? What?"

"There are no results for that phrase with quotes," New Sam says.

I reach out and grab Old Sam's shoulder. "Carly, oh my god, that is quite the grip. Relax."

"Anything else?" I'm biting my thumb nervously.

"There's a Bob Evans song called *Darlin', Won't You Come?* That's wild. Do you think this is the same Bob Evans as the fast food place?" New Sam asks.

"Sam! Focus!" I yell.

"Fine, fine. You really have no patience, Carly," New Sam mumbles.

"Consider the circumstances!" I do not like this level of stress.

"There are a couple other songs about running away, but none of them have those exact words in that exact order," New Sam says, continuing to scroll.

"Holy shit," Old Sam and I say.

"Geez," New Sam says. "What kind of girl is this? Leaving cryptic messages on her Instagram posts when she's supposed to be getting married?"

"The love of my life," I say simply.

"We've gotta find that church." Old Sam grabs his phone and starts furiously typing.

"What?" I look at him.

He laughs, then tries to look more serious. "I'm sorry.

Did you just call this girl the love of your life?"

"Well, yeah." Really, what else can I call her?

"Great, so this girl, the love of your life, just posted a picture of a church with your lyrics as a caption, and you don't think the next rational step is to try to figure out where this church is?" Old Sam's voice gets higher as he goes on.

I open my mouth, but stay silent.

"I swear to god, Carly, if the next words out of your mouth are excuses about why this isn't a sign, then I will hurl this phone at your head," Old Sam says.

"A sign," I say, and my shoulders drop. "How did I not see this before?" Now I'm furiously running my hands through my hair.

"See what?" New Sam asks. "I sure don't see anything."

"I went to see a psychic a couple months ago because I didn't know what else to do. I thought she was a crackpot. She kept going on and on about how I wasn't ready then, but I needed to be ready when this sign came."

"This is the sign!" Old Sam holds up his phone.

"That's your Wonder Woman background."

"This is the sign!" he repeats, this time unlocking his phone and pulling up Mollie's Instagram.

"I honestly think it could be, because she kept saying it would come when the white shirt turned brown!" Now I'm kind of starting to believe that maybe this IS a sign.

"Okay, now you've lost me," New Sam says.

"What color shirt was I wearing when I had the meltdown on the side of the road?" I ask this as calmly as I can.

"White," Old Sam says.

"Right!" I point right at him. "And what happened after I stood up on the roof of my car?"

"You bit it really hard," Old Sam laughs.

"And what color was my shirt after I got out of the puddle of mud after I bit it pretty hard?"

"Brown," New Sam says. "Brown! What the hell? So your psychic was right?"

"Apparently! I trusted her at first because she knew my name without me telling her, but then I remembered I was wearing my name tag from work, so I kinda lost faith. But this, this is the absolute real deal."

"Well, shit," New Sam breathes out slowly. "Color me convinced."

"I call this even more reason to figure out where that church is," Old Sam says.

"Why would she do this?" I wonder aloud. "This is basically like her inviting me to her wedding."

"Only if you followed her, but you don't, so it's not," New Sam says.

We both turn to look at them.

New Sam looks at us with pity. "Why do I have to explain this to you two? Look. If you followed Mollie, it'd pretty much be a guarantee you'd see it, right?"

We nod.

"And if you followed Mollie, she'd know you followed her, right?"

We nod again.

"Okay," New Sam continues. "But you don't follow her, so there was no guarantee you'd see the picture, so it's not an invitation."

"What is it then?" I'm hoping New Sam has an answer I want to hear.

"Something," New Sam says.

"Great," I counter sarcastically. "Not a lot I can do with something."

"Carly, there's some part of her, it's impossible to say how much, but there's a part of her that wants you to show up and break down the church doors," New Sam says. "There has to be. Otherwise, she'd never post a photo like that with a caption like that."

"I dunno." I so want to believe.

"It's not a formal invitation," New Sam goes on. "It's like a message in a bottle. She put it somewhere you could find it if you were looking. If you'd moved on, then you wouldn't be stalking her Instagram in fucking Missouri of all places, and you probably wouldn't care the caption was the lyrics to the song you wrote. Mollie was pretty smart, actually. She threw this out into the void of the Internet and knew that if you managed to find it, that would mean you wanted to show up."

"The fact that she remembers a song you wrote for her in high school says more than enough," Old Sam adds.

"She had a copy of the song," I tell them.

"You burned her a CD?" New Sam asks. "How retro."

"Just an MP3 file I made on my computer. I sang it for her years later with an acoustic guitar. Whatever," I trail off. "There used to be a video of it on YouTube."

"What you're saying is that she could've found the lyrics if she wanted to?" Old Sam asks.

"I mean, check for the video on YouTube before we get too excited. For all I know, she deleted the MP3."

"Already on it, and yeah," New Sam says, turning their phone around. "The Internet never lets anything die."

Sure enough, there I am with Bryan and Heather and Matt and Mark in Cameron's backyard. The image is grainy and shaky, and if you didn't know the song already, it would be pretty hard to piece together the lyrics. But there it is. My heart on the line for all the world to see.

"Dude, you've got a good voice," New Sam says.

"Oh, well, um, thank you." I stutter, and blush a little.

"So this proves what exactly?" Leave it to Old Sam to keep us focused.

"It proves that even if she doesn't have the MP3 anymore, she could still watch this and figure out the lyrics "to get the wording exactly right," I say.

"Which proves that she wants this," New Sam says.

"Which circles us back to finding out where that church is," Old Sam says. "If you people had just listened to me five minutes ago, we'd probably know the name of the church already."

"I will never doubt you again," I tell him.

"Let's find this church!" Old Sam exclaims.

Seconds later, New Sam shouts, "Got it!"

"Okay, are you some kind of tech wizard mastermind?" Old Sam asks.

"Only in my free time." New Sam winks at him.

"So," I say, bouncing on the tips of my toes. "What church is it?"

"Trinity Church."

"Oh my god, like in *National Treasure*," Old Sam says, with reverence in his voice.

"How the hell did she swing Trinity Church?" I wonder aloud.

"Dunno, but I'm on their website, which is ancient, by the way, and I see them," New Sam holds up their phone up. "There they are. Under upcoming private events."

I sink to the ground. "She really wants me to do this."

"Sure as shit looks like it," Old Sam says.

"Well, there's nothing like the sights and sounds of New York City at Christmas, right?"

"Do we know when the wedding is?" New Sam asks.

"December 17. Annie told me. Plus, it's on the website," I say.

"Oh, right. Well I'm in," Old Sam says. "I've been saying that from the beginning."

"I'm in too." New Sam smiles like we're going to my wedding.

"Am I really going to do this?"

"I don't want to tell you what to do with your life," Old Sam offers. "But there's a reason we're in Missouri. There's a reason we haven't U-turned it to L.A."

"It's your life, Carly Allen," New Sam adds.

I feel like it's so easy to forget that our lives are our own. It's easy to see the way things work in the world and feel like we have no say in what goes on around us. I was a scared little kid when I was eight or nine; worried that everything that could possibly go wrong, would go wrong. I felt so powerless against the magnitude of the world.

Thankfully, I got less nervous as the years went on, but that powerless feeling is still inside me. It's like I'm in a tiny boat in the middle of the ocean in a hurricane, and I have no choice but to go wherever the waves take me. Not every circumstance is as dire as a dinghy in a hurricane, but it sure can feel that way. Life offers no guarantee of safety, emotional or physical. Good things and bad things can happen anytime and anywhere.

There's a part of me that's been screaming about this since the day Annie told me Mollie was getting married. The eighteen-year-old reckless optimist in me wanted to get on a flight that very day, knock on Mollie's door, and say "Choose me." But the part of me that felt overwhelmed by the twisting tides of the universe didn't let me buy that plane ticket. It didn't let me understand that the only way out of a situation I don't like is to go right through it. There's nothing to do but keep pushing until I get to the thing I want. It's so important for all of us to remember that we have to hold the things we care about close to us. We have to say no to fear and yes to love, whatever that love is for. The alternative is to end up like I've been for the past few years.

I look at the Sams' expectant faces. "I can't give up yet."

Old Sam's lips curl into a proud smile. "That's my girl."

25

Life Is a Highway
by Tom Cochrane

I wake up earlier than the Sams the next morning. As I'm lying in bed, I remember Annie's text messages about that place online calling for submissions, and I know it's something I need to do. I need to write, even if it's the worst thing in the world, because I need to write again. For myself. It's as simple as that.

"Psst, Old Sam," I whisper.

"Huh?" he asks, only half awake.

"I'm gonna go to the library."

"The library?"

"Yes, the library," I say, tugging on my coat.

"You nerd," Old Sam says into the pillow.

"Yeah, yeah, I've heard it before." I pause at the door. "See you guys in a little. I don't think I'll be long. Just don't leave without me."

He rolls over. "Wouldn't dream of it."

We passed by a library on the way to the hotel, and it's not a far walk. I push open the door and already the old dude at the front desk is shushing me. There's another desk in the middle of the room where a sweet-looking old lady is reading *50 Shades of Grey*. Missouri, you certainly are a wild time.

"Um, excuse me," I say, as softly as I can.

"What did you say, dear?" the sweet lady practically shouts. I hear the old dude shush again, but I don't think his co-worker heard it.

"I'd like to use a computer." I raise my voice only slightly, but it sounds loud in the silence surrounding me.

"Oh, a computer!" the woman exclaims. "Let's get you set up."

She puts down her book and grabs my hand. "You can use computer fourteen. The only website you can't access is Facebook."

I sit down in front of the computer. I can't get on Facebook, but the guy next to me has no trouble navigating around what looks like a porn site. What kind of establishment are these people running?

"If you need anything, just holler!" the woman hollers, and the old guy shushes her from across the room. I wonder if they have this will they/won't they workplace dynamic where he can't stand how loud she is and she hates how quiet he is and their hate blossoms into love. That comment may make you think I've officially lost my mind.

I pull up the website Annie texted and read a little more about the submission call. Basically, they want people to talk about new beginnings with the new year. It's December, so everyone's getting into that bettering themselves mode. Diets are being planned, gyms are being researched, vows to quit drinking coffee are being made. It's the worst time of the year.

I've never made a New Year's resolution. Certainly, there are things I could improve on, but I've just never felt the need to make a big change in my life coincide with the beginning of a new calendar year. Y'all know me. I say time is fake every chance I get. I'm not about to let the arbitrary passage of time determine my actions.

However, this year, making big changes just happens to coincide with the beginning of a new year. The website wants people to talk about love, loss, and moving forward. I roll my eyes. This sounds like a self-help book or a Hallmark movie. I ignore my disdain for both of those things and close my eyes to think.

My life right now is entirely comprised of love, loss, and moving forward. This is another sign from the universe. It has to be. What else could the psychic and this trip and the Instagram photo with the lyrics mean? I open my eyes and watch the cursor blink, waiting for me to start typing. I let my fingers rest on the keys and then…nothing. My mind just stays blank. I slump back in my chair and look at the guy across from me. There's a pair of headphones sitting next to him, unused.

I clear my throat. "Hey, um, can I borrow your headphones?"

He looks behind him. "You talking to me?"

"Yes," I say.

"Yeah, sure." He shrugs and hands the headphones to me. "Left side doesn't work though."

"That's okay. You're a lifesaver."

I plug the headphones into the computer and open a new tab for YouTube. The cursor blinks in the search bar. This time, though, the answer's easy. I type *Born to Run* and press Enter. A playlist of Springsteen's *Born to Run* album pops up and the twinkling piano notes of *Thunder Road* come through the right ear bud. It's distorted and crackling, but it sounds like home.

Once I set the playlist to repeat, I go back to the first tab. The cursor's still there, blinking expectantly and waiting for whatever it is I have to say. I don't know if it's the music or this library in the Middle of America or the fact that there's a very real chance Mollie is expecting me or a combination of all of those things, but I'm ready now. It all comes pouring out of me.

I love words. Not the mundane "Hey, how's it going" gibberish we spend most of our lives in. Not that. I'm talking about the words that have to be screamed from rooftops. The words you send in a text message at two a.m. completely sober, drunk on the possibilities that come with just hitting Send. I love the words that spill out of us because they absolutely have to. No amount of decorum or restraint can keep them in. Words heavier than the weight of the world. Those words, the ones that can't be silenced, are the bravest, truest things on this planet.

What the hell do we know compared to what our hearts know? Our brains make our hearts stupid. They tell us not to buy that plane ticket or not to send that text or not to go to that party or not to do the thing that's terrifying and mesmerizing at the same time. That thing that has a one percent chance of success. Our brains talk us out of it and tell us we're part of the ninety-nine percent. Don't worry, this isn't an extended metaphor about Occupy Whatever. I'm talking about the business of love.

There's a wedding just around the corner that could have been mine. Some other girl's going to stand in my spot, wear my tux, say my vows, and marry my girl. I don't mean my girl in a weird, misogynistic, ownership sense, but in the way we all have a somebody like that. Yours might not be a girl at all. It could be anybody, but the feeling is the same. My girl, your guy, their human. Someone you love more than the world could possibly understand. If you're lucky, one of the luckiest people on this planet, you get to marry that person, ride off into the sunset, have 2.5 kids and a dog named Fido, all white-picket-fenced into the American Dream.

If you're not lucky, like me, your person chose someone else. It's easy to forget about the person for a while. If they're out of sight, you can work at it and keep them out of mind, but then your best friend gets invited to the wedding and everything goes to shit. You remember it all as it slams into your chest like a freight train.

You remember the way she sips her coffee as she reads *The New York Times* over the brim of her favorite mug, while you try not to break her concentration. Somehow, though, there's always a stain on the countertop when she's done. The way her breath felt in your ear, on your neck. The sound of her saying your name, which you might as well change because it will never sound as sweet again.

Everything is ruined. *The Princess Bride* will never revert to being just a movie. Forever, it will be her cold feet tucked under your thigh or the red dress she bought at Goodwill because it looked like Princess Buttercup's. It will be the year you dressed as Buttercup and Wesley on Halloween or the DVD you bought your junior year of college because you were at Target late one night in your pajamas and you missed her. Purely, simply, honestly, achingly, missed that girl. You overdrew your bank account that night because it was a Tuesday and you didn't get paid until Friday, but you couldn't wait. You missed her because it was Tuesday. But it was also one less Tuesday you had to spend away from her.

I've been without her for so many Tuesdays now. I don't even know the last one I spent with her. And I don't know if I'm more upset about that, or the fact that there's no Tuesday with her to look forward to.

That's what the brain does. It tries to beat down the romantic in all of us by saying affairs of the heart aren't practical. It reminds us of the odds. Hollywood and Alfred, Lord Tennyson say it's better to have loved and lost than never to have loved at all. For once, Hollywood is right about something. I don't know about Tennyson's track record.

Open the floodgates. Buy that plane ticket. Run through the terminal. Shout it from the rooftops. Send that message. Go, go, GO.

When I was young, I believed in it all. All the magic in the world. And I believed I had it all at my fingertips. I thought that, when it came to love, there was always one more chance. One last Hail Mary. One last leap-of-faith swan dive off the tallest building. I really thought I could fly, but when the time came, I fell so hard; landed broken and bruised. Not because I flew too close to the sun, but because I was too afraid to even try. I lost my heart.

Now, years later, I believe I've found it again. Finally. After all that time wandering aimlessly around this big rock of ours. My ability to believe in myself was hiding in plain sight: in the Middle of America, on the edge of the Grand Canyon, in an '80s dance club in Vegas, even in Boys Town, Nebraska, of all places. I found it in friends, new and old. I found it on an endless expanse of highway through the heartland of America as I drove toward my one last chance.

I've wanted to be a writer for as long as I can remember. A nice bunch of words strung together in just the right way can be more powerful than any drug. It can make your bones ache or set your soul and body and heart on fire. For the longest time, I've dreamed of writing words that made a difference to someone. I've also failed every single time I've tried. My particular collection of words always came out sounding like overthought, pretentious meanderings. I finally chalked myself up as a failure and quit writing. What I didn't realize until recently was that I couldn't write something someone else needed to hear if I couldn't even listen to what I needed to hear.

So these next words are for me, and I really need to listen closely.

This one's your fault. You pissed away two things in your life that you loved dearly, just because you were afraid. You let your brain ramble on about the odds of success, and it scared you. The odds of you making it as a writer and the odds of your relationship working with her. They sounded too small to ever be real; to even be possible.

Newsflash of the century: YOUR BRAIN IS A FUCKING IDIOT.

There's no such thing as a sure bet, in your

life or anyone else's. That's a fact you might as well accept. That, death, and taxes are the only things you can count on. So stop wasting your time, gather up your chips, and go all in on the things that matter. This article is a start, but don't forget about her.

The world is full of magic. It's in the way people are still shocked by 3-D movies at theme parks; in the way you shakily write your number on a napkin for the pretty girl at the bar; in the way that, in a few days' time, I'm going to burst through church doors and stop a wedding. Odds be damned.

This is being written on a computer that seems to be from 1999 in a library in Missouri at ten o'clock in the morning listening to Bruce Springsteen on YouTube with half-working headphones borrowed from the guy across the desk from me. There's a man looking at porn to my right and a woman looking at cats for adoption to my left. For the first time in the longest time, I feel like myself again. The real, brave me. For the past three years, I've been running through an airport looking for a girl who's already gone. Today, it feels like I can run fast enough to catch that plane. It feels like I'm about to right some wrongs. It feels a lot like love.

So, spoiler alert, Bruce Springsteen: Love is wild and it is so very real.

I lean back in my chair, more exhausted than I should be for just sitting and typing. But it feels like a weight has been lifted from my chest. I do a quick re-read to see if I've made any egregious grammatical errors and find a few that I take a moment to correct.

My next thought is that I don't have to submit it. Just the act of writing was probably enough, but a voice in the back of my head tells me to go through with it. If they choose to run it, great. If not, it's just a harmless shout into the massive void of the Internet, right? The important thing is that I wrote something, right? I let the mouse hover over the Submit button, brace myself, then click. And just like that, my heart's on the line again. In the hands of someone I may never meet.

I'm only moderately hyperventilating, thanks for asking.

26

Walking in Memphis
by Marc Cohn

"I can't believe we're actually going to Graceland!" New Sam squeals from the driver's seat.

It's their first time driving. I know this may sound very dumb because writing is like the exact opposite of taxing, but I'm tired. Listen, it's been a while, reflecting on your life for too long is draining, and Old Sam has driven a lot. So New Sam gets to drive.

"I don't think I know a single Elvis song." Old Sam is flipping through the Graceland brochure New Sam picked up at our last gas station stop.

I scoff from the back seat. "Yes you do. *Viva Las Vegas.* There's one."

"Yeah, the first time I ever actually heard it was when you played it," Old Sam says.

"*Can't Help Falling in Love.* You have to know that song. It's one of the best love songs ever written," I counter.

"Is that so, love expert?" Old Sam teases.

"You've at least heard of that song, right?" I can't believe he doesn't know this song.

"Yeah, I mean I've heard a cover of it." Old Sam shrugs.

"I can't believe you don't think a Bruce Springsteen song is the best love song ever." New Sam looks at me in surprise in the rearview mirror.

"I said one of, so that still leaves room for Springsteen." I cross my arms and squeeze my eyes shut. I don't want this memory.

"You okay back there?" New Sam asks.

"Just peachy," I reply.

"Are you gonna hurl?" Old Sam turns around in concern.

"I'm really okay," I tell them.

"You look like you're trying to take a dump," Old Sam says.

"It's just a memory I'm trying to forget."

"The more you try to forget something, the more it's just going to keep coming back," New Sam offers wisely.

I let all the muscles in my body relax. I know the Sams are right, but I really want to stave it off. Looks like it's not going to work, because the memory's coming at me like a freight train. All I can do is brace for impact.

****

I've only been to Palm Springs once in my life, and it was because Mollie really wanted to go. It's not something I would have chosen. The thought of going into the desert just sounds miserable to me. I'm not a heat person. I like my weather to be cold and overcast. Why I live in Los Angeles is a mystery, but I certainly never want to go to a place that's hotter. However, Mollie Fae had a way of persuading me to do things.

We drove from my apartment and it took almost three hours, because of course we got stuck in traffic. It's California. What're you gonna do? Also, what do people do in Palm Springs? Like, do y'all just go out and sweat by the pool? Literally no one was in the pool at our hotel, but every single pool chair was filled. And it was 100 degrees in the shade. I just don't get it.

Even with all that, it was a fun trip. There's something about the desert, although certainly not during the day. Good god. The desert during the day is literally like the devil's front yard. But the desert at night and at sunset is just beautiful. The sky goes on forever, and the sunset offers the prettiest colors you can't see anywhere else in the world.

I remember Mollie pulling off to the side of the road on our last night, just as the sun was going down. That beautiful chill was coming into the air. I was wearing my favorite denim jacket, the fabric soft from years of use, and Mollie had on a leather jacket that was soft under my fingers.

There isn't really a reason Mollie decided to pull over, but it felt right. Like the natural progression of the evening.

She cut the engine and turned on the high beams.

"Come on," she said, as she opened the door and climbed out.

"Hold on." I pulled out my phone. "I'll meet you out there." I plugged in the aux cord and picked the perfect song. *Can't Help Falling in Love.*

This beautiful girl with windblown hair, nervously holding her hands together, illuminated by the high beams, in the desert...I don't know. It's one of the best moments of my life. It was proof that love is real and magic is real and life is this great and terrible and marvelous thing that means everything.

I turned the radio up as loud as it would go and got out of the car. The sand crunched beneath my boots and goosebumps climbed up my arms.

Can't Help Falling in Love is a three-minute-long song, but that night it seemed to go on forever. A day after forever even. I'll always remember the way the dust floated in front of the car's lights and the way Mollie looked as we danced. She was young and hopeful and there were stars in her eyes. I remember every freckle and every laugh line on her face. I remember the way she smiled up at the desert sky when I dipped her as the song ended. I held on tightly, with never a thought that I would drop her. I still haven't dropped her. I'm still holding on.

"It's a perfect song," I say.

"That's so mainstream of you, Carly," New Sam comments.

"Hey, sometimes the public gets it," I reply, looking out the window.

"You know what's a good Elvis song?" New Sam asks.

"What?" Old Sam and I ask.

"*Kentucky Rain,*" New Sam says.

"Oh, hell yes," I agree. "That's a great song!"

"Don't know it," Old Sam says.

"It's about Elvis walking through the Kentucky rain looking for a girl he lost and can't find," I say.

"Well, I see why you like it now," Old Sam laughs.

"Rude." I kick the back of his seat.

"Unrequited love songs are the best," New Sam sighs.

"Thank you," I say. "Any old schmuck can write a love song, but unrequited love songs. Whew, that's where you separate the artists from the poets."

"I know you hate poetry for some reason, but you know songs are basically poems, right?" Old Sam asks.

"Whatever," I tell him. "It's different with music."

"Everyone's a critic."

"Carly's right. Unrequited love, that just hits you hard," New Sam says, smacking their hands on the steering wheel.

"Tell me you didn't cry to *Teardrops on My Guitar* at least once in your life," I say to Old Sam.

"I would like to plead the fifth," he replies.

"See! Love songs are great, but they're happy, and happiness has limits. Sadness, especially the sadness that comes from losing the love of your life, that shit springs eternal," New Sam says.

"Well aren't you two just a bundle of joy today," Old Sam says.

"Speaking of joy," New Sam announces, "we're here!"

I look out the window. "Why is the parking lot empty?"

"Maybe it's a slow day," New Sam guesses.

"Tourist attractions like Graceland don't have slow days," Old Sam says. "Certainly not slow enough that we're the only car here."

"Are they closed on Mondays?" I ask.

"They can't be closed," New Sam says, the color draining from their face.

We pull up to the guard at the gate and New Sam rolls down the window.

"You kids know the mansion's closed?" the guard asks, and I can't help but laugh.

"We do now," New Sam nods solemnly.

"Emergency repairs," the guard continues, "but the gravesite's open for another 90 minutes or so. You can park here and walk across the street."

"Thank you," New Sam says as we pull away.

"Soooo," Old Sam drawls. "Should we keep going?"

"Nope." New Sam pulls the car into a parking space. "I did not come this far to see nothing. We're gonna go look at some gravestones and the front door and whatever else we can see."

I shrug. "Why not?"

We trek across the road and walk up the massive driveway to the mansion. For good measure, New Sam tries the door, but of course it's locked. I'm picturing that scene in *The Princess Diaries* where the loudspeaker screams at Mia in all those different languages to get off the grass, but nothing happens. It's just us and a locked mansion.

Around the side of the mansion is where the Presley family is buried. New Sam takes a long time reading everything and snaps a few pictures. It seems their grandfather is an even bigger Elvis fan than they are, and he always wanted to come out here. He lives in Vegas and saw Elvis perform back in the day. New Sam's whole family loves Elvis, and there's a rumor that New Sam was conceived to an Elvis song. It's a rumor New Sam has never tried to verify, mainly for their own psychological well-being.

After a while, New Sam says they're ready to go and we head back to the car.

"You good, or is there more you wanna see?" Old Sam asks.

"If we can find a way to break into the mansion, that would be great," New Sam says.

"That would be a good plan, except I didn't work bail money into the budget when I was preparing for this trip," Old Sam says sadly.

"There's always next time, I guess." New Sam grabs Old Sam's hand.

I look closely at the two of them. "Next time?"

"You're not invited, Carly," Old Sam says.

"Don't get excited, Old Sam," New Sam says with a smile. "My hand's just cold."

"You have pockets," Old Sam points out.

"I can let go," New Sam says.

"No, that's alright," Old Sam says with a dope grin.

"Come on, kids. You can flirt in the car."

27

Down on Music Row
by Dolly Parton

"Hey, Annie!" I say into my phone when she picks up. "On a scale of one to ten, how busy are you at this current moment in time?"

It's 9:00 at night, and we haven't been able to find a hotel room we can afford. Now we're in the suburbs of Nashville, sitting outside Annie and Todd's house. I see some lights flick on inside.

"I'm not super busy. Why? Also, you sound weird."

"Yeah, that might be because I'm in front of your house trying to figure out the best way to ask if we can crash here for the night."

"Wait. You're outside?"

"Yeah, c'mon out here you crazy kid." I laugh and get out of the car.

"Carly Allen, if this is some kind of prank I will end you. I already put my curlers in," Annie squeals.

"Curlers? God, Annie, married life sure did age you fast."

I hear Annie laugh through the phone and then the

door's opening and she's on the front porch. I hang up and run to meet her halfway with a huge hug.

"Watch the hair!" she says into my shoulder.

I pull away and flick one of the pink curlers. "What have you become? You were kinda cool once."

She slaps my hand away. "What are you doing here? Why is your car here and who are those people in it?"

I turn around to look. "Sam and Sam. One of them works with me. New Sam we picked up in Vegas. So far so good."

"What? Why were you in Vegas? Why are you here?"

"Good to see you too," I say, then let out a little sigh. "I was moping about Mollie and Old Sam suggested a road trip. Things have been snowballing ever since. Now here we are."

"Right, but why?"

I sheepishly scratch the back of my head. "Uh, I think I'm going to crash Mollie's wedding."

She smacks me in the stomach. Hard.

"Oh, good god," I say, doubling over. "I thought you supported this."

"You *think* you're going to crash her wedding?" Annie asks in a tone that scares me a little.

I gulp. "Uh, yes."

She smacks me again. Only a little bit softer this time.

"Annie!"

"This is one of the biggest days of her life and you *think* this is what you want to do? Think about what this means for her!"

"Geez, okay, I'm sure! I'm one hundred percent positive this is what I want. It's all I can think about. This is it," I say, hands flailing.

"You couldn't have just called her?" Annie asks.

"You know me. I've always been a bit dramatic."

"You don't have to tell me twice," she says, walking past me to the car. "Now let's meet these Sams of yours."

"Wait." I stop her. "That's all you have to say?"

"Carly, I just wanted to make sure you were sure. That's it." Annie takes a step back toward me. "In the spirit of being honest, I've been wishing it was you who was going to be in that church too."

I smile softly. "You think I stand a chance?"

She shrugs. "I don't think you would've driven this far if you didn't think you stood a chance."

"Annie!" I cry, more pleadingly than I'd like to admit.

"Yes," she says firmly.

****

The Sams have called it a night and are sleeping in Annie and Todd's guest room. Annie, Todd, and I are in the living room drinking wine and reminiscing about the good old days of high school. Well, Todd's drinking wine, I'm drinking whiskey, and Annie's got tea.

"Do you have your crashing-the-wedding outfit planned?" Annie asks.

"I feel like that's not a thing people plan," Todd interjects, then adds, "right?"

"I bought a new suit," I tell them, excitement bubbling just under the surface.

"Really?" Todd seems surprised.

"What's it look like?" Annie asks.

"Navy. A nice navy and a white shirt. Foulard tie."

"God, stereotypically less feminine clothes are so boring to describe," Annie complains.

Todd laughs. "You should see her when I drag her out shopping."

"Todd, come on. You've known Annie for forever at this point, and you've just figured out she hates shopping?"

"Marriage is about compromise," Annie says, tucking herself into Todd's side.

"What's the compromise? It's not a sex thing, right? No, wait, definitely don't tell me if it is."

Annie rolls her eyes. "It's *The Real Housewives.*"

"What about them?"

"Annie goes clothes shopping with me and I watch *The Real Housewives* with her," Todd explains, then kisses Annie's forehead.

"That's the secret to marital bliss? Compromising over

The Real Housewives franchise?"

"Remember that when things with you and Mollie work out," Todd says, nodding in my direction.

"Oh, that reminds me," I say. "Why aren't you guys in New York yet? I thought you were gonna go early, have a little extra honeymoon in the city."

Todd answers. "Work. There's a meeting the night before the wedding that was scheduled super last-minute. Our flight's the first thing in the morning on the day of."

Annie nods. "And then we're staying a few nights after."

"Why does something feel odd about that?"

"Come on, Carly," Annie says. "You think I'm going to lie to you about a trip to New York?"

"Maybe."

"Carly," Annie says.

"Annie," I say.

"Todd," Todd says.

"You're gonna make the best dad jokes for your future kid," I tell him. "I feel it in my bones."

"Don't encourage him," Annie pleads. "He ordered a dad joke book on Amazon."

"Awesome!" I say. "Hit me with one."

Todd scoots excitedly to the edge of his chair. "Two guys walk into a bar, the third one ducks."

I stare at him blankly. "Oh, that's it? I was expecting like a knock-knock joke, or more of a buildup."

"You get it though? Two guys walk into a bar. Are you with me?" Todd asks.

"With you," I say.

"Yeah, so two dudes walk into a bar, the third one ducks." Todd is smiling widely.

"I'd ask for a refund on that book."

"Thank you," Annie says. "Now tell us about the Sams."

"They saved my life. Both of them. I was in a bad place after your wedding and Old Sam pulled me out."

"I'm so sorry," Annie says.

"You didn't know. I certainly wasn't making it obvious. It wasn't something you could pick up on over the phone either." I reach out for her. "Annie, you helped me as best you could. You answered every single time I called. That was the best thing."

"I love you," Annie says.

"I love you, too," I tell her.

"I don't know if it's pregnancy hormones or just the fact that I've missed you, but I feel like I could cry enough to fix the drought in California," Annie says as tears start to fall.

I sniffle and laugh a little. "I'm always gonna need you around."

"Same here," Annie says.

"Should I leave?" Todd asks helpfully.

"No, no." I shake my head. "It's fine. Everything's fine. Finally."

"Yeah," Annie grins.

"Whew." I wipe my eyes. "I feel like I've been on an emotional rollercoaster forever."

"What changed?" Annie asks.

"What do you mean?"

"Why are you changing your mind about Mollie's wedding?" Todd fills in, and Annie nods.

"She left this trail of breadcrumbs on her Instagram and I just," my voice breaks a little, "I have to follow it, y'know? It just got to the point where I have tunnel vision and she's all I can see."

"And you're happy?" Annie asks tentatively.

"I wrote something. I *wrote* something. I haven't done that since before she left. And I don't know, I'm not changing all of this for her, but she's there in the back of my mind. It's because of her. And because of you guys and the Sams and this random cab driver I had in Chicago after your wedding. I want to be the person you guys all think I am. I want to be the person I've always wanted to be."

"That's wonderful," Annie says quietly.

"You really do have a way with words," Todd adds.

I blush. "Thank you. I'm going to use it. Or try to, at least. I've finally got so much I want to say, to write."

"Are you going to write a book?" Todd asks.

"I'm gonna try. No, I'm going to do it." This voice sounds so much more certain than the one I'm used to hearing.

"Who knew that driving across the country with a guy from work and a literal stranger would be what you needed to get back on track," Annie says in wonder.

"Yeah, I really wish someone would've mentioned this to me ages ago." I can't help but laugh.

"Welcome back, superstar," Annie says, and I tear up again.

28

My Hometown
by Bruce Springsteen

We hung around with Annie the next morning, then continued our slow ramble toward New York. After Nashville, we make a stop in Lebanon, Ohio. It's home to what should be a national monument, the Waterloo motel from *Carol.* If you want to get technical, the motel isn't actually called The Waterloo, it's just in the fictional town of Waterloo and we all remember the way Cate Blanchett laughed at that town name. I know this is neither the time nor the place, but I would just like to say that the Academy is a bunch of cowards for not nominating that movie for Best Picture.

Ahem.

That night in Lebanon, as we ate off paper plates with plastic utensils, we all lamented about how long it had been since any of us had eaten a homecooked meal. And that's how we got here.

"I knew you were a suburbs kid," New Sam snorts from the back seat.

We're pulling off the Beltway onto the York Road ramp that's been my way home since I first got my license. That stretch of highway around Towson, Maryland, was my life stream. I cannot tell you road names to save my life and I am no geographical expert, but I know this place. It's like my brain has switched to autopilot and I know where I'm going solely based on a feeling.

It's weird being home.

"I'm not even going to pretend I know what you're insinuating," I say, winding us through the streets to my childhood home.

"You probably biked to your friends' houses and snuck into the woods to have parties. Alcohol always provided by an older sibling. Definitely had spin the bottle parties in basements," New Sam says, watching the houses pass by.

"Where did you have your spin the bottle parties in Vegas?" I ask.

"Someone's parents would rent us a hotel room," New Sam says.

"Oh my god," I groan. "That's the most *Gossip Girl* thing I've ever heard anyone say in my entire life, and I had family who lived on the Upper East Side."

"At least you guys got invited," Old Sam complains. "I went to one spin the bottle party and then I was never invited again."

"Were you a nerd?" New Sam asks.

"No!" Old Sam protests. "I was really quite cool. It just happened that I got my braces stuck together with Josie McCay's at the first party. After that, nobody wanted to kiss me."

"I didn't think that actually happened in real life." I try not to laugh.

"Yeah, well, it does, and it scars kids for life, okay? Josie never talked to me again, even though we should have been friends after spending two hours connected at the mouth."

That gets New Sam laughing really hard and I can't help but chuckle too.

"It's not funny, guys," Old Sam complains.

"I mean, it is a little bit," New Sam says, holding their stomach. "I'm just picturing you with a shaggy bowl cut stuck to that poor girl. It's pretty funny."

"Don't worry, I'll put you out of your misery." I pull into the driveway of my home. "We're here."

"Are your parents home?" New Sam asks as we climb out of the car.

"I only see one car, so I don't know. They usually carpool for errands. I didn't bring my key."

"No problem." Old Sam walks confidently ahead of us toward the door.

"Do you know how to pick a lock?" I ask.

"Nope." He raises his leg to do a weird ninja kick.

Before my brain can process what he's about to do, his

leg's swinging toward the door. His foot makes contact and the door flies open. All our jaws are on the floor.

"Dude! You just kicked down my parents' door!" I inspect the door for signs of damage. "Huh."

"Is it broken?" New Sam asks.

I turn to look at both Sams. "No, but it should be, right?"

"Well, shit on a stick," Old Sam says. "I'm a wizard!"

"Shh, there's probably a noise limit set by the HOA," New Sam says.

"We are not part of an HOA. I'm not that suburban."

"Carly? Is all that slamming you?" I hear my mom call.

"Mom?" I turn around and there she is.

"We left the door open for you. Didn't you get my text?" my mom asks.

"See, not possible," New Sam says under their breath.

"Don't just stand there. Surely you're not embarrassed to give your mom a hug in front of your friends."

I let myself be pulled into a hug. There are very few things in this world that a mother's hug cannot fix.

"Now," she says, when we finally let go, "who are these lovely people?"

"Old Sam and New Sam," I say, pointing to each of them. "Old Sam goes by he/him and New Sam goes by they/them."

"Well, it's a pleasure to meet both of you," my mom says, giving them big hugs too.

"Where's Dad?"

"He's out doing some grocery shopping," Mom says. "When we found out you were going to be here, he insisted on going back out to buy something special for you from that strange-smelling grocery store on York Road."

"Oh man, that means we're going to have to eat whatever he brings home?"

"Afraid so," Mom laughs.

"Is your dad a bad cook?" Old Sam asks.

"Not bad, just…Mom, what's the nice way of describing Dad's cooking?"

"He's an innovator," she says.

"Innovator. That's good," I agree. "Oh my god, I don't know how I forgot. New Sam, you're a chef. Please help him cook tonight. Otherwise we're going to be eating something wildly indigestible."

They laugh. "I'll see what I can do."

****

When my dad finally gets back, he drags Old Sam and New Sam into the kitchen to help him prepare dinner. I think my mom planned it this way so she could get me alone to figure out what exactly I'm doing here. I was vague when I texted to ask if they'd be in town and if I could bring two people she's never heard of before to crash on the couch for a night.

She pulls me into the den and has a seat on the couch that's directly across from the recliner I sink into. The rug on the floor is the same one from when I was a kid. It's frayed more now and the color's faded, and even though I have shoes on, I remember what it feels like with bare feet. There's a pattern on it, a royal blue oval in the middle of it. When I was little, I used to stand on the edge of that oval during *Go the Distance* in *Hercules*. Like Herc stands on that cliffside, I stood on the edge of that oval, daring the world to let me go on a hero's journey.

"Are you going to tell me what's brought you all the way out here?" my mom asks gently.

See, I told you. She has no desire to ease into this.

"You have to promise not to be upset," I start.

"You'd have to have done something truly awful for me to be upset with you," she says.

"I'm going to see Mollie." The words tumble out quickly and I can't meet my mom's gaze.

I hear her sigh.

"Is that okay?" I ask. "I know it's weird to ask your permission, but I feel like this is an insanely massive life choice that I haven't ever even mentioned to you. It's a pretty recent decision, but still, I called you two weeks ago because my toilet wouldn't stop running and I didn't how to make it stop, so it seems like this is something I should've at least run past you."

"Carly."

"No, I get it. I'd probably be mad if my kid did something as reckless as drive across the country with two kind-of strangers, only to ask to crash on my couch before crashing a wedding." I finally look up and there are tears in her eyes. "Oh my god, you're crying. Why are you crying? What's happening?"

"I'm okay," she laughs, wiping at her eyes. "I've missed hearing you ramble like that."

That's a swift punch to the gut. I've been living out in L.A. since I graduated from college, and I've only been home a few times, but I just didn't expect my parents to miss me. I thought they'd be happy to get rid of me. In retrospect, I see how idiotic that is, but I spent so much time feeling like a burden to them that I couldn't fathom I'd be someone they would miss.

"So those aren't tears of anger?" I ask cautiously.

"Of course not." She smiles then, and of course my own tears start up. "Now what made you come to this decision?"

I take a deep breath. "I still love her."

"And do you think she still loves you?"

There's that logical, scientist brain of hers, wondering if both sides of the equation are equal.

"I think she might," I say. "And that slim bit of hope is more than enough for me right now."

"You never did tell us why you two broke up," Mom says softly. "You just deflected every time we asked."

I shift a little uncomfortably on the recliner. "It was my fault. I didn't cheat on her or anything, but it was still my fault. I just stopped trying. I stopped trying in our relationship, in my writing, in my life."

"And there was only so much she could do."

I nod. "Uh, yeah. There was only so much she could do to get me to see myself the way she did. She showed me who I was, and even that wasn't enough to get me out of my own head. I was so deep inside of my brain that I couldn't even recognize myself."

"Oh, Carly, why didn't you tell us?" Mom asks.

"I didn't know! I didn't know there was anything wrong at all. I just thought this was how it was going to go for me. Like in a weird way, I deserved the outcome I got."

"That's ridiculous."

"Yeah, well, it didn't feel super ridiculous then, but I can see it now. I was just so sad. I was working at a job I hated and that was only supposed to be for a couple months, maybe a year. I wasn't writing or making friends or going out. I was only doing things I didn't want to do. I thought that was what it meant to grow up."

"And now you've seen the error of your ways?" Mom smiles.

I nod. "It's so dumb, but, yeah. Driving out of L.A.,

leaving all that behind me, seems to have made something click. I don't know, the other shoe dropped, I guess. Finally. It's like someone cleaned my glasses and the world isn't hazy anymore. And so I just had to come out here and fight to get a piece of my life back."

"I don't know if I've ever been more proud of you," Mom says, giving me a big hug.

"You're proud of me for this?"

"Of course." She kisses the top of my head. "You found your way back. That's not something a lot of people can say."

I sniffle. "Yeah, I guess you're right."

"You guess?"

I laugh as she pulls away. "I know."

She kisses me on the head one more time and takes my hand. "Now let's go see what my husband's set on fire."

The scene we find in the kitchen is one of utter chaos. Old Sam is yelling, holding a fire extinguisher and trying to pull the pin. Dad is holding a burning pan as far away from his body as he can. New Sam is standing wide-eyed in the corner, hands on their cheeks, watching the flames get higher.

"I got this," I say. I walk over to Old Sam and take the fire extinguisher out of his hands. Then I pull the pin and squeeze the handle, covering the pan and a little bit of Dad with the foam. Once the crisis has been averted, I put the extinguisher on the ground.

New Sam clears their throat. "I'd just like to say I did not have a part in any of that."

Mom sighs. "Don't worry. We're used to small fires in this household. I have pizzas on the way."

I don't know how, but my mom always guesses right with this. It's truly uncanny, and the closest thing I have to proof of the supernatural. She rarely orders back-up pizza when Dad cooks, but she somehow always picks the right night to do it.

Here I am, eating pizza from Italian Gardens like I have since as long as I can remember. We're all sitting cross-legged on the floor in the living room, and my parents are telling embarrassing stories about my childhood. Their personal favorite is the time I finally got a solo in the elementary school chorus. It was all I'd talked about for months and then, when the big moment came during the grand finale of the nondenominational holiday concert, I peed my pants. Right there, big spotlight shining on me. They bring out the video at least once a year and I personally love to watch it. Hate the story, don't get me wrong. But that video has me waving weakly with a massive dark spot growing on my khaki pants and my dad's howling laughter drowning out the music teacher's piano while my mom's hands wave in front of the lens to try and maintain some of my dignity.

After we've finished eating and laughing about younger me, the Sams and I take over clean-up duty while my parents relax in the living room. It takes us a while since the dishwasher is already full and we have to do it by hand. It took the entirety of our dishwashing time for the Sams to convince me to take them out tonight.

"You guys don't want to stick around and watch a movie?" Dad asks.

"I have a feeling I know which movie you're going to suggest, and I think it's gonna have to be a hard pass," I say, grabbing my coat. "Besides, I want to show them the town."

"That's not going to take very long," my dad says.

"If we get back in time, you're good for the movie," I promise. "But I wouldn't wait up."

"Honey, she knows cooler places than us," Mom says, placing a hand on Dad's arm. "Your tour is just grocery stores."

"New Sam would love that tour, isn't that right?" Dad asks.

"You don't have to answer that," I say.

"Take my keys so you can get back into the house without kicking down the door," Mom says, looking pointedly at Old Sam.

"Sorry, ma'am," he says politely.

"Thanks, Mom." I drag the Sams out of the house.

I lock the door behind us and we all climb into my car. It's become almost like a weird little home for us. There are stickers on the ceiling that Old Sam purchased in every state.

We have a trash collection situation worked out on the floor in the back, and snacks neatly organized in the middle of the back seat. There are sneaker prints on the dashboard in the front passenger seat and my bag of muddy Missouri clothes is still in the trunk. The outside is covered in two thousand miles' worth of dirt, mud, and splattered bugs.

This little four-door Prius feels more like home than my L.A. apartment has in years.

29

Wild in the Streets
by Bon Jovi

"So is this the Carly Allen Grand Tour of Towson, Maryland?" Old Sam asks, hopping into the back seat.

"Can we get dessert? I want something sweet," New Sam adds.

"Yeah, I know this great donut place."

"I should hope so. This is your hometown," Old Sam comments.

"Let's hope it hasn't closed down since I was there last," I say as I pull out of the neighborhood.

"When was that again?" New Sam asks.

"Like three years or something." They groan. "It's fine. I know plenty of places to go for good dessert, okay? Even if the donut place is closed."

"I'll believe it when I see it," Old Sam says.

I point out the window on my side. "You see that building? That used to be a Friendly's."

"Holy shit. I forgot about Friendly's. I loved their sundaes when I was a kid," New Sam tells us.

"We only went there once, and we didn't even eat anything," I say. "We walked in, the greeter asked how many were in our party, and I puked on the spot."

"Oh my god, that's so tragic." Old Sam laughs loudly.

"What is it now?" New Sam asks.

"You planning to expand your restaurant to a second location in Towson?" Old Sam asks.

"No," New Sam scoffs. "Just curious."

"Nothing, as far as I know. Just a weird, empty place."

"It's kinda sad when a place is just abandoned," New Sam says, watching it as we pass by.

"Everything gets abandoned eventually," Old Sam comments in a deep, serious voice.

"Yeah, well, let's just hope no one's abandoned the donut place."

I'm not really sure Towson could actually be considered a city. In the technicality of the government or whoever decides when a city is a city, I guess it fits all the criteria. But if you're picturing a big metropolis, then you're giving it a lot more credit than it deserves.

There's a mall, a movie theatre, a small business district, one or two moderate-rise buildings, and a college, all right in the thick of it. It's enough to always have something to do, but not enough to make teenagers not dream of something bigger and better. Does that make sense? What I mean is that it's small enough to feel like there's a whole wide world just a stone's throw away.

New Sam gets donuts because the place is thankfully still in business. We're sitting at a table by the window, a dozen donuts between us. We fully intend to eat all of them.

"You see the 7-Eleven across the street?" I ask, taking a drink of milk. You can't have donuts without milk.

They both nod, then Old Sam steals my milk.

"I used to go there on my breaks from driver's ed classes. I'd always get Vanilla Coke and Chex Mix."

"You guys didn't take driver's ed in high school? It was a separate thing?" New Sam asks.

I nod. "Yeah, it was some insane amount of money and like three hours a night, three times a week. It was awful."

"At least you guys got a break during it," Old Sam offers.

"True," I agree. "There was one guy who ordered a full pizza during the break once and he sat in the front row and ate the whole thing just staring at our teacher."

"What kind of weird power trip was that?" Old Sam asks.

"That's actually super-impressive, but yeah, also weird," New Sam agrees, grabbing another donut.

Six down, six to go.

"So across the street over there is an LA Fitness. That used to be a movie theatre. I went on my first date there."

"Aw, that's cute," New Sam says.

"First date with a guy, let me clarify. I didn't know it was a date. I showed up and he let me pick the movie. I picked

The Great Gatsby for Carey Mulligan. In my defense, I spent a good five minutes talking about how much I loved Carey Mulligan, so I feel like I was pretty obvious."

"He tried to kiss you, didn't he?" Old Sam laughs.

"I don't know why you're laughing. You tried too." I throw a bunched-up napkin at him. "But yes, he tried to kiss me when Carey Mulligan came on-screen for the first time and I said 'Not now' and pushed his face away."

"Stop!" New Sam is doubled over laughing. "No way you did that."

"I really did. And that's the only part of the movie I remember. We never spoke again after that night, but I think it was for the best."

"Look at you being a teen heartbreaker," Old Sam says.

"You puke in any other fine establishments around here?" New Sam asks.

"Hilarious, but yes. Over in that pizza place and at my high school. Also on the tennis court more than once."

"I wanna see Carly Allen's high school," Old Sam yells.

"Keep it down. We can go after we finish here. It's like two minutes away."

"Challenge accepted," New Sam says, and stuffs a whole donut into their mouth.

"I'm taking the last one," Old Sam says, also shoving a donut into his mouth.

"I feel like I can't take you kids anywhere." I gather our

trash and throw it away.

We pile into the car and I drive the route to school that's ingrained in my memory. I'm pretty sure I could get us there blindfolded, but when I attempt to try, the Sams yell at me. Whatever. I could've done it.

Once we park in the lot, Old Sam starts making his way to the front of the school. It's after hours, but there are a lot of cars here.

"Why are there so many cars here?" New Sam asks.

"Check out those posters on the door."

The posters are advertising the winter musical production of *Grease*. They've been doing *Grease* for forever, but I guess everyone's been doing *Grease* for forever. One time, they took us on a middle school class trip to a local production of *Grease*. It was one of those places where the waiters were also the actors, and I still feel so bad for them having to deal with us.

Anyway, we went because the teachers were assured that it was age-appropriate, but making *Grease* middle-school appropriate was about as successful as Delta Airlines editing the gay love story out of *Carol*. So, next to impossible. But, and this is the last nonsense I'll say about *Grease*, *Born to Hand Jive* is a bop, but nothing's better than *Grease 2* and *Cool Rider*. I ain't sorry.

"Old Sam!" I call out. "Are you trying to catch a show?"

He turns around. "No, but I fully intend to get on the

roof."

"The roof?" New Sam gasps.

"Yeah. I always wanted to go on the roof of my old high school, but all my friends were chickenshit. This isn't my high school, but we're gonna get on the roof."

I can't argue with that. "Fine. Let's do it."

"You're serious?" New Sam asks.

"I mean, the front door's already open, so it's not breaking and entering. It's just trespassing," I say.

"I hate both of you," New Sam says. "I would just like that noted before we start doing this."

"It'll be fine." Old Sam grabs New Sam's hand and tugs them along.

And it is fine. It was actually a lot easier to get on the roof than I think any of us imagined. The view from up here is incredible. I take a seat on the ledge and can almost hear my mother yelling at me to be more careful, but up here, I feel untouchable. Unstoppable. Invincible. Of course, with all of those things comes a fair dose of stupidity.

"Can you believe we're almost done?" Old Sam asks.

"Everything's ending." I look out on the tennis courts below us and the football field a little farther away. "The whole world is changing."

"At least summer's gonna totally kick ass," Old Sam says, sitting down next to me.

"You gotta promise to stay in touch," New Sam says as

they sit down on my other side.

I smile. "You ever think you'd be here?"

"On the roof of a high school I've never heard of, in Maryland, in December? No, safe to say this scenario never popped up in my imagination," Old Sam says. "You're right, though. The world's changing."

"Remember in high school when that was all you wanted? When you would stay up and plead with God or whoever to just speed things along?" New Sam gazes out at the athletic fields.

"And then, all of a sudden, you'd give anything in the world to make it slow down?" I sigh. "Yeah. I'm familiar with the feeling."

"Do you think that ever stops?" Old Sam asks. "Like, do you think we get out of our heads enough to just enjoy this?"

"I'm starting to think it's possible," I say hopefully.

"I'm gonna go back to school." Old Sam nods slowly. "I'm going to be a teacher."

"I'm gonna be a writer," I say. "For real this time."

"And I'm going to continue to be a chef."

"Yeah, how did you do that? How did you do it all so young?" I ask.

"I wanted it. I wanted it so terribly badly that I couldn't imagine my life without it," New Sam says.

"But how'd you get past the mountains of crippling self-doubt?" Old Sam asks. "Assuming you're not superhuman and you, too, face crippling mountains of self-doubt like the rest of us mere mortals."

"I don't know," New Sam shrugs. "I mean, there was a time when I wanted to quit. When I couldn't raise the money and the menu was a disaster and nothing was going right. That was the point where I was done. And then one night I thought of five-year-old me and how this was my dream even back then. And I couldn't bear the thought of telling that kid their dream died just because I gave up. I couldn't bear it."

"So that's the secret to following your dreams?" I ask.

"It worked for me," New Sam says. "I mean, think about it. When you're that young, you think you can be anything. Astronaut, president, chef, writer, teacher, anything you can imagine. We get a little older and we lose the dreamer in us, but somebody's gotta do all those things. People have to grow up to be everything, so why couldn't I be one of those who became a chef and had my own restaurant?"

"WWYFYOSD?" Old Sam proclaims sagely.

"Excuse me?" I check to see if he's having a stroke or something.

"What Would Your Five-Year-Old Self Do," Old Sam elaborates.

"Yeah," I agree. "I like that."

"We should get tattoos!" Old Sam yells.

"Think again," New Sam says.

"Why not?" Old Sam pouts.

"What did Kim Kardashian say about tattoos? You wouldn't put a bumper sticker on a Lamborghini, or something like that," New Sam says. "Although, I have kind of always wanted one."

"You consider yourself a Lamborghini?" I ask.

"Shoot for the stars," New Sam says. "Also, I know nothing about cars."

"But the consensus is no tattoo?" Old Sam asks.

"You know what?" I turn to look at him. "Let's fucking do it."

"Seriously?" he asks excitedly.

"Seriously?" New Sam asks suspiciously.

"Why not?" I say. "But I'm not getting WWYFXYZD, or whatever you said."

"Oh, I know! Bruce Springsteen back tattoo!" Old Sam suggests.

I shove his shoulder.

"Hey! Don't push me! We are on a ledge!" Old Sam jumps dramatically away from me.

"I'm gonna get a chef's knife," New Sam says.

"Well, shoot," Old Sam says. "I'm shocked you guys are really serious about this."

"You're doing it too," I say. "You're the one who brought it up."

"Fine," he says. "I'll even go first."

True to his word, Old Sam is the first one to get tattooed.

We had to go into downtown Baltimore to find a tattoo parlor open this late, but we're here. Old Sam is sitting in the tattoo chair, trying his best to look like it doesn't hurt, but the nail marks in New Sam's hand say otherwise. He's getting "O Captain! My Captain!" tattooed on his bicep in a typewriter font.

New Sam's next and they're getting a chef's knife right by their ankle. New Sam has no qualms about letting everyone know how much this hurts and I can't blame them. The tattoo lady said the ankle is a terrible place to get a first tattoo. New Sam holds my hand and Old Sam's hand, and lets out string after string of expletives until the lady's finished. When it's over, New Sam's all of a sudden sunshine and daisies again.

Now it's my turn, and I tug off my jacket. The tattoo is going right below the bend of my elbow on my forearm. Three words, three different handwritings. The first word is written by New Sam, the next by me, and the last by Old Sam. Five guesses as to what those three words are.

Give up? You're going to be kicking yourself because there's literally only one option – Born to Run.

If you want to delve too much into it, yes, there's a reason I chose the word for each person to write. If anyone asked in real life, I'd tell them it was random, but you guys are basically a part of me at this point, so I'll tell you.

New Sam is "Born" because they reminded me that we

all have that five-year-old dreamer inside of us who doesn't know the definition of failure and has no idea that giving up's a possibility. The kid we tend to forget, to beat down, to silence, because the world tells you to give up on your dreams. But you shouldn't, because if you give up on your dreams, that five-year-old inside of you is going to start throwing temper tantrums, and that's when your life officially stops being your own. That is the honest-to-goodness truth.

Old Sam is "Run" because that's what he did with me. He picked up the shambled mess that I was and took me running. Mollie Fae has already exposed me as a closet comic book nerd, so I'm just going to lean into this explanation. When Superman or Supergirl loses their powers because they exerted themselves too much fighting some evil force, the sun can only do so much. The yellow sun, which is different from Krypton's red sun, is what gives them their powers, but when their powers are blown out, they need something more than the sun to jolt them back. Usually, it's some adrenaline junkie thing like Lois Lane's in super danger and Superman just *has* to save her.

I like to think that's what this road trip is for me. It's the jolt I needed to bring me back to one hundred percent strength. When there was no other option and I had nowhere else to turn, I just had to run. And I have to thank Old Sam for being the one who made it so that running was my only option. I don't mean running in the scared sense that makes somebody run away. I think of it like Superman. That jolt to bring me back.

Which brings us to my word, "to." The word, if you're not familiar with the definition, expresses a sense of motion or acts as an identifier of the person or thing that's being affected. Hence why I chose that one for myself.

And you guys thought I was just getting a simple Bruce Springsteen tattoo.

30

Don't Dream It's Over
by Crowded House

"Carly, get up!" Old Sam hits me with a pillow.

"I thought we agreed to sleep in today," I complain, pulling my blankets higher.

"You're everywhere! Twitter, Facebook, Reddit. Hell, someone I know even captioned their Instagram with a quote from you," Old Sam says, talking a mile a minute.

"Yeah, it makes sense why you went to a library now," New Sam adds, toothbrush dangling out of their mouth.

"What are you guys talking about?" I sit up slowly and try to decipher what they're rambling about.

"Does 'Thoughts from the Middle of America?' ring any bells?" Old Sam asks, shoving his phone at me. "By the way, you are so good at hiding how pretentious you truly are."

I grab the phone out of his hands, and there it is. Clear as day. Big, bold, confident letters spelling it all out. Right underneath the title, there's my name. Carly Allen. Carly motherfucking Allen. I look at the address bar.

"Holy shit. Does that say *The New York Times?*"

Old Sam nods like a bobblehead. *"The New York Times*, Buzzfeed, Huff Po, tiny local newspapers, Vice. I don't even know anymore. I lost track. You did it, dude."

I wordlessly hand him his phone and take mine off the bedside table. I have missed calls, voicemails, texts from virtually everyone I've ever known.

"Unreal," I whisper.

"I can't believe you wrote that in an hour," New Sam says. "I cried because of it, you ass."

"If I wasn't rooting for you before, I'm sure as hell rooting for you now," Old Sam whistles.

"She for sure knows you're coming," New Sam adds. "There's no way she didn't read this."

I take a deep breath. "That makes me infinitely more nervous."

"Why?" asks Old Sam.

"I had the element of surprise before. Now everyone in that church is going to be sitting there, waiting with bated breath for the doors to bang open. Oh my god, I might vomit." I lean down and put my head between my knees.

"Side effect of going viral," Old Sam jokes.

I start pacing around the room. "Okay, so she knows I'm coming. Should I call her? Will she call me and say don't show up? What's the polite thing to do in this situation?"

"I'm pretty sure the polite thing to do is not barge in on a wedding, but you've already jumped that shark," New Sam offers.

"Ignoring that," I tell New Sam. "But think about it, okay? What if there are guards now? Or people waiting to throw me to the ground the second I set out of the car?"

"Mollie is not going to hire security for her wedding," Old Sam says. "You've just gotta make sure you have a good speech prepared."

"Speech?" I squeak.

"Yeah," New Sam says with a strange look. "Did you think you were just gonna walk in there and ask if she wants to grab a coffee or something?"

"I mean, no, but I haven't planned a speech."

"You've got all day," Old Sam says.

"What if I call her instead? You know, instead of royally fucking up her wedding?" I crawl back under the covers.

"Carly, the damage is done. The thing you wrote did that," Old Sam says. "You published it under your own name. You put it out there. No mistaking it for someone else's writing. And unless you have another ex-girlfriend getting married this weekend, it's obviously about Mollie."

"This was the dumbest thing I've ever done," I say into my pillow.

"I mean, let's not go that far," Old Sam says.

I get out of bed and pace back and forth across the room. Thoughts are whizzing around so fast I can barely focus on one long enough to sort through them.

I've been writing to no one about no one for so many years that I forgot the rush of what it's like to give a damn. To have the words be about someone so clearly in the forefront of my mind. Unflinchingly, obviously about. Someone who makes me want to try to change things. I remember being in college and writing non-stop. I wrote constantly about her.

There'd be stories about a girl, like all good stories start, who'd look nothing like her. Serious to her fun. Tall to her short. But she'd have the same coffee order or the same shimmer in her eyes. She'd shuffle her shoes nervously in the same way. Look down and smile through her hair just like she does. How could I foolishly think I was ever writing about anyone else? Every single word written on paper or computer has been for her, about her, *because* of her. I haven't thought about her like this in the longest time.

It makes me feel eighteen again. It makes me feel good again. Just so…good. Great, actually. It feels so alarmingly different from what it's been.

I'm not here to say that one person can save another or fix someone or anything like that. That's some kind of bullshit. It's not anyone's job to save anyone else, but there's something to be said about wanting to be the person someone believes you are.

Mollie saw me simultaneously as who I was and who I could be. She saw the potential of my world. That's a crazy thing to be able to see in someone else. She was behind me full force, but it wasn't enough back then. See, that's what I mean. It wasn't Mollie's job to change me. She had a life and a set of dreams of her own to follow, but she loved me. She loved me as sure as the sun. And I loved her just as surely. Love is enough, don't get me wrong, love is always enough, but romantic love isn't the only love in the world. You've got to love yourself enough to see the potential inside you that the people around you see.

My phone lights up on the bedside table. An unsaved phone number from New York City is calling. My heart is in my throat. It could be her. It could be Mollie Fae. My hands are shaking as I reach out to pick up the phone. I let out a deep breath and answer carefully.

"Hello?"

"Hi, am I speaking with Carly Allen?" a woman asks.

Part of me is relieved it's not Mollie. A larger, more hopelessly romantic part of me is torn apart that it's not her.

"Uh, yeah, this is me. This is she," I say.

"Hey, this is Carrie from Harper Collins," she says, much calmer than I am. "We have your phone number on file from a couple years ago."

"Oh, yeah, the article from before. About lesbians in pop culture," I say, sitting up straighter on the bed.

"Yes! That's the one. After the article you published last night, we had to try and contact you again. You were the talk of our morning meeting."

"Wow, thank you," I say awkwardly.

"We're actually calling about a book deal," Carrie says simply. So casually. As casually as I order coffee. As casually as I just slid off the bed and right onto the floor.

"I'm sorry? What? An actual book? Made from a tree?"

"Yes," she laughs. "Well, eventually. We want you to start by writing a few things for us that'll build brand recognition for your voice and then it'll be the whole nine yards. Hardback, paperback, audiobook, e-book. Any type of book you can imagine."

"God, my voice sounds so weird on voicemails," I say absently.

"We can always get someone else to record it when the time comes," Carrie replies.

"So to be clear, you're asking me to write for you guys?"

With that, Old Sam starts jumping up and down.

"Yes, a memoir, specifically," she says. "We think you have a story to tell. There's something about your voice and your narrative that captivated everyone. Especially with you crashing a wedding."

"I haven't done it yet," I say. "Tomorrow. I'll let you know how it goes."

"Please. We'll be on pins and needles," Carrie replies.

"Join the club." I'm not sure whether I'm laughing or crying.

"We'd also like you to come in and discuss what we see for you in the future if you're anywhere in the New York area," she says.

"Yeah, yeah, that'd be great. I'll actually be in the area very soon."

"Wonderful! Let me give you my direct line. Once you get this grand romantic gesture sorted out, give me a call, okay? Are you ready to write?"

I scramble for a pen and notepad in the bedside drawer. "Yes, uh, ready when you are."

I scribble down the phone number, and after a little more chitchat, we hang up. When the line goes dead, I toss my phone on the bed and look at the Sams.

"So?" New Sam squeals.

"I think I'm going to get paid to write." A shit-eating grin threatens to break free.

"My friend's a novelist!" Old Sam yells, hoisting me over his shoulder.

"Not yet!" I laugh.

"My friend's an eventual novelist!" he chants.

"This is incredible," New Sam gushes.

Old Sam puts me down. "I knew this road trip was exactly what you needed."

"Thank you," I say. "Seriously. Genuinely. Thank you."

He pats my cheek. "That was mushy, for you."

"Speaking of," New Sam interjects, "are we heading out?

We've got places to go. This road trip isn't over yet."

"A wedding." Old Sam elbows me.

"Let me just brush my teeth and say goodbye to the parents," I say.

"Pass along some love from us," New Sam says.

"Will do."

After I get dressed and pack up my things, I head down the hall to my parents' room.

I knock lightly, just in case they're asleep, but that's not really possible. They're usually up before dawn every single day. How I am their daughter is forever a mystery to me. I could sleep until one in the afternoon if I truly wanted to.

"Come on in," I hear my dad say.

"Hey, guys." I push the door open and lean against the doorframe.

"Don't just stand there," Mom says. "Come give us a hug."

"Hey, Carly," Dad says as I move into the room.

"Yeah?"

"Do you remember what I told you when you were in high school?" he asks.

"You'll have to be a little more specific."

"About us Allens," he says.

A wide smile comes over my face. "Oh, that. Yeah. I remember that."

"Go get the girl," he says.

"You'll be the first ones I'll call," I tell them.

"We'd better be," my mom says.

"I love you guys. I'm gonna visit more. I promise."

"We love you, too, kiddo." Mom's smile is full of encouragement.

"I was just telling your mom we need to get a little sun, so maybe we'll see you out there on the...what do they call it?" Dad pauses. "Oh, the best coast!"

"Never again, Dad," I say, smiling nonetheless. "I should go, though. I love you."

"Love you," they say together.

The door clicks closed behind me and I walk to the living room where Old Sam and New Sam are waiting by the door with their luggage. My heart feels full just from being here in the home that raised me. The home my parents built. I see the chip in the doorframe from when I ran full force into it. I see the table I busted my lip on when I had braces. Fun fact, it's the reason that even today there's a little bump on my bottom lip.

It's weird to come back to the home I grew up in and see that nothing's changed. The floor and the doors and everything, they're all still here. It's all exactly as I remember it. Every other time I've come home, I've felt like I was in a place where I didn't belong. Trespassing, I guess. The twin bed I grew up sleeping in would feel like it belonged to someone else. I always felt like I was pretending to be someone I wasn't.

This time around, it feels like home again, like it used to be. It's mine, and I know it so well. Like the way you have to fiddle with the controls to get the shower to give you enough hot water, or which kitchen drawer is for utensils and which is for measuring cups.

I've been afraid of familiarity for a while. Familiarity is what got me stuck in the rut I was in back in L.A., but I realize now that it can be a good thing. It can be warm and comforting and not lonely at all. It's certainly not boring. I think it's important to know there's a difference. Being comfortable isn't a death wish. It's not the end of creativity or your life, it's the exact opposite.

You know when you hear a song from middle school or high school and you just feel electrified? See? That's not bad! That's staying up late at slumber parties making up a dance routine to *Wannabe*. It's that feeling of being let out of your last class early and getting into your best friend's car, turning on the radio on the way to get ice cream, and singing to *Mr. Brightside*. Sometimes, being comfortable is the thing that kicks you into high gear and brings you back.

That kind of familiarity and comfort are what I feel now, standing in my living room. I'm comfortable in knowing that as soon as I walk out that door, my life is about to turn upside down. I'm okay with that. That's all I've ever needed.

"Ready?" Old Sam asks, picking up his bags.

I nod. "We need to make a stop along the way."

****

We drive through Philadelphia because New Sam insists that, as a chef, they need to taste a true Philly cheesesteak. Old Sam wants to see the Liberty Bell and what he referred to as "the rest of the film locations from *National Treasure.*"

But Philly is just a pitstop to the real destination.

"Why the hell are we on a boardwalk in the dead of winter?" New Sam asks, pulling their jacket tighter. "What happened here that's so important?"

"What happened here?" I repeat. "Are you serious? Music was born here."

"See that borderline psychotic look in her eyes?" Old Sam asks. "That means this has something to do with Bruce Springsteen."

"I resent being called borderline psychotic," I say.

New Sam pats my shoulder. "It's fine, Carly. It's the exact same look he had at the stamp ball. This is definitely more understandable."

"Stamps are cool!" Old Sam protests.

"You don't even collect them!" I retort.

"Doesn't make them less cool," Old Sam huffs.

"C'mon, let's go inside." The awe in my voice takes over.

To say I'm overwhelmed is an understatement. I don't

think there's a word grand enough to communicate what I'm feeling. It's like I've come home, where home is the world inside a Springsteen song. There's a massive Welcome to Asbury Park postcard mural painted on one of the walls and a Springsteen cover band playing on stage at the back of the bar. If I close my eyes, I can pretend it's really him.

"Want a drink?" Old Sam asks.

"What?" I honestly forgot they were here.

"A drink?" Old Sam mimes drinking out of a straw.

I shake my head. "I'm okay. I'm just going to find a spot and listen for a while."

The band is playing all the hits. *Rosalita, Growin' Up, Born in the U.S.A., I'm on Fire, Dancing in the Dark, Badlands.* I could stay here forever, singing along as loudly as I can. I love this. It reminds me of the band I was in back in high school. Granted, One Direction is nowhere near the same as Springsteen, but I miss being on stage. I'm shaken out of my daze when the lead singer leans close to where I'm standing.

"Hey, did you hear me?" he asks.

"What?"

"I asked if you like Springsteen," he says with an easy smile.

"Oh, uh, yeah, a lot," I answer sheepishly.

"You sing? You look like you sing."

I gulp. "Sometimes."

"She used to be a singer in a band," Old Sam yells from

somewhere behind me.

The singer raises an eyebrow. "Feel like singing tonight?"

"Oh, I don't know about that."

"Don't worry," he says, reaching out his hand to pull me onstage. "We're all friends here."

When I was briefly in jazz band in high school, I played the piano. When we all eventually quit jazz band for our One Direction cover band, it was decided we didn't need a full-time piano player, so I'd only play if the song called for it. It should come as absolutely no surprise to you that the first real song I ever learned on the piano was *Thunder Road*.

My mom made me take piano lessons when I was a kid, and I hated it. Playing *Jingle Bells* and *London Bridge Is Falling Down* forever sounded like a fate worse than death. In my young mind, those were the only two songs in the world that had a piano in them. I decided I wouldn't be caught dead playing that nonsense, but it was those weird years of my life where I only knew kiddie music and whatever nonsense my parents played.

Of all the musicians in the world, I still don't know what made my dad pick Bruce Springsteen to inspire me one day. I remember him interrupting my piano lesson and turning on the record player. I didn't even know it worked. I thought it was some weird antique radio. The needle dropped, and when the first piano notes twinkled through the speakers, I felt like I was in a trance. I'd certainly never heard anything like that in my life. I don't know if I've ever heard anything like it since.

Thunder Road was the first song I learned how to fully play on the piano, and also the first song I taught myself how to sing along to. I like to think of it almost like a guardian angel that showed up when I needed a push in the right direction and whispered in my ear, "Show a little faith."

I grab the guy's hand and he pulls me up, my legs wobbly.

I point to the piano. "Can I play that?"

He nods. "I'll plug you in," he says, kneeling down and fumbling with some wires. "What's your name again, kid?"

I sit on the stool and take a deep breath. "Carly. Carly Allen."

He finishes up with the wires and makes his way over to the microphone. "Ladies and gentlemen, Carly Allen and the E Street Band."

The keys of the piano feel exactly like the keys of the first piano I played as a kid. The piano at the bottom of the stairs by the desk my mom used to work at. I remember the way the basement carpet felt on the tips of my toes because I was too short to have my feet firmly planted on the ground.

I've probably played this song a thousand times. My fingers could play the notes blindfolded and backward, but I've never played it with a band before. That first kick of the bass drum sets off a wildfire in me. Springsteen may have written this song, but tonight it's mine. Tonight, Mary and I are the ones who have one last chance to make it all real. I have a million more words to say and a million things left to do in this life, but right now, with the band and the audience and the electricity radiating from the magic of it all, it feels like *Thunder Road* has all the words I'll ever need.

I feel like describing an auditory experience in a distinctly non-auditory medium is next to impossible, so I'm not gonna do it. And you can't make me. But playing *Thunder Road* onstage at The Stone Pony is the closest thing I've ever had to a religious experience. If you're sitting there rolling your eyes and murmuring "Okay, Carly, stop exaggerating," I'd ask that you find yourself a record player, a copy of Bruce Springsteen and the E Street Band's *Live/1975-85* album, and close your eyes. He starts the show alone with *Thunder Road* and it's honest and urgent and incredible.

In *Almost Famous*, they say that if you light a candle and listen to The Who's *Tommy*, you can see the future. That's one hundred percent true. If you listen to *Born to Run* in its entirety on a highway at sunset in the middle of the desert, you can drive to the edge of the universe. And if you sing *Thunder Road* onstage at The Stone Pony, it can save your life.

31

New York State of Mind
by Billy Joel

After our detour to The Stone Pony, we're back on the road. We get into the city late. I'm a little buzzed off that performance, alcohol, and just the air of the city. I beg Old Sam to drive us through Times Square and he humors me.

"I used to live in New York," Old Sam tells us.

"I didn't know that," I say.

"It was for college. The best time of my life. I still hate Times Square though. You're lucky I like you."

"I've never been here." New Sam is staring out the window at the blinding lights.

"Never?" Old Sam and I ask in shock.

"Never. I'm a West Coast kid. We barely ever left Nevada. I went to Disneyland once and we went to L.A. for a day. L.A.'s too spread out, though, to really feel like a city."

"That settles it," I say. "Old Sam, we're staying at the Marriott Marquis."

Old Sam's eyebrows shoot up. "Are you serious? That's not in the budget."

"Yeah, it's not in yours, but it's in mine. Come on," I urge him. "New Sam's never been here. We're gonna do this right."

"We don't have to stay in an expensive hotel. Just being in the city is more than enough," New Sam says.

"Nonsense. Think of it as a thank you for everything. For both of you. For doing this with me."

"I'd do it again in a heartbeat." Old Sam reaches back to pat me on the knee.

"Same," New Sam says.

"Well, I really appreciate the sentiment, but let's hope we don't have to do this again."

"Let's go then! I'm not going to try and talk you out of paying for us to stay at the nicest hotel I've ever set foot in," Old Sam says.

"You've stayed there before?" New Sam asks.

"Oh, honey, no, no, no," Old Sam laughs. "I said set foot in. Not stayed in. I would just pee there all the time."

"Gross," New Sam says.

"Listen, it's impossible to find public bathrooms in New York City. I learned to walk into hotel lobbies and act real cool and collected like I was staying there, then just use their bathrooms," Old Sam says.

"That's what I do too!" I say.

"You don't do it in Vegas?" Old Sam asks.

"No, but I'm going to start," New Sam says. "That's

actually pretty genius."

"Thank you. I am quite the revolutionary," Old Sam says proudly.

"Take the next right," I tell him.

Old Sam pulls up to the valet stand. It took quite a lot of arguing for him to agree to valet park the car. He insisted he could find a parking spot, to which I said, yeah, that might be true uptown, but not in midtown. He's got to learn to love valet parking. We all pile out of the car and I tip the valet, who takes the keys from Old Sam.

"I can't believe Times Square is right here!" New Sam gasps.

I laugh. "Yeah, it is. Old Sam, show them around a little. I'll go get the room."

Even though it's late, the hotel and the streets are bustling. I feel nervous. It probably has something to do with the fact that there's a wedding tomorrow. The wedding this entire road trip has been leading up to. GUYS, I'M FREAKING OUT. And sweating. I think I'm sweating. Reality is setting in and it's a lot to process.

I walk up to the front desk.

"Hey, how's it going?" I ask.

The girl at the desk looks up. "I'm doing well, thank you. How are you?"

"Good, good. I, um, I'm looking to check in. I don't have a reservation, though."

"Okay, let me see if we have anything available," she says, but she doesn't look encouraging. "How many rooms do you need?"

"Two. Honestly, though, I'll take anything. Even a cot in a stairwell. I'm not a picky person. I just need a place to stay."

"Just one moment." She looks at me suspiciously, then starts typing.

"I'm not a terrorist," I blurt out.

"What?"

"That was probably the wrong thing to say, but I'm not a terrorist. I'm only acting like this because there's a wedding tomorrow that I really need to be in town for."

She perks up a little at that. "Oh, is it a friend's?"

"Ex-girlfriend's." I can't decide if that makes me look more or less insane.

"Oh."

"Yeah, so this is either a massive waste of money or the idea of the millennium," I say.

"Well, I hope for your sake it's the latter. The least expensive room we have available for tonight is $885."

"That's not so bad for two rooms."

"It's the price for one room," she explains.

"Oh," I sigh. "Okay, fine. I'll take it."

"Wow," she comments unprofessionally. "I honestly thought you were gonna bail."

"Me too."

"It's a mini-suite," she says.

"I'm sorry. Are you telling me the only room you have available for tonight is a suite?"

She nods. "New York at Christmas is very popular."

I lean down and rest my head against the counter. This is absolutely crazy. After a few moments I straighten back up. "Y'know what? It's worth it. Just do it," I say, handing over my credit card and license.

"At least you and your party will have separate rooms," she says.

"There are separate rooms within the room?"

The girl looks at me like I'm an idiot. "I really don't think you have any idea what to expect, do you? It's a suite."

She was one hundred percent correct. When I open the door, I realize I had absolutely no idea what to expect from a suite in the Marriott Marquis in Times Square. The suite has a living room!

Old Sam's jaw drops. "Oh my god."

"This is bigger than my apartment," New Sam murmurs.

"Same," I say.

"Same," Old Sam says.

"I feel like I can't even afford to breathe in here, let alone sleep," New Sam says.

"Well, for two nights, we're living like royalty," I say as we walk in.

"Two?" Old Sam asks.

I shrug. "Tonight, and then who knows what's going to happen tomorrow. I just booked it for a second night."

"You know what's going to happen tomorrow," Old Sam says.

I let out a sharp laugh. "I actually don't, and that's making me beyond nervous. I thought I was going to shit my pants when I was checking in."

"Because of the price of the room?" New Sam asks, sprawled on what looks to be a very comfortable couch.

"Yes," I say, pointing to New Sam. "But also, I think it's really just weighing on me. Like, it's here, y'know?"

"Less than twenty-four hours," Old Sam says.

"Not helping." I let out a deep breath. "It's just like when you were a kid and there was something you were really looking forward to and when it's finally about to happen it seems terrifying. I feel like that. I've pictured tomorrow morning a million and one times, and I just don't fathom how it can possibly go well. I've been aching for this day to come, and now that it's here, I kind of wish it wasn't."

"Because you're scared?" New Sam asks quietly.

"Yep, pretty much," I reply. "Everything in my entire universe is going to change tomorrow. Everything. I'm either going to walk out of there with the love of my life or I'm not, and wow, that is a lot."

"You should get some sleep," Old Sam suggests.

"I think I'm going to go for a walk first. It'll be nice."

"Are you sure you should go alone?" Old Sam looks very concerned.

I smile weakly at him. "Sure. I've missed New York. It'll be nice to be back."

"You're from New York?" Old Sam asks.

"No, but my grandparents used to live here, remember? We'd come all the time." I pull on my jacket. "You should take New Sam to see the windows on Fifth Avenue."

"Yeah," he nods, then looks over at New Sam with a small smile on his face. "That'd be nice."

"I have no idea what that means," New Sam says, returning Old Sam's fond smile, "but I'd like to go with you."

I open the door. "I'll see you guys tomorrow."

"See ya, Carly." Old Sam is talking to me, but his eyes never leave New Sam's.

Times Square is a tourist trap. It's loud, overpriced, crowded, and one of my favorite places in the world. Maybe it's because I've always been just a visitor, but I'll never be over this place. Remember how I said I loved Los Angeles because of the people who are out there because they *had* to follow their dreams? Well, that's why I love Times Square. It's the East Coast equivalent. If your face is up on one of these billboards, it's definitive proof you've made it. You beat the odds.

I take a seat on the TKTS steps. There are people around me from all over the world, speaking a flurry of languages I don't recognize. An older couple gestures to me and holds out a camera. We don't speak a lick of the same language, but I know they want me to take their photo, so I do.

"Cheese!" I say, and their smiles shine brightly, even amid all the LED lights that make this stretch of the city seem like it's broad daylight. I hand the camera back to them and we go our separate ways. Me, back to my spot on the steps. Them, off into the night of their New York adventure.

For the past few years, I've been lonely. I've felt sadder and more isolated than at any other time in all my years of life. It's easy to forget there's a big, wide world around me. If I wanted to, I could probably exist without ever interacting with another human being again. I pay my rent online, I live alone, I can order my groceries and everything in the world from Amazon, I could find an online job. I could be entirely isolated. There was a time I would've happily taken that life, but I know now it's not what I want.

I see these people in their bulky marshmallow coats and their beanies pulled down over their ears, arms tucked against the ones they love, and I realize how absolutely stupid I've been.

Listen, I'm not going to pretend I have even the tiniest clue about what happens to any of us when we die. Do we get reincarnated? Is there life after death? Is there a heaven? What about hell? What about purgatory? I have no fucking clue. All I know is that what I have now is real and tangible and in front of me. And, yeah, one time my seventh grade math teacher was like, what if Sebastian's in a coma and we all only exist as part of his coma. That messed me up for a while, but even if it's true, even if all of this is just Sebastian Jones' coma dream, it's still real for me. And if it's real, all that matters is love.

Love is the only worthwhile thing humanity has ever done. It's the only thing that can change everything. Love cracks us open and lets us see things the way they're meant to be seen. And I'm not even talking about romantic love. It's just love. Love for humanity because we're all here in Sebastian's coma dream together, and the only way to make sense of any of this is to love. Love your neighbor. Love your friends. Love nature. Love your partner. Love this beautiful planet we call home. And it's just like Lolo said. You wanna shake people and make them realize how dumb they're being when they take all of this, any of this, for granted.

Love is sitting in Times Square in December, surrounded by strangers but not feeling alone. Love is Old Sam and New Sam with their arms intertwined, meandering along Fifth Avenue. Love is Annie and Todd in the suburbs of Nashville, asleep in bed, their legs intertwined, holding each other close. And love has always been Mollie Fae.

It's the way she used to kiss my cheek when she would wake up before me. It's the way I used to hold her hand during fancy dinner parties because I knew how nervous they made her. It's the way we knew what the other was thinking before we ever said anything. It's the way her glasses would slide down her nose when she forgot to order new contacts, and the way I used to kiss her nose and push them back up. It's the way she never sang the right words to *Rich Girl,* and the way I never wanted to correct her. It's the way I think about my future. There's a hand in mine, and I don't even have to look down to know it's hers.

All I know is that the only true currency in this world is love, and I'm so over people thinking that if you love, you're weak. There are people who say that being in love makes you pathetic and needy, but I know that being in love is the bravest thing any of us can do. Being passionate about something is brave, because there are always obstacles and so many people just waiting at every turn to tear you down. To be in love and to be passionate in the face of all of that isn't pathetic. I will never accept that. It's the only thing that keeps this world turning.

I don't think I'm nervous anymore. Well, I mean, I know I'm still nervous, but it's a different kind of nervous. I'm more nervous about putting myself out there like that. I'm not nervous about how I feel. That, I'm ready to shout from the rooftops.

32

Fool for Love
by Lord Huron

I'm standing in front of a mirror trying to straighten my tie, my hair going in a million different directions. My breathing is shallow and my fingers can't get the knot right. I look a little like a frazzled mess.

All I can think of is the last time I struggled with a tie and how it was prom night. Todd was there with me and we were waiting for Annie and Mollie. We were eighteen and the whole world was in front of us. I think we put too much pressure on ourselves when we're eighteen. We expect our lives to jump light-years in milliseconds, but that'll never happen. You don't just get to wake up in a new world, you have to make it.

It's nice, though, to look back on little moments like prom night and know that nights like that were the building blocks for the future.

There's a knock at the door and I walk over to open it. I see Old Sam through the peephole, standing outside with a paper bag in his hands.

I open the door. "What's up, Old Sam?"

He sighs. "It's just us. Can't you call me Sam?"

"If you insist. What can I do for you?"

"Is this a business meeting? Do you get all formal when you're nervous?" He takes a seat on the bed.

"Until you've stood in front of a mirror on the morning of the day you're about to interrupt a wedding, I feel like you can't judge my coping mechanisms."

"You've got me there," he agrees. "Speaking of got, though, I got something for you."

I take the paper bag he's holding out to me. "What is it?"

"Open it and you'll find out."

I reach in and pull out a pair of socks. Bruce Springsteen socks, to be exact, with his famous *Born in the U.S.A.* cover stitched all over in miniature. I absolutely love them.

"Where on earth did you find a pair of Bruce Springsteen socks?" I ask in wonder.

"Oddly enough, at a gas station near Boys Town, Nebraska." He looks very proud of himself. "I saw them and I knew you'd eventually need them for a special occasion. Today seems like as good a time as any."

"Did you plan all this?" I ask softly, after a moment.

"Plan to give you Bruce Springsteen socks? Of course not. I didn't even know such things existed," he scoffs.

"You know what I mean," I say seriously. "When we left for the Grand Canyon, did you know we'd up here? In New

York. On her wedding day?"

He shuffles his feet a little and looks down. "I hoped."

Tears prick at the corners of my eyes. "All along?"

He nods his head. "That night when we were in your apartment, talking about her, I just thought you didn't seem ready to lose her. And you were in such a funk that I wanted to do *something*."

We're quiet again while I pull on the Bruce Springsteen socks.

"It was a little selfish on my part too. I've always wanted to do this. You know, have a road trip story to tell my kids about someday. My parents would always tell me about when they drove across the country with friends right after they graduated from college. I've never had friends I wanted to be cooped up in a car with for thousands of miles. I'm not the best at making friends," he adds with a laugh. "I mean, I basically forced you to be my friend."

"I remember," I agree. "I'm glad you did."

"Me, too." He gives me a serious look. "So it was for both of us. I didn't want to push you to show up to the wedding, but, god, I wanted you to. The way you talked about Mollie that night, it was like I could see you as the old person in the retirement home who goes on and on about the one who got away. I couldn't bear to let that happen to you. But I still wanted you to figure out for yourself that this," he says, gesturing out the window, "this is where you're supposed to be. Doing what you're supposed to be doing."

"Thank you," I say. "Thank you for getting me here."

"You got yourself here. I just paid for half the gas."

"Thanks, Sam."

"Thank you, Carly," he replies.

"So, you and New Sam?' I ask, wiggling my eyebrows.

"Nice change of topic. Real smooth. Yeah, I uh, I like them. A lot. Last night, walking down Fifth Avenue and looking at all the Christmas stuff was pretty cool."

"You felt like you could picture the two of you walking down city streets when you're old and gray?" I ask.

"Yes!" he exclaims. "That's exactly it. Almost like a future déjà vu."

I remember the night in San Francisco with Mollie where I felt exactly the same way.

"That's a good thing. It's a really good thing."

"Is it crazy that I want to see them after all this ends? New Sam was just a random person and now here they are and this crazy experience is over, but I want to still see New Sam every single day," Old Sam rambles.

I look at him fondly. "I think you should tell them that."

"Does this mean I should move to Vegas?" he asks. "Or should New Sam move to L.A.?

"I mean, that might be jumping the gun a little bit, buddy. But when the time comes, I think you'll figure it out," I reassure him. "First you have to tell them how you feel."

"Oh, yeah, I'd just like to fast forward through that part," he says.

"They'll think it's cute you're nervous."

"I never said I was nervous," he protests. I raise an eyebrow and he sighs. "Fine. I'm nervous."

"That's good. That's really sweet, actually. Use it to your advantage."

"Whew, okay." He wipes his hands on his jeans. "I'm gonna go tell them."

"I'm rooting for you," I say as he walks toward the door.

He turns to look at me, walks back to where I'm standing, and scoops me up in the tightest hug.

"I'm rooting for you, too," he says. "You're gonna get the girl of your dreams. You've come too far not to."

I let out a shaky breath and nod.

Old Sam lets go of me. "Go get her."

I blush and shove him toward the door. "Go get them."

"I'm really glad you made us stop for that suit back in Vegas. You look great." He gives me a wink and then he's out the door.

I turn to look at myself in the mirror again, and for the first time in a while, I like the person I see staring back at me. The bags under my eyes aren't from the haggardness I've been unable to shake since Mollie Fae left me; they're from staying up too late in the city that never sleeps. They're from being in a car with people I care deeply for. They're from being in love with this life.

If I could go back, I'd do it all again. Everything. From high school to college to the chaos of being an aimless postgrad to almost being shot in Boys Town, Nebraska, to singing at The Stone Pony, to standing here right now in front of a mirror in a hotel room in New York City.

My phone's playing music through the hotel alarm clock speakers. It's Led Zeppelin's *Going to California,* and there's that line about the girl in California with flowers in her hair. That, to me, is just the most magical sentiment. The promise of a girl to love. The way he sings it stirs my bones, makes them ache.

We're all perpetually chasing girls across the country. Metaphorically or literally. And it may very well be insane, but it's all we have. A girl nearly 3,000 miles away. A girl waiting out there. A chance at feeling alive and in love. Something about that wording of the lyrics gets to me. I don't know how to explain the way it makes me feel. It just instantly makes this picture in my head. Old grainy footage, sepia, but still bright, saturated colors. And there's a girl with her back to me. We're in a field of sunflowers swaying in the sweet summer breeze. Her hair's dancing lightly. Then she turns around and smiles the most ethereal smile just for me.

That's the image I get whenever there's some weepy, romantic, lovestruck boy from the '70s or '80s plucking away on a beat-up guitar. He sings wistfully about a girl and I'm sure in his mind, he's seeing the equivalent of the sublime girl in my magical sunflower field. It could also be a wife, or a boy. Somebody. We all see somebody. I know who I see, though. Clear as day. Mollie Fae. Always.

I look over at the clock and realize it's time. I put my phone and wallet into my pockets and check my hair one last time in the mirror. It's not like I'm being narcissistic. It's just that I want to look like I'm worth taking this risk on. I want to look like someone Mollie would want to run away with.

The next few moments pass in a blur. Before I know it, I'm out the door, in the elevator, and crossing the lobby to ask the front desk to call me a cab. Now I'm sitting in the back of a cab that smells like Christmas, and my leg is jumping and my heart feels like it's going to burst and it won't even matter if Mollie would run away with me because I'll have spontaneously combusted from nerves in the back of the best-smelling cab I've ever been in.

The cab driver hits more traffic than I anticipated, so I'm running later than I'd hoped. But here I am. I'm on the way there. I'm in New York and it's Christmastime and there's a decent amount of snow on the ground and I can't help but be in awe. Being in L.A. for so long made me forget about how pretty snow makes cities. New York with all the snow and the people bundled up could make lovers out of every single one of us. It's exactly what I need on my side because it just hit me that I'm about to potentially ruin a wedding. I understood it in the abstract, but the weight of it all is settling in a pit in my stomach.

Have you ever wondered why people don't interrupt weddings in real life? I don't know a single person who's stopped a wedding, or even given serious thought to stopping a wedding. Why is that? Is it because it's wildly impractical? Or do real-life people not feel as passionately as they do in movies?

Maybe it's just the realness of it. There you'd be, running into a church or synagogue or nondenominational field full of people gathered together to watch their friend or brother or sister or just someone they love marry the person they love. Weddings cost very real thousands of dollars. If you want to stop a wedding, you have to be pretty fucking confident the person is gonna run away with you, or just be fine with potentially ruining what's supposed to be the most perfect day of their lives.

For the first time since setting out for the wedding, I think of Mollie's fiancé, Jessie. If I were in her shoes, how would I feel about somebody ruining this? Like, it's one thing for the person in Mollie's shoes, because no matter if she decides to choose me or not, she's got somebody at the end of the day. But Jessie could end up without anybody on her side. So could I, but I didn't have anybody before today. My life I don't mind ruining, but it's another thing to ruin an innocent bystander's life.

I don't know what it says about me, but I'm not turning back now.

The cabbie's turning the corner and I can see the church. My knee's jumping even faster and I can't help but smile just the tiniest bit at the last time I felt like this. I was eighteen, sitting in Mr. Hall's English class, chasing after a girl I'd lost. The girl I've lost now. The girl I'm never going to lose again.

I'm tired of losing.

I throw the fare and a generous tip onto the front seat and push the cab door open. The wind ruffles my hair and I wonder why I even bothered to brush it. There's a lump in my chest and I'm jogging to the door before the smarter part of me can talk me out of this. There's snow and ice everywhere and I'm taking the stairs of the church too quickly. I end up arriving far less gracefully than I'd imagined when I pictured this moment during nearly every single mile of the cross-country road trip that led me here. But the doors are opening and my shoes are sliding on ice, and I'm tumbling into the church. Finally, after the three longest months of my life, I see Mollie Fae.

33

Every Little Thing She Does is Magic
by The Police

The first thing that hits me is that there's no one in the church except Mollie Fae. The pews are empty, there's no organ music wafting through the rafters, just Mollie Fae sitting on the steps of the altar. If ever there was a person who could make me believe in divine intervention, it'd be her. Legs crossed in front of her, softest blue blue jeans, and a loose sweater. My mouth finally catches up to my brain.

"Mollie! Where is everyone? Why are you alone?"

She smiles a little. "I called the wedding off."

"Wait, you...the wedding...I don't understand. You canceled it?" My head is shaking like a bobblehead.

She nods, standing up. "Right after Annie's wedding. But this church was the only thing that was non-refundable."

I stare at her incredulously. "I'm sorry, I'm just still very confused. I anticipated bursting through those doors and seeing a whole bunch of people who were really pissed at me and there's no one," I stammer, running frantic hands through my hair. "I don't get it. What are you doing here?"

"I had a feeling you'd come tumbling through those doors. I hoped you would, at least. That's why I'm here."

"I don't understand. What happened to Jessie?"

"It's your fault, actually," she says. "Remember that speech you made at Annie's wedding? The one about living in an '80s music video? It terrified me, because when I got off the plane and saw Jessie standing there with a cute Welcome Home sign, I didn't feel anything. I waited for the lights to dim and a synth track to echo in my ears, but there was nothing. No haze of hairspray, no leg warmers, nothing. The world kept turning. It never even stuttered. Not for a second. But today, you came through those doors and I felt it all. Time standing still, the spotlight on you like it's been since we were eighteen." And then she says the five simplest, best words I've ever heard in my entire life.

"It had to be you." She says this with a shrug, like it's a completely unrevolutionary fact. But in reality, those five words are going to alter the course of life as I know it.

"Nothing to do with that article?"

"Well, that didn't hurt your case."

"I had some things I had to get off my chest."

"Did you," Mollie starts, but falters and looks around. "Did you mean it? What you said? Did you mean to come here today?"

"Not really, no. I just saw the church as I was walking

through the neighborhood and thought I'd check out the architecture. And I'm a sucker for stained glass."

"Carly," her voice breaks.

"Everything. I meant everything," I say quickly, with as much conviction as I can muster.

"Everything?"

I nod. "Every. Little. Thing."

"Because you said a lot." She takes a step toward me.

"You'll come to find that I meant a lot too." I move a step closer to her.

"I mean, you said a whole lot." She takes another step toward me. "A lot a lot."

"Want me to say it again?" I'm finally toe-to-toe with her.

She shakes her head no, lip between her teeth. "There's something else I'd like."

Then, and I really can't emphasize enough how simple this all feels, she kisses me. She leans toward me and kisses me like it's the only thing either of us was ever meant to do. It feels like nothing's changed since that first kiss in the hallway of Bethany's parents' house, but I'd be an idiot to believe that. Everything's changed. The universe is entirely different. When she kisses me, it's like the earth splits open and everything I see is as it should be.

I wrap my arms around Mollie's waist, pick her up, and twirl her around. She smiles against my lips and lets out a laugh that echoes all the way up to the tip of the steeple.

"I love you," I say, looking right at her.

She runs her fingers through my hair and skims the lipstick off my lips with her thumb. "I've never stopped being in love with you."

I smile and put her down. "I had a speech planned."

"You did?"

I nod furiously. "Of course! I was ready to fight for you."

"You're a tough lady, Carly Allen. Can I hear it?"

"My speech?"

"Yeah. You can't just say you had this big romantic speech ready, and then not give it."

"Never said romantic," I cut in.

"I sure hope there's some romance in there. You were planning to stop a wedding for purely platonic feelings?"

"Okay, you're right," I concede.

"So," she says quietly. "Let's hear it."

"Somehow this feels more intimidating than doing it in front of an entire church full of your closest family and friends, and fiancé slash almost wife," I say. "Okay, um, go stand up on the altar."

Mollie walks back up to the altar and I turn in the direction of the church doors. "Are you going to start with your entrance again?"

"I mean, if you want me to do this, then I'm gonna do it right," I say. "Be right back."

I jog lightly to the back of the church and slip outside.

My brain is too overloaded to process what's happening. I let out a deep breath and push the doors open once again.

"Stop!" I yell, and the biggest smile crosses my face because there she is, looking at me with all the love in the world. It always felt like it was Mollie waiting at the end of the line. Like this was our inevitable conclusion. I start walking toward her. It feels like I'm walking home.

"I know this is wildly inconvenient and probably also wildly inappropriate, because no one in real life does things like this, but, Mollie, you make me want to do the craziest things. Like this, for instance. Or driving across the country with a stranger and a semi-stranger. You make me want to believe in myself, which is the craziest thing in the world. I love you. I've never stopped loving you. There are times when I've loved you more than I love myself. It took two-thousand-some-odd miles to make me see that the only way a girl like you could love someone like me is if I loved myself. So, yes, I'm perpetually running late and I don't eat enough vegetables and I drink a little more than I probably should and I'm filled with so much self-doubt that sometimes I'm paralyzed and I am in *love* with you. I tried not to be. I tried to forget about you and let you live your life, but I couldn't. I couldn't let go. I love you because loving you made me love myself. So I know this is inopportune, but I just want to ask one last favor," I say, tears pricking at the corners of my eyes. "Choose me. Marry me instead."

"Wow," Mollie whispers, her hands reaching out to me. She wipes the tears off my cheeks.

"Like run away with me wow?" I ask.

"Oh my god, definitely," she says in a rush, then kisses me soundly.

I'm sure the logistics of this relationship will be insane, and I probably should have thought about them before now. Mollie lives on the East Coast and I live on the West Coast. How's that going to work? There's also the fact that Mollie had a very real fiancé mere months ago, and just the general shitty state of my life up until a few days ago. None of these feel like big things, though. They feel manageable and wildly irrelevant because right now, the love of my life is kissing me. It feels like the first kiss of the rest of my life.

"What the hell were you doing in Missouri?" she asks when she pulls away, a big smile dancing on her lips.

"That sounds like a story best told over brunch," I answer. "Would you, uh, want to have brunch with me?"

"Carly Allen, are you asking me out?"

"I think so?"

She laughs. "You think so?"

I can't meet her eye. "You still make me a little nervous."

"Me too," she says. "A good nervous."

"The best kind." I take her hand. "Come on, let's get out of here."

34

Uptight (Everything's Alright) by Stevie Wonder

Five Years Later

"Get a move on, everyone! This family is not late!"

"Love, it won't kill us to be a little late, will it?"

"Are we killing people? That's bad."

"No, it's just an expression. It's fine, don't worry about it. Just find your other shoe, kiddo."

Mollie Fae smiles and sits on the bench by the door. "This is our life now, huh? I should just accept the fact that we're going to run late sometimes?"

I peek my head out of the shoe closet, grinning. "Would you want it any other way?"

I already know the answer. She doesn't say anything because we both know she doesn't have to.

We look over at our son, Freddie, whose feet are kicking in the air, half in and half out of the shoe closet. One foot has a Wonder Woman light-up shoe on it, the other is wearing a sock covered in cartoon monsters. My hair's a little matted with glue from arts and crafts this morning, there are crayon marks on the wall, three dismembered LEGO people are lying in the middle of the hallway, and Mollie's purse has a purple handprint on the strap. Freddie lifts his other shoe triumphantly, and Mollie claps and pulls him into her lap. She undoes the Velcro and whispers jokes in his ear. He giggles as she slips his foot into the shoe. My entire world is embodied in those two giggling idiots on the bench. I'm sitting here, in the home Mollie and I built together, and the scene in front of me proves again that magic is real. Possibilities expand and bend and grow. I don't think I could've dreamed up a better path for us if I'd tried.

"You ready to go, Mama?" Freddie asks, peeking up at me through his curly bangs.

"Yeah, Mama," Mollie Fae echoes, her eyes twinkling and gleaming. "You ready to go?"

I nod, my heart filled to bursting with love. "I'm ready."

Bring it on, world. We're ready for you.

ACKNOWLEDGMENTS

First of all, I'm sad that Carly Allen's story has finally come to an end. She's a good kid and I've really had fun hanging out with her all these years. And yeah, sometimes I did just want to shake her and tell her to stop being such an idiot. I say that as though I wasn't entirely in charge of her life and her story, but I think she found her way in the end.

This book was written after I'd just driven across the United States to move my life to Los Angeles. Carly and I took different routes and we had wildly different motivations for crossing this country. My journey began on the day of the Women's March in 2017. I remember driving past buses full of women with signs in their windows going to use their voices to make a difference. That's the country I love.

Driving long distances puts things in perspective. Watching the sun rise over the big Texas sky with one of my best friends and almost being murdered in more than one hotel in the Middle of America made me want to help people realize this world is so very small and our lives are so very short. At the risk of sounding like an Afterschool Special, all of our differences are important, yet at the same time, they're meaningless. We're so insanely different, and that's what makes us great and good and worthwhile. Let people live and love in peace. Drive across the country. See the sun rise over the Grand Canyon. Drive through the Painted Desert listening to *This Land Is Your Land*. Give a damn and love each other.

I'd like to say that I'm aware of the factual inaccuracies of this book. I know there's no season of *The Bachelor* or *The Bachelorette* that occurs in December. However, I'm gonna play my artistic license/creative liberty card and say Mollie Fae just seemed like a winter wedding kind of girl, so that girl was gonna get her winter wedding. I loved the concept of Old Sam and Carly bonding over *The Bachelorette* too much to part with it. Everything else in this book is 100% true, including the indisputable fact that *High School Musical 3* is the best film in the *High School Musical* cinematic universe. (Yes, Melanie, that was directed at you.)

To my mother and father, thank you for marrying each other. Not only have your art and copywriting skills been truly invaluable, but also, you guys are the reason I'm here on this planet getting to write these books. Thank you for choosing to go to grad school in Middle of Nowhere, North Dakota, so you could meet each other.

To my sister, I know you never read these books, but thanks for letting me use your Spotify account.

To Chinua Achebe, who knew yams could be so romantic?

To Bruce Springsteen, thank you for being a guiding light in my life. There's not a lot I've done without you by my side. Your music is the closest thing to magic on this planet, and maybe one day I can thank you in person. If this book does nothing else, I hope it makes someone listen to *Born to Run* for the very first time and feel their whole world crack open.

This book was written in hotels in Clinton and Gallup; on Graceland stationery in Memphis; on the Notes app on my phone in a hotel in Nashville; in IKEAs in Costa Mesa and Burbank; at Dinosaur Coffee in Los Angeles; in the living room that was my bedroom of the apartment I shared with two of my best friends in Tustin; cross-legged on the floor in Glendale in the first apartment that was truly mine; in more Target parking lots in more cities than I can remember; on the 5 using the voice to text feature because when inspiration strikes, it strikes; in movie theatres before the lights went down in Long Beach; and overlooking the world from Griffith Observatory.

That's all for now, folks, and as Bruce Springsteen's mighty mom says:

Lace up your dancing shoes and get to work.

Like what you just read?
Leave a review on Amazon and Goodreads.
Reviews help other readers find this book and
put a smile on the author's face.

Thanks!

Want to be the first to hear about Tina's latest books? Just
send an email to BurnBeforeReadingBook@gmail.com
and we won't let you miss a thing.

Still can't get enough?
Check out TinaKakadelis.com

Turn the page for a sneak peek of Tina Kakadelis' new novel *American Dreamy*.

Chapter One

As an adult, it's easy to hate summer. It's all traffic, crowded supermarkets, and cicadas. Summer is stifling. It's humidity, sweat-drenched suits, kids everywhere, crowded beaches. Everything reminds you that it's no longer the magical season it was when you were a kid. For adults, summer is one of the easiest things to hate.

For kids, summer is one of the easiest things to love. No school, no homework, no getting up early, no doing all the things you don't want to do. Summer is freedom. It's later bedtimes, ice cream trucks, popsicles after every meal, pools, sunscreen, beaches, fireflies, and every good thing about being young. For kids, summer is one of the easiest things to love.

For Ryan Denning, summer meant sleep-away camp. She'd been going to the same place every year since she was a kid. Camp Whispering Pines in the Catskills. Her mom went there before her, and her grandmother before her, and a whole lot more hers before her. Ryan didn't feel like a summer camp legacy, especially when her family picked up and moved to Missouri. But every June, without fail, Ryan was packed into a car and driven to Camp Whispering Pines.

The only other camper who'd been going there as long as Ryan was Princess. Despite this shared history, their paths rarely crossed. No one knew Princess' real name, and this didn't seem unreasonable to Ryan. The rules of the outside world didn't always apply at camp, which was one of the things that made it so magical. As far as Ryan could tell, not a single person at camp knew this girl's name. To Ryan, and everyone else at Camp Whispering Pines, she was simply Princess, no questions asked.

Princess was exactly that, a princess. She came from a wealthy family, but no one knew how wealthy. The specifics of her richness were the subject of camp debates every year. Some claimed they saw Princess dropped off and picked up by a chauffeur in a Rolls Royce. Others said her family owned the camp and that's how she could get away with whatever she wanted. There was a rumor that one of the camp buildings was named after Princess' grandmother, but no one could agree on which building it was. And no one would ever dream of asking Princess about any of this. She didn't treat people like she ruled the place, but they treated her that way. Every time she walked through the mess hall, so many kids got out of her way that it looked like Moses parting the Red Sea. All the cooks loved her. They'd been sneaking her extra cookies since before she could walk, and long before she was a camper.

The year they were thirteen, the first time Ryan's family wasn't there for family day, Princess found Ryan alone on the dock, eyes red with tears.

"Families are here," Princess called from the edge of the water. "Aren't you coming?"

"No," Ryan sniffed.

"No parents?" Princess asked, and Ryan gave the slightest shake no. "Me either. Can I sit with you?"

"If you want." Ryan wiped her eyes with the collar of her shirt.

Princess walked to the edge of the dock and sat down next to Ryan. She'd just gone through a growth spurt, so her toes skimmed the top of the water. Ryan's feet weren't even close. It was the summer Ryan's camp nickname became Ryan the Runt. No matter how much you try to fight them, camp nicknames, like Goonies and legends, never die.

"So why isn't your family here?" Ryan asked.

Princess shrugged. "They've never come before. I don't think they're gonna start anytime soon."

"But they basically own the place," Ryan said.

"Yeah," Princess sighed. "Why aren't your parents here?"

"We moved to Missouri," Ryan said. "They're just coming for the talent show at the end of camp."

"Aren't there any summer camps in Missouri?" Princess asked.

"Sure, but my family has been coming here forever," Ryan explained. "Gotta keep up the tradition. That's what my mom always says."

"Can I stay with you here until family day's over?" Princess asked.

"Of course." Ryan smiled, then looked back at the lake.

"You're Ryan, right? The one they're calling Ryan the Runt?" Princess asked.

"Yeah, that's me," Ryan said.

"Doesn't it bother you that they're calling you a runt?"

"Not really," Ryan answered softly. "At least they know who I am. Do you like people calling you Princess?"

"It's okay," she conceded. "Like you said, it's better than nobody knowing your name."

"But Princess isn't your name," Ryan said.

"Nope," Princess said.

Ryan cleared her throat. "What is your real name?"

"I could tell you, but then I'd have to push you in the lake," Princess said, throwing Ryan into the water. Her head went under and she sputtered as she came back up.

"Not fair!" Ryan cried, pushing wet hair out of her face. "You didn't even tell me your name."

Princess smiled widely. "Oops?"

Ryan shook her head, a smile on her face too. A smile that wasn't totally innocent. She grabbed Princess' ankle and pulled her into the water.

"Oops," Ryan smirked when Princess surfaced.

Each summer after that, they'd meet at the dock on family day. It was a tradition all their own. Princess' family continued to ignore her and Ryan's family continued to not be able to afford to visit more than once a summer.

Ryan's nickname became more ironic as time passed. She grew taller, broader, and stronger, fell into basketball, and led her high school team to three state championships. She became confident and charming, and girls at camp noticed. That noticing started out innocent enough, but then feelings began to grow and grow and grow before being unleashed during the magical months of summer. They were freshly teen-aged kids who had minimal adult supervision and wanted very much to figure out what the deal was with that kissing thing they kept hearing about. Although Princess wasn't the first girl Ryan kissed at summer camp, she was the first girl Ryan felt the *need* to kiss. Not just a simple want, but a constant, underlying *need*. It all started that evening at the docks, but Ryan wouldn't fully understand it for a few more years.

Despite their annual tradition, Ryan and Princess didn't socialize during the rest of camp. Ryan fell in with the athletes and the rock climbers and the ones who spent their free time playing capture the flag and pick-up soccer. Princess lived up to her name. She spent her free time braiding hair, painting nails, and taking teen magazine quizzes.

All that changed the summer they were sixteen.

About the Author

Tina Kakadelis is the writer of the book you just read.
Find her on social media as @captainameripug.

Other Books by Tina Kakadelis

Burn Before Reading
I Didn't Start the Fire
American Dreamy (coming soon)
Shadowed Doorways Anthology

38273706R00203

Made in the USA
Middletown, DE
07 March 2019